THE BLACK FOX

THE BLACK FOX

A Novel of the Eighteen-Seventies

GERALD HEARD

With an introduction by

AARON WORTH

BRITISH LIBRARY

This edition first published in 2026 by
The British Library
96 Euston Road
London NW1 2DB
bl.uk

1 3 5 7 9 10 8 6 4 2

The Black Fox was first published in 1950 by Cassell and Co., London.

Represented in the EU by Authorised Rep Compliance Ltd., Ground Floor, 71 Lower Baggot Street, Dublin, D02 P593, Ireland. arccompliance.com

Cataloguing in Publication Data
A catalogue record for this publication is available from the British Library

ISBN 978 0 7123 6905 3
e-ISBN 978 0 7123 6275 7

Image on page 6: Gerald Heard, circa 1960. Courtesy of the Estate of Gerald Heard.

Cover and frontispiece design by Mauricio Villamayor
with illustration by Mag Ruhig
Text design and typesetting by Tetragon, London
Printed in England by CPI Group (UK) Ltd, Croydon, CR0 4YY

CONTENTS

INTRODUCTION

The Black Fox, the brilliant polymath Gerald Heard's final novel, has a reputation among aficionados of the macabre as The Ghost Novel M. R. James Never Wrote.

It certainly has all the ingredients one might expect to find in such a tantalising counterfactual text: a fictitious cathedral close in late-Victorian England; a clergyman-scholar lusting for preferment; an experiment in black magic that awakens an ancient curse; an occult retribution which unfolds with the slow, creeping inevitability of nightmare, conveyed or heralded by a slinking animal Nemesis. Indeed, this particular constellation of narrative elements points especially to a specific tale, as Rosemary Pardoe hints in calling the book a 'superb Jamesian novel of the "Stalls of Barchester Cathedral" type'. And anyone familiar with James's seminal 1910 story (with its ambiguously feline rather than vulpine creature) will likely agree that Heard borrowed from it much of the underlying scaffolding for his novel. Nor can it be a coincidence that both authors give their clerical central character a sister-companion called L(a)etitia. Nonetheless, and even taking into account the fact that Heard's best-known novel (*A Taste for Honey*) and its two sequels are Sherlock Holmes pastiches, *The Black Fox* is not simply, or at least not solely, an exercise in Monty-Jamesian pastiche. The late anthologist Hugh Lamb called the book 'almost, but not quite, M. R. James at novel length'. This isn't necessarily a criticism. For while *The Black Fox* certainly has enough of a 'ghosts and scholars' vibe to scratch that Jamesian itch, it also has other qualities—they might be called

'Heardian'—that give the novel its own unique character, meriting its own special place within the canon of the Weird.

'Unique character' is the epithet *juste* for its author as well. Heard is one of those figures who, while all but entirely forgotten today, was to his contemporaries a central, even indispensable, part of the cultural conversation—a major player in the intellectual debates and discussions of his day; and this despite, or perhaps because of, the restless, protean catholicity of his interests, mirroring his own transformations throughout his life: from an interwar version of David Attenborough or Bill Nye, to influential cultural and social prophet, to bestselling mystery novelist, to charismatic New Age guru and early psychonaut who championed LSD as a 'sacramental' doorway to other realms. Born in South Hackney, London in October 1889 (a decade or so after the events chronicled in *The Black Fox*), Henry FitzGerald Heard, also known as Gerald, was both son and grandson to (Irish) Church-of-England ministers of strongly evangelical bent. He meant, or was meant, to have followed in their footsteps, but he only got as far as their alma mater (Cambridge, where a portion of the novel is set), where his faith, or at least his attachment to orthodox religion, faltered and fell. An old, old story, of course; it's as if young Gerald were belatedly living out one of the 'faith and doubt' novels so popular in the Victorian age. Yet in the end he did not so much lose his religious impulses as redirect them into different channels; as the *Dictionary of National Biography* puts it, 'his subsequent career as a peripatetic mystical preacher may be viewed as the fulfilment of his spiritual vocation'.

In his thirties Heard lectured on various topics and began to write seriously, mostly for periodicals. And while he does not seem to have made much of a splash with the general public in these early years, the fact that he was tapped to contribute a volume to the celebrated 'To-Day and To-morrow' series of speculative essays published by Kegan Paul suggests that the right people had already identified Heard as an embryonic public intellectual, a thinker to be taken seriously. Accordingly, his first book, *Narcissus: An Anatomy of Clothes* (1924) took its place alongside texts by such heavyweights as Bertrand Russell, J. B. S. Haldane, Robert Graves, and Vera Brittain. But it was in the following decade that Heard emerged fully onto the public stage, as a science commentator for the nascent BBC—the first such figure, and one of the most popular and prolific ones in its history. Heard was able to distil a host of wide-ranging topics for a large general audience, including (in the words of Heard scholar Alison Falby) 'telescopes and refrigerators; pituitary and thyroid glands; radiation and seismology; ophthalmology and bacteriology', and became, Falby tells us, 'virtually synonymous with popular science broadcasting'. H. G. Wells, whose early scientific romances Heard had devoured as a child (and to whom he would be frequently compared by critics in later years), confessed that Heard was 'the only man I ever listen to on the wireless. He makes human life come alive.'

Heard stopped broadcasting in 1934, but his writing pace only accelerated. A relentlessly interdisciplinary thinker (his close friend Aldous Huxley called him 'that rare being—a learned man who makes his mental home on the vacant spaces between the pigeon-holes'), Heard churned out a steady stream of intellectually ambitious non-fiction books on topics including psychology, evolutionary biology, spirituality, sexuality (*Pain, Sex and Time* is a title for the ages), and speculative science, as in his late book *Is Another World Watching?: The Riddle of the Flying Saucers*. In 1937 Heard migrated, with his partner Christopher Wood, as well as Huxley and his family, to the USA, settling permanently in Southern California, where he would live until his death in 1971. In retrospect the move seems inevitable: where else, at that moment in history, could he have reinvented himself as a countercultural psychedelic advocate and self-help guru; as (in Falby's words) 'conservative religious prophet [and] gay spiritual leader', all at once?

In the 1940s, Heard turned to fiction writing, producing, in the course of a decade, a quartet of successful mystery novels (the above-mentioned *A Taste for Honey*, admired by such readers as Vladimir Nabokov and Raymond Chandler, is considered a classic of the genre, if an idiosyncratic one), the dystopian science fiction novel *Doppelgangers*, and two collections of strange stories, *The Great Fog and Other Weird Tales* (1944) and *The Lost Cavern and Other Tales of the Fantastic* (1948). On the strength of the first of these collections Vincent Starrett heralded Heard as 'A New Master' of speculative fiction, one who 'plays as daringly with the test tubes of science as did the early H. G. Wells', adding, 'The title story is a remarkable fable for our times.' (For those interested, this apocalyptic tale of mould-induced climate change can be found in the British Library Publishing anthology *Spores of Doom: Dank Tales of the Fungal Weird*.) At their best, these stories succeed on multiple levels—intellectual or philosophical as well as emotional—at once, developing ingenious conceits which unfold within an atmosphere of steadily mounting dread. Reviewing *The Lost Cavern and Other Tales of the Fantastic*, literary critic Robert Gorham Davis wrote of the typical Heard protagonist: 'Sooner or later, on some dark night in a village lane or a deserted Norman chapel, he becomes aware of a Presence breaking through an "awful rent in the safe net and curtain of the everyday world." This Presence is not only terrifying in the usual ghostly, Gothic way. Its terrors are also of the soul. It gives mind-shattering evidence of the spiritual warfare which underlies creation and of which material reality is merely the symptom or consequence.'

These words apply equally well to *The Black Fox*, which was first published in 1950 and was positively, if not perhaps quite as widely, reviewed. Anthony Boucher, who considered Heard 'a writer as unclassifiable as he is entrancing', declared it to be 'Literarily and spiritually, the outstanding supernatural novel of at least the past decade.' Both adverbial modifiers, I think, are important. 'Literarily' would seem to pick out the same qualities for which *The New York Times* also praised the novel, albeit in a 'caviar to the general' kind of way: '"The Black Fox" will never be a best seller. But for those who like to sip of subtlety in style, wit and idea... it will prove to be a gracious vintage.' There is, to begin with, its impressively scrupulous reconstruction of a vanished time and place: from the novel's first page we are plunged into a Trollopian world of surplices and lawn sleeves, vergers and choristers, and above all Canons and Archdeacons and Bishops (and their female adjuncts) jockeying for position and prestige within a highly stratified ecclesiastical hierarchy (a world that Heard, descended from Victorian clergymen, depicts as a claustrophobic, paranoid terrarium, a panoptic and panaural space where any action might be overseen, any stray word overheard). Unashamedly (shamelessly?) 'literary', too, are the novel's stylistic flights and frolics, its baroque tropes and descriptions, and its Jamesian (Henry—not Monty—this time) parsing of shades of feeling and thought. Then there are its countless intertextual connections, both real and fictitious (Heard's metafictional

Travels of Ibn-Barnuna suggests a mash-up of Jorge Luis Borges and H. P. Lovecraft's *Necronomicon* by way of the historical writings of Ibn Battuta).

Some readers will appreciate these elements of the novel. (Some of us even enjoy the chapter featuring a fez-wearing Disraeli.) Others may find themselves growing impatient during the slow-burn early chapters: with the mannered prose, the recondite allusions and quotations, the characters' sallies of intrusively ingenious wit. To this second group I would say: persevere. And I think you will find that the tone and style of the first part of the novel are deliberate, tactical choices on Heard's part, calculated to intensify, through contrast, the existential horror of the obscene Thing which Throcton has summoned, when it finally comes for him. Implacable as one of the demonic familiars in Sheridan Le Fanu's 'The Watcher' or 'Green Tea', as suppurating with rank corruption as anything in Arthur Machen, the entity represents a horror that is moral and spiritual as well as physical. And here is where the second of Boucher's modifiers, 'spiritually', comes into play. For ultimately *The Black Fox* is not only a tale of occult experimentation and its consequences, of transgression and punishment. It is also a story of repentance and redemption, of expiation and selfless sacrifice, and of the triumph of good over evil (its sympathetic treatment of Islamic mysticism, rooted in Heard's own religious studies, is one of the novel's more striking features). It is an impressive achievement, and a testament to Gerald Heard's singular vision. For all its borrowings from other classic weirdists, I think it is fair to say that, in the tradition of supernatural fiction, it occupies a place all its own.

AARON WORTH

AARON WORTH is professor of Rhetoric at Boston University. For the Tales of the Weird series he has edited *The Night Wire*, *Out of the Past* and *Spores of Doom*, as well as introducing the neglected classics *Randalls Round* (Eleanor Scott) and *Medusa* (E. H. Visiak). He is also the author of *Imperial Media*, a study of how advances in media and technology shaped the British literary imagination in the late nineteenth century.

A NOTE FROM THE PUBLISHER

The original stories reprinted in the British Library Tales of the Weird series were written and published in a period ranging across the nineteenth and twentieth centuries. There are many elements of these stories which continue to entertain modern readers; however, in some cases there are also uses of language, instances of stereotyping and some attitudes expressed by narrators or characters which may not be endorsed by the publishing standards of today. We acknowledge therefore that some elements in the stories selected for reprinting may continue to make uncomfortable reading for some of our audience. With this series British Library Publishing aims to offer a new readership a chance to read some of the rare material of the British Library's collections in an affordable paperback format, to enjoy their merits and to look back into the worlds of the past two centuries as portrayed by their writers. It is not possible to separate these stories from the history of their writing and therefore the following novel is presented as it was originally published with minor edits only, made for consistency of style and sense. We welcome feedback from our readers, which can be sent to the following address:

British Library Publishing
The British Library
96 Euston Road
London, NW1 2DB
United Kingdom

To J. M. B.

CHAPTER ONE

'Ah, Canon, you too are taking a turn.'

'Yes, My Lord, I thought I might make a little draught without adding to my own temperature.'

'A nice art on a night like this!'

'Well, the air in my house seemed to have become another element or, shall I say, a gas non-luminous but of sufficient heat that one is surprised that it does not glow.'

'A Miltonic notion of Hell! But, really, I do not recall ever experiencing a more suffocating night. And were we not of what friend Trollope calls The Cloth, I'd wager that the atmosphere in the Palace is still more dense than that in your residence. You know what a wag once said of this environment—"The city is the sink of the countryside, the Close of the city and the Palace of the Close."'

'We are certain to have a storm to-night?'

The answer came in a sudden flicker on the blackness. The two speakers were silent, listening. They even stopped their slow promenade. They had to wait for a considerable time, and then their ears in the stillness only just caught the growling confirmation that the flicker had been the reflection of a flash.

'Well, that shows,' the first voice continued, 'that it is still under the horizon. We shall have no relief for hours. I certainly shall not insult sleep by lying down under my baking leads and asking it to accompany me. A turn or two here, and then, perhaps, if one sits somewhere in the Close a little rest may be won even if slumber cannot be wooed.'

'Your prescription is so sound, may I follow you in your dispensing of it?' Evidently assent was given—at least leave was not refused. For the two pairs of feet could be heard in slow step pacing out the flagstones. The dark was not absolute for somewhere outside the Cathedral Close gate, the faint light of street lamps made the upper stories of the surrounding houses appear like an almost transparent over-painting of grey against the sky's dense black. The two walkers could just tell that they were on the pavement and each be aware of the form of the other looming beside him. It was probably this protective darkness, this intimacy and yet seclusion, even from each other, that gave the second speaker a certain boldness. They had made hardly more than half a dozen of their slow turns, when he remarked:

'The Archdeacon's indisposition seems to have proved stubborn?'

The curious condition of the night—giving, as it did, a double sense of being alone out in unobserved space and at the same time closeted in an intimate privacy, had evidently much the same effect on Bishop as on Canon. Bishop Bendwell was known to be what the Book of Common Prayer likes to call—it is one of its highest terms of commendation—'a discreet man.' He knew how to mind his own business and to see that others respected that frontier. But now it seemed to him that there was no reason for not sharing what the doctor had told him that noon. Accustomed to sleep well, to use most of the night for that useful if mysterious exercise, and able to forget his dreams the moment he woke, such a man, the more capable he is in his day, the more he should guard himself when awake in the night. For the night can enforce its rules even on those who feel that by wakeful watchfulness they can remain creatures only subject to the laws and reasons of the day.

'All too stubborn, I fear,' he replied. And when the other asked, more definitely, 'I trust his condition does not give rise to any alarm?' he repeated verbatim the doctor's verdict. 'He may linger for a couple of months—he might still be alive at Advent—but that would be the limit.'

'Poor man, poor man.' The Canon's voice, of course, even in the day-time, would not be expected to show more than courtesy condolence. The Archdeacon was almost over-full of years. There can't be preferment without predeceasement and, after all, there is Heaven. Even Purgatory, thought the Canon, has been conveniently removed from the spiritual prospect of Protestants. So there was not the slightest reason for not wishing the failing '*bon voyage*.' Archdeacon Travers had enjoyed, even to that four-score years which the Psalmist thought could only be 'labour and sorrow,' a nice taste for Greek, a fine library to sustain that taste, a considerable ear for music and an equally sober appreciation of port. Life had done him well at its huge and very variously garnished board. He had had a good place. And most people felt that he had given as good as he got. 'A thoroughly nice man,' nice people had been saying about him for close on sixty years. They had found little else to say—neither had even the not thoroughly nice. Yes, things had cancelled out quite well, and well—everyone now felt, without impatience but with no wish for delay, that a thoroughly quiet death would be nicely in keeping with such a life.

The in-step pairs of feet beat out another couple of turns before the Canon's voice closed the Travers's career with 'A thoroughly nice man.' The Bishop antiphoned and the Canon felt the chance had come for a more intimate condolence that could lead to further confidence. 'The real burden falls on you. These choices must indeed be part of your heavy burden that you would most gladly lay aside!' It was a bold thing to say, of course, but the unique conditions of the night seemed heaven-sent. They also made their hearer's defences relax. Few people really object to being sympathised with. But, as with flattery, the object of it must be sure that he is not being fooled.

'There will be time to think it over,' the Bishop replied warily. 'Of course the doctor may be right—perhaps we should presume it. But after all with men who have lived long and quietly, death seems to approach them with an equal patience. There's an old country saying! "Long in living, long in dying." Here, in the Close, we generally have a couple of examples of that—the Dean for instance. He certainly isn't dying but like a clear evening sun he is declining. "Sufficient unto the day..."' He paused and then added 'But, you are right, these are the real burdens of high office.' 'And,' the voice beside him added, 'With the highest quality of conscientiousness, the longer the choice has to be considered, really the greater the strain.'

The 'True' with which this was allowed encouraged a further test, 'Especially when so many people will expect an appointment that one with really intimate knowledge might feel compelled to disappoint.'

The footsteps became slower, then paused. The Bishop's dim large form was bent back. Apparently he was looking up at the wall of the house that skirted the footpath on which they were walking. 'You are right,' he finally conceded, having evidently decided to go on with the issue. His voice sank. 'I must bind you to the strictest confidence. I have long suspected that you realised the situation which was bound to arise, sooner or later.' He paused again... 'Everyone will expect me to appoint Canon Throcton. I had not intended to raise the matter with you, but the doctor's news to-day and our meeting here to-night... Well, I need not wish to disguise from you that only two people are, as is said, in the running for the post—the scholar outside whose house we are now, and yourself. I need hardly say that you must realise how important it is that no one should suspect that we have even discussed the issue. It must reach no other ears!'

'I assure you it will not,' Canon Simpkins gave his word with solemn and indeed grateful expectancy, and certainly with every reason for keeping it. But he was answering for more than he could command or know. The wall, under whose side they walked, was tall and blind. None of the windows of this Canon-Residentiary house gave onto this quiet footpath that linked up one part of the Close with another. But not all of this high unbroken wall was that of the house itself. The house wall had been carried on to make, without break, the wall of the house's garden. And on that dark suffocating night, another of the Cathedral body had not been able to sleep. He was sitting silent in his garden without a light, sitting precisely on the opposite side of this high wall. In the stillness and with the smooth stone to carry every sound, he could hear the conversation as clearly as the two speakers heard each other. Like that ancient sound-trap, 'The Ear of Dionysius,' that prison quarry in which the Syracusan tyrant kept his prisoners so that, overhearing their words, he might have evidence to execute them, these high garden walls conducted every word spoken in the lane without, to anyone sitting within.

'Canon Throcton,' the Bishop continued with the quiet relief with which we break a long-kept self-confidence, 'is a scholar of which any Chapter might well be proud...' The Canon beside the Bishop cleared his throat with a slight expectancy making at the same time a conventional assent. The Canon the other side of the wall smiled in the dark a smile that if he had seen it in a mirror might have caused him as well as his unsuspecting colleagues some little misgiving.

'But even scholarship can be excessive and nowadays office can no more go to the pure researcher than to the purest of blue blood. And yet, and yet he will be expected to be the next Archdeacon. I wish people realised how little power the man at the top has. Frankly I would like you for the post. Social conscience and practical administrative capacity are what are needed to-day. But I don't know that we really can go against what is, you might say, "in the succession." I trust that if the social conditions of the diocese make it advisable for me to fall in with what is expected you will understand it is due to my desire to meet everyone's wishes and not to override general feeling.'

There was a pause, the two men had stopped walking. The third on the other side of the wall had risen, the better to catch every word as it came over. Obviously, Canon Simpkins felt the moment had come when he must not accept defeat with victory still in the balance. His voice when he spoke was steady, reasonable, detached.

'I know you will realise how difficult it is to be frank when oneself is a party involved. But now you have spoken to me I feel in honour bound to tell you that, whether or no you should feel it wise to choose me for the post, Canon Throcton is not the man who could be to you with the diocese what an Archdeacon should be to his Bishop—his sheep-dog. I am not referring to his perhaps excessive scholarship. Of that it might well be said I am no judge. What I do know is that he disturbs many people's convictions. I must bear witness to the fact that he is not orthodox. This is not the time, My Lord, as you know, to play fast and loose with principles. As I have said, I am no scholar but I know my way in the theology of our Church and to that I am unwaveringly loyal.'

'Of course Anglicanism being the *via media* does allow of a certain latitude.' The Bishop was speaking in almost a questioning voice. He had often escaped from such issues by pleading that he was too busy for controversy.

'And no one would support that more than myself, than ourselves if I may say so,' Canon Simpkins answered. 'But you know Canon Throcton's speciality?'

'Hebrew, I thought?'

'And Arabic—indeed one might say that the Hebrew was merely a bridge to the Arabic. He is, as Aquinas would have said, a better Arabian than a Christian.' There was another and even longer pause. Then the Bishop's voice said slowly but with perhaps a shadow of relief in it, 'I think we must pursue this further. This is an aspect to which I see I have not given sufficient weight. Come, let's go down and sit by the Cathedral lawn. Out in the open there may be a breath more air. This wall seems positively to absorb what little air there is, as pumice soaks water.'

'Certainly, certainly. As I was saying, considerably more of an Arabian than a Christian.' And the feet moved off to the silence of the lawn. At the other side of the wall the standing figure whispered to itself, 'More of an Arabian than a Christian! Well, if that is Christianity thank God I am!' Muslim or Christian might however have felt a doubt as to what God had been addressed, when a moment after the same whisper continued, 'If ever I forgive that cunning snake... if ever I get a chance...' But at that moment there came from the horizon a sudden flicker like a signal. He paused, and while waiting, there came a roll of thunder sufficiently dramatic that with a shamefaced smile he made for the house. When, however, he had reached his study and turned up the blue point of the gas-jet till the room was lit, sleep still appeared as out of the question. True the air was already cooler but the storm, which was already driving a wind before it, had taken over from the stagnant air the task of sleep-banisher.

'I'll read', he remarked to himself. 'Thunder won't distract me. Better keep up my Arabic. They say I'm nothing but a Saracen. Very well, it's clear I can hope for no preferment in the Church. So I'd better keep up my linguistic studies. Perhaps one of the Universities might yet give me a Chair.'

He looked along his densely populated shelves. The Sufis? Junaid, Al Gazali, Rumi? They were the best and the least orthodox! 'It's too late though for even the most poetic and least dogmatic of theologians. Ah,' his eye had lit on The Travels of Ibn Barnuna. 'That's the book to calm the mind. The blind anger of the elements, the equally stupid malice of man, he can take one away from both. A man who globetrotted half a millennium ago through cities that are now dust heaps; and adventures that are now only exciting in his ruminative prose. Yes, that's my medicine.'

Like most highly-trained linguists in a little-known tongue Canon Throcton was a deliberate self-talker. The reader was soon engrossed. As the storm rose above, all its distractive power was spent in vain, at least in this room. Indeed as it reached its peak of violence, so that through the curtains came flashes bright enough to compete with the gas-light, the Canon seemed to become roused from easy distractive reading to real study. He reached out to his desk, took a pencil and jotted down some page notes. At last, as the sudden glares and roars grew more distant, the reader rose, stretched himself, more like one who has been asleep than in vigil, put away the volume, lit a candle and left for bed.

CHAPTER TWO

The following morning a certain abstractness might easily be excused. The day was fresh and sunny but those who had gone through a night that first suffocated and then stormed could hardly be expected to show an equal resilience. Canon Throcton was no longer of the age of which a shining morning face can be expected. The surface was what photographers call matt, the profile handsome without being good-looking. The nose was a little too large but so little that it looked commanding: the eyes on the small side, yet so slightly that they appeared shrewd rather than suspicious. And this morning both nose and eye showed signs of the late weather, the one a little more bent and the other a trifle more drooped. Miss Throcton, who presided over the Residence, observed these past-weather signals as indicating her brother's need for silence. She had observed that need (in the observational and observant senses of that word) for fifty years and therefore had a hold upon his house that the rest of her virtues—which were considerable—might never have won her. 'We know each other below speech level,' she remarked with some finality to Canon Simpkins's wife. That lady had been employing condolence as a vehicle for inquiry—a common Trojan-horse method in the female strategy that manoeuvres across cathedral-close lawns. Miss Throcton added as a quietus—for the condolence was on the grounds that too much silence was really worse than too much speech—that she was an unwavering upholder of the gold-standard.

Her brother, however, after speaking no more at table than courtesy and family prayers prescribed, when he gained the shelter of his study became more communicative to himself than he had been last night, carrying on his concern a further step. The weather's recovery, too, was echoed in his whisperings.

'Of course, the Bishop was simply being cautious, letting libel have its lip and pretending for peace' sake to agree. Bendwell doesn't belie his name! That pompous bulk is at heart, if not soft, wonderfully supple. He spoke the truth, too! he just can't go against public opinion. *The Times* would give him a flick of its whip if he dared to appoint such an...' He paused and changed just below speech-level 'oaf' into 'anomaly'... 'as Simpkins. All I have to do is to be a little more punctilious at matins and evensong and put a slightly more precise and narrow an accent into the theology of my sermons, for the next quarter. That should not be too severe a strain and I have now an added incentive—what does Rumi say? "He to whom Allah discloses the designs of his enemies, by this revelation does the Most High reveal His intention to scatter their machinations".'

Nevertheless the Canon had made a triple misreading of the situation. He was wrong in his application of Rumi's general remark to his particular case. For he was wrong in his estimate of his Bishop's action. And what added an intolerable sting to the matter was that he was wrong also about public opinion. The injury seemed doubly intolerable when he saw the clerical and congregational equanimity in the face of the new appointment. Practically no comment was made when it was announced that the next archdeacon would be Canon Simpkins. Indeed, the Bishop showed now his complete indifference to seemliness by remarking to Canon Throcton that, naturally, his scholarship demanded freedom from all administrative cares. Further, this shepherd of shepherds so ill-read the countenance of his sub-pastor that, after such a left-handed compliment, he remarked, to Simpkins: 'Though Throcton may have desired the small step in preferment, it is fortunately clear that he can accept his passing over for a more practical man with the philosophic detachment of the scholar when he might have lacked the true resignation of a Christian. Perhaps also the fact that the public have accepted this solution as the right one, weighs with him.'

Whether there might have been still another reason did not occur to either of the speakers. That was not surprising for the disappointed man certainly did not communicate it even to his closest relation. He asked no sympathy from his sister. Partly because it seemed to offer one of those rare opportunities when she might dispense herself from the self-denying ordinance, which was more her defence in public than her comfort at home, partly because she not unnaturally felt some clan resentment (Mrs. Simpkins would now in Cathedral society take precedence), Miss Throcton told her brother, 'It was a shame.'

'Put not your trust in Princes, nor in any child of man.' His reply from one of the more worn liturgical antiphons did strike her as being sufficiently out of character to send her back into her silence. One of the few religious confidences which he had ever reposed in her concerned what he called the gross overuse of the psalter. 'One hundred and fifty psalms of very mixed morality and many of minor, yes, even minimal, poetry—why, even the few which are masterpieces could not sustain the incessant careless traffic of our tongues! Bad and good, savage dance of revengeful triumph, lashing vituperation, paean, lyric, threnody—they have been "cast out and trodden under foot" until, truly "there is no savour in them."

Why cannot we use some of the incomparable—I say it advisedly—poems of Rumi and Furdusi? Why Miriam and Jael when we could have Rabbia?' She had spoilt that promising philippic against the inadequacy of the Western liturgy by remarking that neither the outbursts of Moses's sister nor the praise of Heber's wife because she broke the sacred law of primitive hospitality, were part of the Psalter. He had gazed at her as Balaam had regarded his ass. Miss Throcton was far from 'dumb' but her brother was almost as far from knowing it. Concentration on books requisite to inform the mind up to the standards of high scholarship often leaves the finished scholar signally ignorant of minds whose information and insight are not bookish. The sister remembering more clearly than the brother this former event did not recall it to him. But for her own use noted the anomaly—the wise woman's rule canonised in the text 'She hid all these things in her heart'—not repressing them nor assuming as yet she could understand them, but waiting. She did not even repeat her protest of loyalty.

When left alone her brother, however, sought his usual relief of self-whispering. He was taking up and out a strain of thought that had evidently been flowing for some time. 'Fantasy is a relief. The fairy-tale has its place. The wise man is surely he who knowing all ultimate truth is myth or only to be stated so, orders his mind by distracting it from the hard fact of defeat by turning it deliberately to wishful fantasy. So we by-pass our passions.' He had actually turned to the bookcase to take out again the volume of Ibn Barnuna, when the sound of the evensong Cathedral bell interrupted him.

'They shan't think of me as an Achilles sulking in his tent.' He left his study and went toward the Cathedral pleased with his power to disguise his real feelings. Often, however, when we decide to brave things out for fear successful rivals should think us cowards, we find they test us more severely than we had assumed we should be tried. When he entered to robe in the inner clerical vestry, Canon Simpkins was already there. Of course, he should have recalled that Simpkins's quarterly term as Canon-in-Residence began this week. His becoming Archdeacon would not affect that? His unspoken question was answered by his successful rival—always a little unsettling even with a neutral acquaintance. The suspicion that another has looked into the speaker's mind is never pleasant. The whole thing was made worse by a mock friendliness. No doubt Simpkins was feeling three things: guilty, sure that his guilt was unknown to his victim, and, therefore, contemptuous. Certainly his opening would have been unhappy even if his second feeling had been sound.

'Well, well, deserting the Arabians to join us of the narrower path.' Then having shown his desire to snub, he added, 'The Bishop thinks the installation should take place on the eve of All Saints, so I shall remain as plain Canon Resident till then. After that my duties being wider may limit the time I can spare for this intramural routing.'

Had Canon Throcton not had interior knowledge of the other's duplicity no doubt he would have been startled at least into irritability. A scratch may sting intolerably: a deep cut not even be felt for the first few minutes. But now he was in the position—provided he showed no sign—of being superior to the man who was able and quite willing to show contempt for him. The other was behaving with coxcomb vanity, proud of an office because he thought his defeated rival thought that he, the winner, had won the promotion through obvious superiority. To the man with interior knowledge there was offered in consequence the more dangerously satisfying role. He might now feel, in return for the other's raillery, a contempt so deep that it could afford to be silent. The defeated could actually relish the feeling of being so alien to this fool—clumsy even in his deceitfulness, so that even if it were possible and wise he would not stoop to expose him. For exposed he might be driven to the grace of shame. The bitter delight rose from the thought of, year by year, being able to watch this fool in his hypocritical exhibition of piety and all the while naked to his foe. Without of course being aware of his condition Canon Throcton was beginning to feel that cold hate which is of all passions the most soothing, that sedative which offers its opiate as the one escape from a condition of frustrated insult which otherwise renders the proud man in danger of madness—the ultimate disgrace, in his own eyes, of nervous breakdown. The relief is so intense that recovery from such an addiction is rare: when a high fever suddenly drops, though the patient is going to die, he feels better, and so with a severe haemorrhage, there is a sense of refreshing rest. He felt suddenly calm as he turned to take his surplice. When he had pulled it over his head and arranged its folds he saw that Simpkins, who already had donned his, was now standing before a small glass rebrushing his hair which was thick, wavy, black and worn rather long. His attention was evidently wholly engaged by this and the watcher found his own unanalysed peace of mind was growing as he looked on at the grooming. He was faintly aware that he had never felt anything quite like this, some subverse of the joy that is felt by the scholar at some singular felicity of phrase. He caught a hardly focused glimpse of himself year after year collecting ever-accumulating evidence of this creature's copious invariable disgustingness. Why think of trying to get some post at one of the big universities, the great laboratories of understanding, when here, in this quiet nook, the true field-naturalist of that odd insect man, could find a species so fascinatingly repulsive. He had always felt his fellow clergy to be invariably dull—now he had found a colleague who might be worth the most devoted attention. The more he permitted this stream of unreflected thought to flow deep down the more the vague impression quieted him. He saw with something like tranquil relief that he need never—indeed, must never do anything about it. That would spoil all. The attempt to push the creature into some further absurd ineptitude might rouse it from its instinctive trance of grotesque exhibitionism. His role was that of the fully appreciative scientist, too content with his superiority even to laugh. Further, at the penumbra of his thought was the realisation that this new pleasure was to be essentially personal. He might—if he kept his secret really to himself, letting no one suspect it—go even further; rise to a higher point of contemptuous detachment than that of the lonely naturalist who has chosen as his study dung-beetles. He might become the master of this object as no naturalist can control the species he studies. He might, he felt sure with an unanalysed certainty, come, if he were patient, to control this creature's destiny, as a hypnotist controls the after-behaviour of his trance-patient. He did not feel that he was thinking these thoughts, putting them together. Rather they flowed out quietly as from some dark source, as ripples on a pool at dusk spreading out, welling up from a palely lit centre and then spreading till lost in the sedge limits of its shore. Though quiet, these thoughts must have been moving fast. The thinker felt that he had surveyed years, but he saw with his eyes that the hair-brush had only been wielded for a few strokes and was now put down smartly. Hardly troubling to face his listener, Canon Simpkins remarked over his shoulder, 'I must see that the choir is ready,' and disappeared into the outer vestry. The clock showed 2.57.

Canon Throcton walked slowly down to the end of the narrow room, alongside of which were the wardrobes, at the end of which was a small table with a carafe and two glasses on an electroplated dish. Above that was a small cupboard and on its door hung the mirror. Canon Throcton, however, did not approach it to inspect his face, nor, had he done so in his present mood, would he have noticed a change in it. He swung open the door. On the shelf inside lay the hair-brush with its attendant comb. He took the brush out. Its dark stiff bristles were fringed and festooned with hairs as dark, but curly like suckers from a hedge too long unpruned. He turned the brush in his hand. 'Thick as autumnal leaves that strew the brooks in Vallombrosa'—the worn line was not apt but the falling-leaf theme evidently pleased him. Then he raised the brush nearer his face and wincing, smiled—the smell of macassar oil was as coarse as the hairs. He put the thing away, wiped his hands on a small towel and going out into the main vestry joined his colleague who was already presiding over the choir and the vergers drawn up to process. He and Simpkins walked together, dividing when they reached the stalls each entering his own on opposite sides.

The Anglican Evensong—'To be said daily through the year'—centuries of use has smoothed from a stately decorum, in which a style of perfect urbanity had from the beginning made vivid conviction somewhat unlikely, to a routine that now rendered fully-conscious attention improbable. Certainly, to a mind as profoundly concerned as Canon Throcton's had now become, the counter-appeal of the service was insignificant. Indeed, not till they all sat down to listen to the First Lesson was he aware of any words. The Lessons change (and so offer occasions for misreadings) more than any other part of this strictly confined liturgy: the Old Testament is at its strongest—and indeed almost unsurpassed in its strength, when it deals with dramatic narrative. The folk-story being retailed that afternoon—as an illustration of the epoch of Law as contrasted with that of Grace—was the curious and brutal tale of the Hebrew Hercules—a tale of magic and violence, lust and trickery, as suited for melodrama and opera as it is incongruous with ritual and worship. Liturgy can however render the human ear and mind wholly impervious to the most obvious and shocking sense. And no doubt Canon Throcton with many years of inurement and an immediate and rapidly growing obsession, would have caught nothing of the story had not in one verse the sing-song voice of the lector informed the quietly wool-gathering congregation, 'If my head be shaven then my strength will go from me.' Hardly knowing what to do, Canon Throcton glanced over to the opposite stall, only to find that its occupant was glancing away, glancing away with that hurried appearance of unconcern which tells us how near we had been to surprising another's inspection of us.

CHAPTER THREE

A Cathedral Close is in itself no protection from the atmospheric effects of autumn—quite the contrary. The climate, on its part, adjusting the balance after the intense early August heat, had become dank, and the small gothic-girt world of the four canonical residences, the deanery and the palace, illustrated the Bishop's quotation about the whole site being a sink. Spring might waken the inhabitants to a certain lively asperity and expectations of summering in the Alps; autumn could only sink them in reminiscence at best, recrimination at worst and rheumatism as a constant, middle and provocative term. Canon Throcton's short-cut hair was greying and in the darkening mornings as he shaved he saw a stubble bleaching toward hoar-frost whiteness reaped from his chin. When shaving—especially with that weapon which in his time was *de rigueur*—a Kropp hollow-ground razor—the skill of hand and steadiness of outward attention let free, he had often noticed a clear thaw of reverie. The deepest emotional layer would rise at that time and almost, one could imagine, would stand, like the uncanny 'Red Cap Sly' of the sinister Ring Stone Ballad, at one's shoulder and almost in the corner of one's vision. Of course, one could not look it straight in the eye, and so make it vanish. For to do that, he would have to take his eye off the sweeping stroke of the flat-laid blade and that would be penalised by a neat but free bleeding line. 'Satire should, like a razor bright and keen, wound with an edge that's scarcely felt or seen.' He could not resist ever so slightly yielding to his habit to mouth the line and, sure enough, a moment after, a fine line of crimson showed where the razor's last stroke had swept away the white foam and the almost as white stubble. The faint sting of the fine wound a moment after confirmed his eye. Vexation spread like a small haemorrhage over his mood. It might take a week to heal and for a day or two he'd have to wear a silly little dab of cotton wool on it. 'I care for my appearance,' he muttered to himself as he dabbed the spot very uninclined to be staunched, 'As though I were that greasy, ignorant, crooked fop...' He checked himself and swivelled his eye round the mirror's field. It was physically safe now to do that, and indeed almost a mental necessity, so external had seemed the malignancy of the hatred. Simpkins was a fool, yes, and a knave, too. But one's privilege and pleasure was not to rage at such a creature—his role was to watch the jackanapes while it was blindly unaware that it was eyed and known by the one person it would be most anxious should never know. Really it was Hawthorne's *Scarlet Letter* all over again. Then reflecting (as he went on dabbing) that that story hardly showed the wronged man, who took his revenge by being an onlooker, in a pleasant light, Canon Throcton in his 'voluntary' modulated into self-pity. He was getting old—the quick scarring and slow healing of his skin proved that. And he had nothing to look forward to, because his rightful advance had been barred by a mean, greasy little rat. Again he was so shaken by the over-boiling of his rage that he could hardly believe that the scalding jet of it was not striking him from an external source. 'I mustn't live so much in reverie,' he counselled himself as he adjusted a final patch of cotton. 'I'm a lonely man,' self-commiseration again turning his major anger into a minor key. 'Well, all the more need for objectivity,' he summed up.

The Calendar caught his eye, as he turned round to finish his dressing. It hung on the wall to mark the terms in which he was specifically 'in Residence' and so responsible for presiding over the Cathedral duo-diurnal services and any other days—such as preaching dates—which were 'of obligation.' He had had none of the latter lately: the former would not start till the New Year. Since the last unhappy attempt not to be accused of 'sulking in his tent' he had not felt equal to facing Simpkins's smug superciliousness, however much he had thought he was certain of his own superiority. 'I might,' he sanctioned his withdrawal, 'be startled into telling him the truth.' As both his judgment as an obvious gentleman and his passion as a repressed hater confirmed this advice it was naturally taken. So the days had gone as they do, slowly each to each because of their monotony but for the same reason when looked back upon with uncanny speed. He gazed at the Calendar, that oblong of numbers headed by the seven pagan names, and then realised where temporally he was. The Installation would be at evensong to-day. As he settled down to breakfast, his sister, breaking the silence with the same words, showed that she too felt that further avoidance was impossible. She was relieved, if the relief had in it a cast of surprise, when he replied. Though a quotation, it was both apt and objective—indeed almost humorous. 'And the days of mourning being accomplished then shall the mourner anoint and tyre himself and go forth again among men. You see I have complied to the date and the letter,' and he pointed to his cotton-dabbed cheek, adding, 'The usual accompanying smile is pretermitted in the hope of discouraging further cutaneous haemorrhage.' Miss Throcton felt her surface relief spread at the obvious gaiety while being aware of an almost disquieting doubt as to its cause. There was something in her brother's tone of voice that did seem to say that not smiling was not at all difficult.

Throughout the service, however, Canon Throcton felt a certain gladness due to a feeling that was odd but curiously pleasant—he felt quietly numb. True, the dark end of the cold last day of the wettest month of the year was chilling enough in all conscience, in the vast dank gloom of the huge weatherworn archaeological fossil in which these few survivors kept on their minimal service. But the numb that the Canon felt was not physical, though it had about it the relief with which we feel a nerve anaesthetised by an injection. To say that he didn't seem to be wholly present would itself have been only half the odd truth. He felt himself, he realised, present in space, in the Cathedral. It was about time that he found he had doubts, coldly pleasant ones—the date, that seemed quite irrelevant. Yet he did not seem to be present in any other alternative date. Time itself did not seem properly important, the ordinary unquestioned importance and supremacy of the present—and Canon Throcton was proud of his punctuality—was somehow reduced to a commonalty with past and future. Hence, he found he could amuse himself by perceiving a moment or two before it became actual what was about to happen. He felt in the dusk of the vestry as if the Bishop had always and would always be saying, 'Just like a small family...' Indeed, before the sentence rolled out in its slow boom he had completed it in his own mind... 'Met together for a birthday party of their youngest,' and the throat episcopal followed the prescient dictate of his foreseeing mind. So he was equally prepared for Simpkins's smirk and small spatter of sub-sarcasms. Even the happy sally that his cotton-wool whisker was a budding if premature tribute to St. Nicholas, did not stir the slightest resentment for he was already waiting to hear the moderately nasal snigger continue, 'Of course, you have been away from our dull routine, lost amid the Arabian alembicks and astrolabes, studying another calendar and alien feasts.' He even took the conclusion of the sentence out of his satirist's lips by replying, 'So, you would repeat that, as you are now to be out and about our father-in-God's wider business, I should now aid properly in the domestic duties.'

He did not even smile frostily at the new Archdeacon's look—half childish disappointment at the aborted boast, half nervous surprise. Indeed, Simpkins was sufficiently disconcerted to turn nervously to the small mirror-faced cabinet and picking out the brush from behind it, to give a touch or two to his coiffure. Perhaps the flourished surplice sleeve and the brush disturbed some dust—there was certainly enough about. Suddenly he gasped, fumbled in his robes, just in time dragged out a large pocket handkerchief, and into its crumpled mass discharged a sneeze that shook even his compacted curls. A second and a third explosion followed, leaving the sneezer gasping but with the offending particle of dust evidently discharged. He fumbled to replace under his surplice the handkerchief which had had to face and contain the three charges. Feeling a not displeasing disgust, Throcton turned away to don surplice, hood and scarf. Once more his interest had started outrunning the present and glancing at the future, as sight-seers run ahead of a procession so as to see it pass some particular street corner. And again he was able to produce for his private pleasure five-second-ahead prophecies. He whispered under his breath, in front of the Bishop's confirmatory boom. 'Come along, Archdeacon. The Dean, you know, can't be here. Gout again—it sounds like Dickens. But it's the real thing and hurts, well like what Catholics believe about Purgatory. I must see that everyone knows his position. Quite a time since an instalment. Never neglect detail: see to it yourself. Canon, follow us as soon as you are robed. The two juniors are already with the choir. Special Lesson...'

The Chief Shepherd, pushing his new sheep-dog before him, went through the door dividing the shepherd's retiring room from that of their singing sheep. As the linen and lawn enlarged figures left the inner room vacant and silent, for a moment the one left to himself found his mind blank. The next sentence, which he had been reading one line ahead, that dialogue sound-track, was vacant. Then his attention was caught by the hair-brush that had been left lying by the drinking glasses. A shudder of disgust, as strong as a rigor, shook him. He went over and lifted the object. The disgust rose to nausea, as almost under an external compulsion he touched the tangle of black hairs that now matted the bristles making a loose web in their stiff woof. It was with the relief that a sleeper feels a nightmare being broken by a noise in the house, that he heard the Bishop's boom, 'Canon Throcton, Canon Throcton.' Putting the brush into its place behind the mirror he hurried out, was quickly marshalled and the processional rite began. Again he found that he could not bring himself to attend to the words, but played instead the game of petty prevision—'Now the organist will cough: now the litany clerk's wife will sneeze.' This time, then, it was not at the First Lesson but not till the second that he suddenly found himself back at present-minded attention. The words that had roused him seemed to be the middle of a sentence and insignificant, if not quite senseless, 'Paul, having shorn his head, for he had a vow.' Again he looked up blindly aware of attention. Again he found that he had been a moment too late. The now fully-installed Archdeacon was examining with an interest more archaeological then religious—considering the time—the carving of his stall's canopy.

The rest of the service, Canon Throcton's mind spent wondering what was going to happen when it was over. When he tried to stretch his previsionary insight that far he could observe that it refused to work. Then his mind turned to consider his emotional state. He had heard that men severely disappointed or overstrained could get heart attacks or chronic indigestion. But it was really ridiculous for a sound scholar left to exercise his gift, to let a petty piece of caddishness not merely sour his temper but actually disturb, yes, addle his mind! Like all intellectuals, this fine linguist could hardly bring himself to believe that his emotions might not obey rational instruction. None the less it was his automatic reflexes that took his body safely and in seemly movement back again into the vestry. It was almost the same level of consciousness that, with the proper tone and the right excuse—the one which he had not called up and the other that he could not recall—extricated him from the Bishop's quite kindly invitation that they should all warm themselves before the big fire in the Palace hall with a cup of tea. Again the same levels evidently ordered that he should disrobe so slowly that by the time he was again in his outdoor clothes he found he was alone. He could just hear the sub-verger pacing about in the transept waiting to lock up when he should come out. Then his surface consciousness came back with the same unpleasant vividness that it had had, when, half an hour before, he had last been alone in this narrow, dingy, dim room. He felt at the same time the rising revulsion and compulsion—the drive that sent him across to the dirty little cabinet and the closing of his throat that was almost a retch. The brush was now in his hands. He raised it till he could see the flakes and clotted specks of dandruff and smell the blend of the cheap scented macassar oil and stale perspiration. Then he seized the comb—itself a small laocoon with the coils of hair that had wound round its prongs—and curried strongly the brush's bristles. The comb became nearly choked. He threw the brush back onto its shelf and with a piece of paper drew off most of the tangled hair that he had reaped. Dropping this on the table he peered again into the cupboard. In a corner he discovered a small bottle of the hair oil. The dust had made a kind of mud round where drops had spilt down the neck. He put the bottle on the table by the piece of paper and investigated again. This time, in the very corner of the shelf (it must have been hidden behind the bottle) he found a small screw of soiled tissue paper. Untwisting this he saw with a fresh disgust a number of flakes like minute clippings of parchment. For a moment it seemed as though he would fling the whole of this routage into the wastepaper basket. Indeed, he looked under the baize-covered table to find it, but doing so his attention was distracted. He bent down further. His face, when he rose, was flushed, though the exertion had been slight. What he had retrieved was the pocket-handkerchief that had had to endure such a storm of the nasal elements, and then, when it should have been stored in its sub-surplice pouch, had fallen and evidently been kicked under the table. He held it between his thumb and finger. Disgust was clearly very strong, but some positive passion was stronger. He no longer tried to find the wastepaper basket. For a moment he hesitated, then was caught by a choking cough and with his disengaged hand put his own handkerchief to his mouth. He retched for a moment and his face went livid. Then, as though it were as natural a semi-conscious gesture as was putting his own handkerchief back into its pocket, he thrust this other handkerchief, the small wrap of combings, the little almost dried-up oil bottle and the paper twist of nail parings into one of the big side pockets of his overcoat. The last wheeze of his cough modulated into coherent whispering, 'The Dean is now all but a dotard. The Cathedral's becoming a rubbish-heap. And now we'll be ruled by an Archdeacon ignorant or contemptuous of the very rudiments of hygiene. If I leave this garbage in the wastepaper basket no doubt he would cite me before the Chapter for insubordination... trespass on his rights and the dignity of his office.'

CHAPTER FOUR

Back in his almost stately residence, kept throughout as though it were a museum-piece, his disgust abated. Without a return of the odd, fascinated revulsion he took the barber-and-laundry debris from his overcoat pocket as he hung it up in the hall and, going up to his study, threw the clotted bottle, the two twists of stained paper and the handkerchief into his big waste-paper basket. He left the room. On returning, he lifted his hands to his face. The inspection was evidently satisfying. The bell rang for tea, and his sister as she handed it to him in her sitting-room where he generally took it, noticed that he seemed less tense than for some considerable time. He even began to speak to her about his current work. 'I think during the rest of the winter I might settle down to a tractate on the Arabian Globe Trotter. Our parvenu Protestantism assumes that till the Industrial Revolution made Anglican Canons mobile, ecclesiastical scholars—save for such charming eccentrics as the eighteenth-century Bishop of Bristol—had never travelled just for geographical curiosity and not under the impetus of theological invasion.'

Perhaps, as in post-hypnotic patients, the remark was a rationalisation to explain or excuse to the patient his irrational subconscious urge, perhaps the source of the drive lay elsewhere. In any case, Canon Throcton when he regained his study certainly took the first step toward fulfilling his word. He went over to the bookcase, the shelf and volume where he had found relief when that August night his peace of mind had been so disturbed by what the unnatural stillness had allowed him to overhear, and, next, bodily rest had been rendered impossible through nature's noisiness as she had readjusted the preceding tension. Indeed, Canon Throcton was so careful to resume his reading that he first looked up the page reference he had made that inauspicious night and then, sure that he had found the place, settled down. That was the precise word. Like most accurate scholars he was never a rapid reader. Yet it was noteworthy that a quarter of an hour had been tolled off by his desk clock and loudly confirmed by the 'Westminster Chime' in the south-west cathedral tower and still he had not turned the page. It was clear that he was repeatedly reading the same passage as though he would learn it by heart. At last though he began to smile, the smile broke into a laugh and the laugh set him talking again to himself. 'Well, I could at least do something to buttress my decayed orthodoxy by rebutting the Arabian! And to do so I must not be content with words but with acts. I must prove him wrong by experiment. And to experiment I have to hand the required materia medica!'

He was silent for a moment after that. The only sound in the room, beyond the quiet lapping of the fire and the discreet clock ticking, was the small rasp as tentatively the flattened fingers of his left hand stroked his chin rough with its evening stubble. Then the laugh broke out again: but this time more peremptorily, defiantly almost:

'Well, heavens above, if really I am so absurd as to think such a farcical pretence of an experiment could have any result but a negative one, surely that shows that I ought to perform it—just to establish beyond any possibility of doubt that it is the grotesque nonsense that I know it to be. If you wake up in the night because you've dreamt too vividly that a burglar is under the bed and your one wish is to get to sleep—well, a sensible man doesn't waste time trying to argue his sleepy mind into sense—and so driving away sleep or simply bringing on again the nightmare. He settles his silliness in the quickest, most sensible way by looking under the bed and making the fool in him see that there isn't any concealed robber waiting for him to doze off again!'

The words evidently convinced him he should take some similar action. For he rose quickly and swung round, as though not quite certain that he was alone. As he stood he held the big volume against his chest, keeping his place with a finger thrust between the pages. For a moment he looked like one of those melodramatic Protestant illustrations of The Reformer Surprised and called 'The Forbidden Bible.' Then, putting the book on a small lectern by his chair he bent down by his big desk and lifting the wastepaper basket stood it on the seat from which he had just risen. His movements now were quick and methodical. His words confirmed that his mind was as clear. 'It's no use fooling with foolishness. The shortest way with a sham is to take a superstition at its own pretence. So you expose it, as you best expose a liar, not by laughing at him but by asking him quietly, seriously, to perform what he boasts. If I am to do this I must do it properly.' It was his usual whisper but delivered succinctly as some one speaks who, with a clear insight as to how a muddle may be cleared up, rearranges the data in right order. And, as though suiting the action to the word, at each sentence's close, he brought out and laid in line on the small fire-side table, that flanked his chair's other arm, the wastepaper basket's upper layer. There was no longer a trace of his former revulsion. He was tidying up a small nuisance—such as a spilt ink-bottle or an overset pin-tray. He turned to some inbuilt drawers which formed the base of the bookcases that panelled the walls. On coming back he was carrying a candle and some matches, remarking as he returned, 'If I am really sane, then I am only accountable for five foolishly wasted minutes. If, on the other hand, I am under more strain than I recognise, I am sure I do not know a better way of relaxing. When young, and before our frocks became so long that we were afraid of any gesture that might question our decorum, we used to "blow off steam" with abuse. As we are too pompous to be allowed that sensible relief—well, I must have it out here in private!'

He went over to the fire and raked it. It glowed cheerily. But the bed of incandescent coals was too well set to blaze, as, under provocation a well-nourished elderly man smiles an easy after-dinner smile when a younger would flash with resentment. The Canon stopped his stoking for a moment to listen, then crossed quietly to the door and locked it. Coming back, he scanned the rubbish lying on the small table. Released by the warmth of the newly roused fire, a whiff of the macassar oil rose to his nostrils. A flare of rage leapt up in him. 'That oily-faced hypocrite—that...' A spasm contorted his face. A moment after he smiled wryly. 'If I get so exercised it shows that I need to exorcise myself! An *auto-de-fé*, an act of faith, as the Spaniards euphemistically called cremating the living. Well, I'll perform it with my occasions of outrage. Now for what my Arabian anthropologist has to tell us.'

He began to read aloud in a low-rapid voice, '"When I was travelling on the inner border of Cathay, I found much witchcraft, or should I not say, the fear of it, lying like a fog over the countryside. Every village lived in terror of wizardry. All these distant parts being still at the very frontiers of the Faith, where, on the very boundaries of the inhabitable world, and not far from the final ocean, the

Power of Evil makes its last stand against the dawn of Allah's Light, the spear of Islam is piercing but as yet its sword does not wholly rend the shroud of Iblis. I confess that when in the cultured world of the Prophet, where the clear lamp of the Koran shines, I had often doubted whether such things could be true. And even when among these depraved creatures, I still thought that all they said was but foul imagining—the horrid wish of their darkened hearts. Falling in, however, with a learned Sufi, who had lived for years, wandering in these deserts for the sake of the Faith and the honour of his Order, he assured me that the local magicians, called Bon, commanded powers of evil now by Allah's Mercy unknown to us. They commonly and as a matter of professional traffic, practised the overthrow of their enemies, and indeed the destruction of those whom they accept payment to molest, even to death, through their skill in sorcery." Of course, that's sheer nonsense.' The Canon paused to comment on his text, 'Childish superstition as far as hurting any other person is concerned. But I see it could well be quite a sound if rather a quaint therapeutic method for destroying a grotesquely repulsive and compulsive idea that has rooted itself in one's own mind. Like as not, our poor verbal inspirationist Sufi and our charmingly credulous Ibn Barnuna mistook, when studying the superstitious and despised Chinee, an advanced psychology for an atavistic magic.' He continued to read aloud to himself, '"The general method whereby they compass their evil end is through a process of two parts. They first collect such personal fragments of their intended victim as they may secure. If they may not obtain his blood, then sputum or a seminal or menstruous cloth is much favoured. Should even these be lacking, they will make shift with skin, hair, nail-parings, or indeed any object that has been about the person of their prey. Then they wait until the moon is gibbous..."' The reader smiled, remarking, 'Well, I'm so ignorant of astronomy or astrology that I can't answer at this moment as to where or in what phase Selene may be. Indeed, am I quite sure that I could say off-hand what gibbous actually indicates—the waning moon, I rather think? Anyhow, let's get over our catharistic play. It certainly won't depend for its efficacy on precise knowledge of the lunar calendar.' He continued, '"The first night that this is so, they take their spoil, dividing it carefully into two parts. For I should say that their theory being that the citadel of man must be assaulted warily, because God has strongly defended the seat of the soul, their blind ingenuity leads them to try—and I fear full often to obtain—a first purchase on the exterior parts of their victim. They therefore put in one division anything that may have to do, or has had to do, with the external area of the body. This is generally—for it is obviously most easy to secure—some hair. And they give another reason for this, which I will set down later, and which has reason, were we to allow—as I must—the method in their madness. As I have said, then, they place in one parcel every hair they have secured and any skin, from the scalp especially".' Canon Throcton glanced sideways, touched gingerly the ranged debris, putting on one side the soiled handkerchief. While doing this his voice hardly checked in its flow of commentary: '"They take this wisp and with the aid of some aromatic gum—my informant told me that he himself had generally found them using (for which they paid highly, as they well might, considering the distance it had to be brought) the oil shipped from the city of Macassar, out of the spice island of Celebes. I say, with this gum or oil they will make out of the hair, nail-parings and such skin as they may have secured, a small object, a model, rough and miniature, of the human head. This made, they burn it, claiming that thereafter, as the moon begins to wane, so the hair of their enemy—or victim—will fall, and his scalp will become not only naked, but afflicted. Further, they assert—as above I said I would show at this point—that this, though seeming a trivial punishment, and a surface affliction, is a preliminary and essential step in their larger and implacable design. For, by destroying the hair, the vital strength of man is assaulted. And the power of the mind—which it is their ultimate intention to overthrow (and thus lead their victim to destroy himself, so flinging his own soul into Hell) cannot be struck at, until the vital strength has been undermined and sapped".' Canon Throcton ceased for a moment his recital, in order that, smiling to himself, he might whisper, 'We may be thankful that our Church has retained for us so much folk-lore through its fancy that the Old Testament is a divinely inspired collection. Why, it cannot be so many days ago that our liturgy was recalling that queer sun-myth of Samson shorn of his hirsute halo. I'm sure I recall it—a pretty illustrative coincidence.'

He shrugged his shoulders, as though already feeling more at his ease, 'Yes,' he added, a rising note of content coming into his voice, 'Yes, one knows enough of superstition to know that particular mistake. We are now on the firm and open ground of manifestly false analogy. At this pace we shall be well out of the wood by bed-time. This now is certainly nothing but subjective symbolic therapy—destroy the object associated with your irrational but not wholly unhygienic disgust, and you will find the clear, male reason once again easy master of the female, vapourish emotions.' He turned at that. Leaving the book, he snatched up the combings and taking the candle, flung it, the clot of hair and the contents of the small bottle onto the glowing bed of coals. For a moment the red flush, chilled by the new objects, went an angrier, deeper tinge. Then, with a sudden splutter, the candle wax melted, the oil caught fire, the hairs sizzled and flamed. A dense mass of oily smoke poured up. At that moment a cold draught, perhaps set in motion by throwing the objects on the fire, came down the chimney. All the soot-charged fumes poured out into the room, an impenetrable whirling fog.

The smoke-pall, striking the ceiling, spread, and began to curl down over the whole room. It sank to the level of his eyes and stung them till he could hardly keep them open, stung also his nose and throat so that he began to gasp and cough. The green-shaded colza-oil reading lamp and the low red light of the fire—the only lights in the room—glowered through the murk like the port and starboard lanterns of a ship that suddenly looms ahead running you down in a fog. Feeling almost panic, and having to choke back the impulse to shout, 'Fire! Fire!' he stumbled past his desk, ran into a table, but at last reached the window, tore aside the curtains and dragged up the sash. Outside the night was cold and clear. He looked across the quiet, wide Cathedral Close. The great lawn and the sheer front of the Cathedral's west facade were clearly enough lit. He raised his eyes to the sky. The mist of the afternoon was quite gone—there would be a frost. The moon was fairly high up and of fair size—in fact, he noticed, about three-quarters big—it would be full in a few days. Now it looked as though it were made of two convex curves. You might have fancied that it was a white vizor held by an invisible hand obliquely before an invisible head. A verse, he couldn't remember reading when or where, floated through his mind:

'That Presence which broods in the gloom of a Yew,
Or in vacant glades at the sun-soaked noon;
That unseen being that looks at us, through
The Ivory Mask of the Moon.'

'Of course,' he remarked to himself in his usual whisper, 'Of course, "gibbous" is the late second quarter. That means that in a few days it will be full—and after that waning.'

These obvious remarks seemed to settle his mind. He pulled down the window-sash and turned again to the room. The smoke had settled back almost as quickly as it had poured out. Evidently opening the window had sent a good draught up the chimney. Except for a smell of singeing and here and there a greasy spot of soot, the room appeared normal. He blew a couple of these smuts off the open pages of the Ibn Barnuna volume, closed the big book and put it on his writing desk. Then, turning to the fireplace, he somewhat hastily picked up the box of matches and put it back in the drawer where he kept such 'ignitia' as he called them. As he shut the drawer, he glanced back at his desk. He saw that the small fire-side table still had on it the dirty bottle and the soiled handkerchief. He strode back, snatched them up and, for a moment, seemed about to throw them on the quiet, glowing bed of coke that the fire had now become.

'The bottle would break in the heat and then might cut the maid's fingers. Besides, she would ask herself, Why should I be incinerating flasks? Queer gossip, specially in a place of such perfect acoustic properties as a Cathedral Close, can start up from far less significant sources.'

While this was said above them, like a committal service, both bottle and handkerchief found themselves stowed with the match-box.

Obviously, if a burnt bottle could start rumours, *a fortiori* an unburnt one accompanied by someone else's overused handkerchief, might be the fruitful seed-bed of enough suspicion to incriminate an archbishop. The drawer then being finally shut, was locked and the very key put behind a row of quartos standing sentry above. Then he went over to the door and with the other key which had guaranteed his privacy for all this psychological therapy and catharsis, he released the lock, turned quietly the handle and looked out into the passage. He felt quite strongly that he did not want anyone to know that he had locked himself in. He sniffed the air, too. He wanted to test if any of the fume had stolen out ahead to rouse olfactory suspicions. The first inhalation seemed to signal, All Clear. The second reassured him that there was no hint of burning. Thank heavens for that. 'Fire is always an excuse for suspecting smoke', he smiled to himself. He sniffed a third time. No, there wasn't a hint of anything scorched. But wasn't there a smell of some sort—a tang—a whiff of... what could it be? Ammonia? The passage was only lit by a lamp on the stairs, round the corner and hidden from where he stood. He could see however the main objects, and indeed, at the upper end near the floor he could pick out a couple of gleams given off no doubt by some facet of the well polished furniture reflecting the lamp, itself out of sight. 'Laetitia certainly has the house kept admirably' he remarked with that sudden appreciation of the manifest security given by a well-run home. Then the twin points of polish moved and a shadow behind them. He chuckled—'the cat—perhaps her keen nose suspected that I might be incinerating a mouse.'

CHAPTER FIVE

Closing the door of his study behind him he went down the passage and joined his sister in her drawing-room. He paid this last call often enough for her not to be surprised, seldom enough for her not to be unpleased. The sense of settled security, as he knew, here reached its serene table-land. He never inquired about her views or feelings but, though he did not even turn the matter over in his mind, he was aware in an uninterested way that she had grounds—of course profoundly irrational and incapable of logical expression—for her peace of mind and that these might be valid, though not for the reasons she would undoubtedly give for them if asked. So he excused himself from finding out anything more about her spirit. She was profoundly convenient and conveniences are better not tampered with. He looked at her with something approaching appreciation but he was sensibly selfish enough to stop short of admiration, for that might end in a sense of obligation. She was a picture of uncritical peace and that was enough. She was knitting, with a volume—pretty certainly of sermons—on her lap. A bright copper kettle, seated on an equally bright brass trivet, attached to a polished steel grate that held a bright well-kept fire, made a flash of warm but not vulgar colour while it hummed its simmering tune no more monotonous and far more restful, he thought, than the intoning of a minor canon. Her feet were on half a large hassock. The other half was made even more comfortable for her toes by being occupied by a large cat just not too sleepy to purr an accompaniment to the kettle.

'You look the picture of domestic peace.'

'Will you then sit with us over a last cup of tea? Tissaphernes...'—that was the cat, given, in honour of its owner, a classical Persian name—'will take hers with us, but without the China leaves to spoil the cream.'

The miniature tiger seemed to understand for it stretched, extending formidable claws. 'The cat is a savage at heart,' the Canon remarked, sitting down and taking the ball of soft fur on his lap. 'A moment ago I glanced her a-prowl round the upper wainscots for any unlucky mouse.'

'Oh, you couldn't—No, I don't mean that Tiss wouldn't rather have meat than milk. But, as it happens, she's been with me all the evening.'

'But I saw her, I'm sure...'

At that moment a violent hubbub broke out in the servants' quarters. 'Laetitia! What are they...?'

But the Canon's inquiry was answered by one of them.

'Oh, mam!' cried a domestic face pushed round the door before the knock of requested entry could be answered. 'Oh, mam... Excuse me, Sir... The Cook's had quite a turn and Carlo is beside himself.'

This was clear from such wild barkings that even Tissaphernes felt that she must put her back up at such disturbance. 'Cook says that she was just going to the pantry down by the back door, when suddenly she saw it ajar and that at that very moment, as you might say, as she had her hand on the latch, something pushed past her and ran quick into the yard and then Carlo suddenly dashed out of the kitchen and as good as took her off her feet and did take the door out of her hand and he giving tongue (if you will forgive the expression, for cook was with hunting people before she, if I may say so, come up in the world) as though he were on a breast-high scent (another word from cook's past and again I ask your pardon), and cook avers as she was with hunting people (and of that there's never a doubt) there was an, an aroma as nothing, but—it's her word not mine—but a dog-fox could give.'

The reflex narrative and its actual image began to subside together. Angry dog and loquacious maid were abating. Laetitia Throcton closed the subject and so, too, the door by making the head withdraw, dismissing it with, 'The incident might well have waited till my visit to your quarters to-morrow morning. Goodnight, Kate. Remember, put Carlo on the chair.' Tissaphernes' fur tippet sank to its proper proportions. The Canon said nothing until his sister handed him his cup. Before tasting it, he paid the tea the compliment of breathing its bouquet. 'Almost too fragrant.' He bent his head to catch again the vapour; then smiled almost apologetically.

'I didn't think', his sister forestalled him, 'it could be the tea. When last in London I told Hawkins that we cared only for a little Orange Pekoe and not to put any Jasmine with the black Ichang.'

'Yes, yes,' he agreed, 'Hawkins might almost be called an artist in his blending trade. He knows how to give personal service for individual palates.'

He sniffed again, this time raising his head, as animals will when questing, and his smile became even more agreeable, even to the borders—usually far away even from his amiability—of confidentialness.

'Of course, it wasn't the tea! How odd our sense of smell is? Do you know, the despised and hardly civilised Arabians—denied spirituous liquors and such palate-destroying drink—actually made an art of scent—as our tea-tasters, on a lower level, have of course made a trade of a lucrative one—an applied science. I recall when in my studies I first came across this Moslem refinement I began to notice my own ignorance—the first step to any knowledge.'

His sister, delighted at this double sign, of ease in himself and with her, ventured, 'Yes, I've often been amusedly surprised by something like that. Once I thought that my ever-so-precious rubber hot-water bottle must be scorching through the housemaid leaving it too close to the kitchen range, and hastening out to save my treasure, I found that cook was preparing a delicious veal Milanaise! The frying red-peppers did, as it happens, smell just like burning rubber. Yet the moment I saw the succulent dish in a flash I liked the smell which till then I'd thought disgusting!'

'Very interesting: very apt.' He took her domestic illustration not only well but generously, and added: 'and have you found that a weak, bad scent may actually be pleasant and vice versa?' Not waiting for her confirmation he concluded, 'I thought it was the tea that was too scented. But now I perceive that the smell did not come from the cup and was not a too-strong spice of tea, but a mercifully weak aroma of fox!'

'I didn't catch a whiff, I'm glad to say.' 'I'm the door side of the fireplace, you see.'

The amiability flowed on, each playing each easy card as it was offered—both, behind their placid pleasure, a little surprised, questioning, almost uneasy—'Why is he being so intimate?' 'Why am I almost courting company?' Her question remained merely an undefined doubt for she could not in any way confirm her misgiving with a reply. To the best of her knowledge, and she certainly had not been unobservant, the service had gone off without exacerbating her brother's sense of humiliation. The whole atmosphere of the moment, the feeling of irrational intimacy, seemed in its way as odd and meaningless as a fox managing to get into the back premises of the house. His question disturbed him more because he was not sure there was not an answer. Could he be chatting away in this aimless manner because he really felt some need for her company, because he didn't want to leave, because he didn't want to be alone?

He had only to raise the question where it could be cross-questioned and it was promptly dismissed as absurd.

'Perhaps you're right,' he broke the silence in which they had both been searching their minds so as almost to have forgotten one another, 'Perhaps you are right, I don't really see how I could have caught the *odur vulp*; the brute could only have poked his nose round the unlatched back-door, trying to have a look at the larder.'

'Yes, I will tell Mrs. Binyon she must see that the door is always locked after dark—a tramp might have slipped in. From the back lane it is quite easy to approach unnoticed even during the day.'

'I expect,' her brother resumed, 'it was just a small case of mind-influence, as the benighted Arabians call it. They claim, and claim it with a persistence perhaps worthy of sounder support—that if a Sufi Sheik—one of their Mystics, a sort of abbot of a free-moving flock of monks—if he tells one of this his flock to smell a rose and the object he points out to his disciple is in reality a dead dog, the trained novice, even, will draw deep and appreciative breaths of the foul gas of decay certain that not attar itself could be as fragrant. Contrariwise, the disciple can be presented with a cloth dipped in attar itself but told that it is a cerecloth of a leper and reeking of corruption he cannot restrain his nausea—a pretty example of faith!'

'How repulsive!'

'But surely highly convenient! I hope next time I come too close to a fox I shall be able, as our organist would phrase it, to modulate its ammonia into rose-water.' He chuckled, 'Superstitions, if they work, we should be ready to reconsider. Then we are not dealing with a pharmacy filled with empty bottles with nothing but high-sounding labels. But with drugs, perhaps of great potency, the trouble about which is that the labels have become mixed.'

'I am not sure I follow you.' 'I am not sure you should. No doubt the essence of the tea and tang of the wild have combined, making my fancy take leaps which reason would say are impermissible.' He felt there was a certain quaintness in accusing himself of fantasy and approving her rationalism. It was a good note to close on. Any uneasiness that he had felt seemed to have evaporated in the good humour with himself that his mild joking gave him. He rose and wished her goodnight and, leaving the room, went along the wide-panelled gallery which led to his bedroom. Once or twice, as he walked with his candle, he did stop and sniff the air. Nothing came to him but the faint smell of the pot-pourri placed by his sister in a large Crown Derby bowl on the broad window-ledge that ended the passage.

Next morning his sister did not expect the almost-intimacy of the night before to have endured. Nor was she incorrect, but the retreat was not so far as she had prepared herself to face—there was nothing that could be called a reaction. The lightness, true enough, had gone, but when he spoke, after they had finished their formal greeting, the family prayers, the glance at the mail and the choice of food—all which procedures always were gone through before any general remarks were made—what he said was both confidential and cheering:

'It would be most unhappy if to this strange and possibly mistaken appointment I should contribute the additional mistake of an ineffective and obvious disapproval. Even when there is a right to protest, it may and I believe should be waived when in order to lodge it the protestor would have to seem to advance his own claim and urge an injured prestige. You would, then, oblige me if, even at a little inconvenience to yourself, and maybe some slight affront to your personal feelings, you would, as I purpose to do myself, attend regularly evensong, at least every day until the new Archdeacon goes out on his visitation.'

Miss Throcton agreed, again pleased in her intelligence and slightly disturbed intuitively. It was right: it was generous even, considering her brother, but considering him she was bound to own that it was out of character. She was aware that characters can change, and some with a sudden *volte face* which may almost be called instantaneous. But that, surely, belonged to Methodists and other Nonconformists—people given to emotion and not, as her communion was rightly framed, to reason, good sense and good taste. She had never known of anyone 'converted'—indeed the very phrase had about it something alien: deeply religious herself, she had, when their partnership was younger and she less learned in that 'discreetness' of which their Bishop was so perfect an example, tried sometimes to question her brother on spiritual questions. Indeed, she had once ventured to ask him what he would call his own religion—High, Broad or Low—the three types recognised in the Church of England. He had replied, 'That wise old banker-poet Samuel Rogers, a true critic of good-taste, once said when asked that question, What is my religion?, "The religion of every sensible man." And, when questioned further as to what that might be, he concluded the matter with, "That is what every sensible man keeps to himself".' Well, that was 'mate' in their quiet game of conversation and like a cornered chess-player, she had 'resigned.'

Evensong, in late autumn, seldom mustered a quota of the Cathedral garrison. Several evenings (except for the 'skeleton crew' of vergers, choristers, organist and minor canon) the new Archdeacon, his unsuccessful 'runner-up' and Miss Throcton composed the entire congregation. Even the new Archdeacon's wife, who might have been expected to attend if only to manifest her elevation, was absent, pleading the nineteenth century's more precisionist title for the 'vapours'—a palpitation. This small team of regulars, however, was bonded strangely. It had not assembled more than a couple of times before the two men became aware that they were covertly observing one another from their canopied stalls—each uneasily aware, yet not absolutely certain that he was being watched and that his counter-watch was perceived. They were even more uncertain as to which had started it. To decide that would have been as difficult as to prove which of two powers began an armament race. All that the Archdeacon could be sure of was that some strange surveillance had started. And, almost as soon as he came to recognise that, he realised that he disliked the sensation with an irrational intensity. He felt a rising exasperation because it was ridiculous that he should be disturbed by such a matter, even if it were true. It was his own helplessness that vexed him so sorely—that he could not help stealing a glance time and again; and now always as he did so, he could not help feeling that the Canon had just finished taking a quick look at him. Once or twice he looked at the third member of their trio-congregation. But that only sent him back to his old covert peering. Miss Throcton, whenever he looked at her, was watching her brother. He began—as the service wore on, to feel absurdly like a cat which, becoming conscious that it is being stared at, is driven to groom itself to demonstrate to itself its own unconcern. Suiting the act to the fancy, he began to smooth his hair with his palm. It seemed only to focus his nervousness—his whole scalp began to feel uneasy—creepy was the unpleasant word—yes, it was a kind of crawling itch. He longed to be able to scratch the skin. Irritation of that sort can be more exasperating than pain.

In the vestry, even before unrobing, he went straight over to the mirror-faced cabinet, took out the brush and groomed his curls heavily. That not proving enough, he added a vigorous combing. Indeed, he only stopped, when, looking past his own image in the glass, his eye was caught by the sight of Canon Throcton watching him from behind. That made him swing open again even more hastily the little door to replace brush and comb. But as he put them back, his observer saw him hesitate and glance a moment. Then, hastily, he disrobed and, only murmuring 'Good evening' over his shoulder, left the room. Canon Throcton had also reclothed himself but paused a moment. His colleague clearly had excused him from any necessity to accompany him. And, by attending evensong, he himself had certainly shown that on his side he was doing all that could be required to keep up appearances and avoid any show of offence. As he waited for the retreating footsteps and their sinking echoes to signal that the Archdeacon had left the vast echo-haunted building, he himself took a turn along this narrow duct of a room built in the giant carcass. Coming to the end he flicked open with his finger the mirror-cabinet and glanced inside for a moment. Then remarking to himself, 'It served no purpose to clean those utensils. Thick as ever. I had better have minded my own business and been content to disregard our sanctimonious squalor,' he swung to the hinged panel, turned and left.

Such was the afternoon pattern of the next fortnight. Except that Canon Throcton wisely observed his resolution not to add to his own inner irritation by looking at the objects that roused it so strongly, the rest of the routine repeated in curious detail that set in the first two days—the congregation of three that played throughout the thirty-minute service their silent unacknowledged game, 'I'm watching you: are you watching me?' The steadily mounting irritability in the senior in rank and junior in age, and that tension's conveyance to the skin and its expression in ineffective hair-stroking: the whole rite ending in an ever longer and rougher brush-and-comb drill the moment the freedom of the vestry was regained.

The last of the autumn had now yielded to manifest winter. The last gleam of incongruity had passed from the term evensong applied to a late afternoon service. Canon Throcton noticed as he walked back from the closed Cathedral, as the second week also approached its close, that the grove of tall lime-trees on his left were now so completely defoliated that he could see the rising moon sailing clear, its disk only laced by the bare thin twigs. The round, full, silver face had already on it what suggested a light bruise on a damaged fruit.

A couple of days after, a slight contretemps disturbed or relieved the office, attended by so few and by them so slightly attended to. The minor canon had a slight catarrh. To spare his voice which had to sustain the chanting and prayer-intoning, he asked Canon Throcton whether he would help by reading the lessons. It was, of course, the duty of the head verger to find, open at and mark, on the great Bible, the lesson to be read. Still wondering whether from the lectern he would be able to see whether the Archdeacon were watching him, the Canon adjusted the pair of reading candles, his pair of spectacles, and began to read where the marker with its red crimson stitched arrow pointed that he should begin.

'And Satan said to God...' He glanced at the top of the page. Yes, the beginning of the Book of the Patriarch Job. Was Job now being read? Late in the Sundays after Trinity? He had doubts. But his far wider incredulities, regarding the whole of the ancient system that gave him his ample daily bread and so few (he glanced at the gaping black stalls—like a cavernous mouth all of whose teeth are nearly gone) so few their spiritual bread, his extensive doubts that no doubt helped to keep the place empty, had long ago made him doubtful of such detail in ritual correctitude. He went on, in that echoing aloudness, so much more empty than any silence.

'Skin for Skin! All that a man hath will he give for his life.' 'Did anyone?' ran the unspoken commentary in his mind, 'Could anyone now believe in the Devil? A principle of active evil that plagues man and thwarts God?'

'And God said...'

'For that matter,' added the inner commentator, 'Did anyone now in that way believe in God? Values, no doubt. And, maybe, Platonic ideas. Yes, just possibly the Aristotelian Theos, "moving all, Himself unmoved." But a Being you came across personally in your individual life, who confronted you, who individually, tested, tried, wrought, fashioned and tempered you for Himself?'

The sound of his voice again caught his wandering thought: 'And Job cast off his garments.'

'Satan the cause of cutaneous sepsis! Yes, such was superstition's unhygienic mis-explanation.'

Suddenly his attention, left unguarded by his speaking one thing and vaguely thinking of another, received a twitch. His eyes seemed to be flicked up from the lit page. Faintly, in the threequarter gloom of the candle-dotted choir he could see in a coffin-shaped panel of black a pale disk. Of course that was the archidiaconal stall and that palish blob was the present occupant's face. And that face, he was sure, was fixed on his with far more attention than anyone who had listened to 'the Order of evening prayer to be said throughout the year,' for a score of them, could be expected to muster. Then, as a waking man comes to a moment when he realises that a 'glimmering square' is his bedroom window, Canon Throcton remembered that he'd been caught red-handed or, at least, wide-eyed. He lowered his head and fixed his eyes firmly on the page and continued gently to rouse the echoes with the superb prose in which a past magic and folk-lore have, like Oligocene ants in amber, found a translucent, jewelled, ceremented immortality.

As he left the vestry that evening, after the other's grooming had been perhaps a little longer and the departure more hurried, in the gloom of the transept, a shuffling step came beside him:

'Very sorry, I'm sure, Sir, very sorry indeed. I permitted the sub-verger to find the places and would you believe it, Sir, for some reason that only Heaving can say, he chose wrong! Of course, Sir, it couldn't be Job's beginning now, as everyone knows. One only hopes to Heaving no one noticed. Though I had, I must own to you, Sir, an upsetting moment when I spied his new Venerableness a-peering across at you. And you obliging Mr. Minor Canon what with his catch in the throat—and those things must be watched at a time of year such as this with your post depending on your voice, as one might say—and I don't know man and boy but I might count on the fingers of one hand when such a thing has fallen out. And I can't say how I feel over it; 'n p'rh'ps you was too gen'rous to note, but there was a like slip over Samson not so long back either!'

The voice wheezed along beside him in the dusk, full of a vague solicitude, a wounded *amour propre* at the breaking of a record of so many years, and these sad moods floating like mists on a rich tide of malt aroma. By the time they reached the south-west porch door he was able to dismiss the familiar, who stayed behind to lock up into its millennial silence the decayed building.

He breathed with relief the damp cold air smelling only of wet grass and fallen leaves. The latter were now so thick on this path that ran under the lime-tree grove that the old close gardener had not been able to keep up with their descent and his feet threshed through their drifts.

'As is the race of leaves, so is the race of men,' he quoted. Yes, perhaps after all, when the Hebrew Canon will have ebbed to the inner shelves of the depositories of dead languages and archaeologist's files, and these great crumbling arches that the worship of that odd assortment of books erected will have fallen down, and Canons and Archdeacons gone too, Homer and his story of man, budding and falling incessantly from the dark Tree of Life, will remain. And Homer's deeper, darker faith of Blind Fate? 'I wonder,' said the Canon. He hesitated for a moment in his hall—for as far as that had his habit-trained steps taken him while his mind floated back and on along the dark river of time. 'I wonder.' Then with that sigh which is released life turning away from thought, he went into tea with his sister.

CHAPTER SIX

The Archdeacon was to have gone for his first visitation round the diocese when the two weeks were up. It was important that he should. The diocese was a small one and so one Archdeacon was enough, but he needed to keep busy to complete his rounds. But he did not go. Neither, however, had the Canon to keep up his courtesy choir-attendance. Archdeacon Simpkins went neither on visitation nor to choir but to bed and on doctor's orders.

Laetitia Throcton gave her brother his tea and this information, when he came in after evensong on the thirteenth day and before he could ask her, as he was meaning to do, whether the Archdeacon's absence from the afternoon service meant that he had been called away to start his new rounds a day before that appointed. Laetitia, of course, heard Close news earlier than he. His inaccessibility warned gossip-loaded minds that this was no nest for their egg of information. His sister was no more anxious to be kept up to date: but the mere fact that she was reserved, in her case meant that her silence exposed her to such deposits, when the drive of her brother's egotism blew away the alighting rumour.

'The doctor,' she began in the conventionally cheering tone with which medical information is generally dispensed, 'declared that it was nothing serious... a Stitch in Time... Prevention the truest Therapy... Just one of those little troubles that yield best to care and rational foresight... Quite likely the symptom of a general condition... Indeed quite possibly the end-process of some all-over...'

'That surely wasn't his word, my dear, if you wish to employ *oratia recta*.' 'Could it have been Syndrome?' 'No. Oh, I do remember now—some disturbance of the Circulatory System provoked, just possibly, by fatigue, nervous in nature. Rest indicated. Travel contra-indicated.'

The Canon showed his sister that comment, too, was contra-indicated. Indeed, in silence he took his tea and then himself off to his study. His sister listened to his retreating steps, then bent and took Tissaphernes on her lap. The cat responded with obvious pleasure.

'I suppose that's why we old maids keep pets.' She counter-pointed the purring. 'If you try to please them they are nearly always pleased and when they are pleased they don't mind showing it. How complex are our refractions. If Charles were a wild animal he'd be pleased that the score is being adjusted now. If he were a tamed animal he'd be sorry now that one of his group is lamed. As it is? Perhaps he's sorry that he's sorry or even pleased that he's displeased. And they call women baffling! Oh, why are we so complex and always tangling and matting everything?'

The cat on her lap began to groom itself contentedly. Its self-assured ignorance soothed her. She settled down to enjoy her limited content—'Sufficient unto the day.' Might one then not add, Sufficient unto the place, this quiet place by the fire? A knock at the door disturbed her growing calm. The interruption was too apt.

'Mrs. Simpkins, Ma'am, and are you At Home?' The maid looked quite neutral. It would have been quite safe to say the magic word 'Out' that would banish not only the maid but the caller—and 'Out' when you were really ensconced by your own warm fire in precious solitude did not involve a fib. It was the acknowledged courtesy way of saying, without hurting feelings, 'Need we meet to-day?' She had indeed almost said No, when the thought of her brother checked her. His aloofness—it had not made him less immune—rather more. The further he retired the more he was vexed by possible intrusions. If she herself wanted to have calm simplicity, why not produce it herself? You either raised the crop yourself or went without. Besides, Mrs. Simpkins might be worried and this was not the time to be distant with her.

'Please ask her to come in, and bring another cup.'

She had been right. Archdeacon Simpkins, as the Close was fond of commenting, owed everything to his energy. The 'recessive' phrase to this 'dominant' was, of course, that he owed nothing to 'breeding.' And, to breeding, the Close held, with considerable truth, the rest of the Cathedral dignitaries owed considerably more than to brains. Further, Archdeacon Simpkins, when he had chosen a helpmeet, himself chose, or was chosen, not by breeding but by energy. The dress of the day suited Mrs. Simpkins; she bustled. But to-day the vigour had largely gone out of her fuss. Nevertheless she kept up, for the initial courtesy exchanges, the required comments on general events. Had Miss Throcton seen the Opera Troupe that had been performing at the city's small theatre? Yes, she herself had gone to *Figaro*. The music and acting carried you along, didn't it. 'One does not need to know actually what the words mean, does one? Indeed, I sometimes think foreign languages were invented for Opera. Such tongues, so unlike our English, were obviously just made for singing when what you say doesn't really matter. It's all sentiment and no real sense, isn't it?'

Miss Throcton smiled at the philological theory. She could now surely inquire. 'I hope the Archdeacon is feeling better?'

'Oh, well, that would be a little sudden, wouldn't it? The doctor thinks it may have been coming on for some time, you know?'

'Sometimes, however, when such things come out, the worst is really over—in jaundice, for example?'

'Yes, yes, you're right, and jaundice is a horrible upset, isn't it?' Mrs. Simpkins paused, 'Jaundice, the old wives used to say, is caused by jealousy...' She hesitated again. 'But Wilkins—I mean Mr. Simpkins—was never a jealous character...'

Miss Throcton could not check her mind's noting, 'Surely no grounds?' Then her thought glanced again. Can she be suggesting that someone else's jealousy has wished on her husband his attack. She felt inclined to titter and so turned the topic slightly by remarking aloud, how fortunate they all were in having a doctor so up to date and free of any ancient medical dogmas. 'Tradition is needed in the Church but not in the hospital.' But the attempt to shepherd the conversation onto the comparatively safe ground of physiology failed. The slight coolness that she had felt, she was now sure was growing.

'I am glad that you feel that in these times we should be very firm about our Faith.' Laetitia Throcton felt that the 'you' was meant to except 'him who is not in this room but in this house.' She was annoyed with herself to find that she was getting annoyed and then smiled in a nettled way to find her mind up to those complex refractions and counter reflections that so disturbed her in her brother. Her guest obviously could not follow these ramifications. But she sensed well enough that she was vexing her hostess. And being tired, with some slight anxiety on her mind making her less guarded than she might have been, and with a long record of inferior feelings towards this lady who was very clearly one, while she was herself so uncertain about her own status, she rose stiffly. The other rose quickly enough to convey a certain relief. Even the real cordiality with which she tried to let things part on a note of amiability, did not carry over. Her 'You will let me know how things go, won't you?' was met with 'The Archdeacon really doesn't like any indisposition he has talked about. He is so singularly free of such weaknesses—in a spot where ill health seems all too common.' The maid had answered the bell to show Mrs. Simpkins out. They shook hands but Mrs. Simpkins as she smiled and bobbed to the other remarked to herself, with no wish to censor her reverie, 'She thinks herself so well bred that we have come to report to her instead of her calling to inquire.'

On the floor above, Canon Throcton had been at work arranging some references for his promised essay on Arabian Religious Travellers. He had often found that so doing set his pen running and his mind could get launched from the Close, to-day so dank that you felt you were at the bottom of a pond. Well had the Bishop christened it a sink. It was hard to believe that only a few thousand feet above their heads this moment the evening sky was sparkling clear and the sunset gorgeous still in the far west. His reading could take him in the tracks of those adventurous men—out over the Hindu Kush, the Altai, the Kuen Lun and others of those fabulous frontier-ranges which those indefatigable walkers had scaled and passed and left far behind. He himself had climbed among the Alps fairly often as a younger man and had found that the poet who was contented with his Sabine Farm was wrong in one of his most quoted psychological remarks. Changing your sky—at least if you do it in the right way, vertically—you can quite often change yourself, or at least that which most people take you for, your mood, temper, spirits. 'Of course, it's all a matter of oxygen,' he remarked in his usual soliloquy whisper, 'In this place there isn't real air, but something that wants to change into water but hasn't either the weight or the clarity to do so.'

He picked up another index card; it gave cross-references to Holy Places visited by most of his sojourners, 'For people whose one faith was One God and One far more inaccessible than the apex of Everest, these Medieval tourists did quite a lot of shrine-grubbing. I suppose they had to believe that holiness was an atmosphere rather than an attitude. Our Muscular Christianity could beat them there, if we weren't so damned narrow.'

The word in the final sentence slipped out driven by some expletive force. And for a moment, as that worn epithet still had at that date and on such lips some tang of its former sulphurous awfulness, he checked.

'Well, anyhow,' he appended as an apology, 'there's no atmosphere now in this socket of a burnt-out religion—only the mustiness of a book given over to silverfish, or a tree eaten out by dry-rot. Even this house, in spite of Laetitia's constantly directed polishings, has mould in its bones.'

He shrugged his shoulders, as if with his own shoulder-blades to chafe his spine: then sniffed the air. Was the fire smoking? No: and the smell wasn't ordinary smoke but smoke more like the cheap incense of a Roman Catholic chapel—smoke, fume, with an undertow of some ammonia flavour. How typical was incense of that corrupt religion—the blend of mental fog, cheap emotionalism and the rank *sudor* of the unwashed ignorant masses. He got up and raised the window. Yes, it had turned mild. The room was too hot and the air had become stagnant. Perhaps the fire had smoked a little. Mary, when she laid it in the morning, to save herself trouble may have put a little paraffin on it, though she had been told repeatedly not to do so—it was dangerous, might set the house on fire. Perhaps part of her forbidden oblation was only now vaporising. He stood at the open window using his lungs more than his eyes. However, as he gazed idly on the narrow, empty road that separated the line of the Canons' residences from the broad lawn that spread right across the West Front of the Cathedral, his eye was caught by one small moving object. A large cat—too low-slung for a dog surely—was slinking along near the kerb—'seeking whom he may devour.' He could just pick out the prowler as it appeared a faint black blur wherever the light of some window made a pale band across the little road. His lungs full of air, at least cold if not clear, he felt cooler, and, pulling down the sash, went back to his seat. 'Seeking whom he may devour'? What was the quotation? Who devoured? Oh, the Devil, of course. Well, God no doubt existed. But the Devil? Yes, he certainly was a projection of the very unhygienic horror, hate and holiness of that queer mixture the medieval mind—and the latter fought the former with septic holy water and fusty incense. Well, scholarship is our weapon. If we can keep the Tractarians at bay—and they fear history as the devil is supposed to hate holy water—in another twenty years just the weight of evidence will have carried us to a lighter, cleaner religion.

It was his turn next morning, when he was coming in from a short walk in the midget city, to run into the doctor. Dr. Wilkes, like most small-town physicians, was not unwilling to be seen at talk with one of the persons of importance.

'Our new Archdeacon,' the doctor began at once, 'Well, I've seen that kind of attack before. D'you know, Mr. Canon, that quite often when a man comes into new office—even when admirably suited for it'—and he glanced for a moment to see by this sounding whether he had sufficient depth of water to sail nearer the rocks—'even when particularly suited'—and he saw it was safe to smile, at least with one's eyes, before passing on—'often, far more often than a layman—if I may use such a term—would suspect, shows, what I might call rightful diffidence, especially...' There was a question, no doubt, in his voice, a request whether he might go still a little further. It was clearly not granted in the face he was watching and warily the wise leech withdrew. He might not know much more than what he called 'his friends of the Cloth' knew about that mysterious bag the body. But his profession had taught him much about the characters that hover over that uneasy still. Naturally his chief study—for on it depended his livelihood—far more than on the accuracy of his physiological diagnoses—was the nice judgment as to when truth—when you happened to know it—was wanted or could be borne, and not the fib which generally brought the fee—and, odd but true, sometimes the patient's recovery and gratitude. And the even nicer judgment when, off the comparatively safe ground of physique and on the dark quag of the psyche, flattery, condolence or congratulation should be dispensed. He often remarked to his wife that Sugar of Sympathy administered to one who was suffering from what the Psalmist calls a 'proud stomach' would often cause a violent acid reaction, that would then be thrown up in your face as though you had administered a bitter insult. Pride lives in fear of Patronage—he remembered the saying as he watched. True enough, the Canon did not wish to be sympathised with. Well then, he must be informed. Even a Pope will listen with attention to a spy.

'Yes, yes, as I was saying, quite a normal reaction. And, to a medical man, interesting in one way, and clear sailing in another. Just a cutaneous reaction.' 'You mean that you will have him on his feet and out on his rather larger rounds, quite soon?'

'Oh, Mr. Canon, please don't quote me as a prophet. That, again, is your province.'

'Humph: The prophets and the priests never got on well, as far as I know. And, in the end, we seem to have put them out of business—to put you in!'

'Oh, no! *Non dignus sumus*. Besides, all science shuns forecasting.'

'But you can foretell somewhat—after all, you do have to gauge probabilities, don't you?'

'Well, if I were a betting man, I'd take a modest wager that if the patient will follow the regime I have proposed, he'll be out and about in a week, ten days or a fortnight. You see I can't be definite, but such are, I'd put it, reasonable hopes. Things run their courses, you know, and illness and health have their cycles.'

They parted with that. The Canon was therefore a little surprised and almost as much displeased when that very afternoon as he was crossing the Close he should be buttonholed again by Dr. Wilkes. A distant bow was quite sufficient. Because they had had a fairly long exchange on what was almost a matter of business there was no need for a man hardly a gentleman to try and enlarge the acquaintance.

'I feel I owe you an apology.' The well-chosen words smoothed a little his not really very ruffled mood. And when to them was added,

'I really wanted a word with you because, I own, this morning, in good faith, I made a mistake. You asked me to forecast; and, within the limits to which you permitted me to confine my views, I did feel fairly sure. But it shows how dark the future is even when one tries to be informed.'

'Yes, yes?'

'In fact the Archdeacon's state puzzles me. And I'm speaking in confidence, because, as the Bishop is up in London and the Dean is so largely bed-ridden, you are the person in control.'

The appeal had gained attention. The 'I trust there is nothing grave to report?' certainly showed interest and—the doctor was glad, with his quick eye and really kind if cautious heart, to notice—something like real concern. 'That's fine,' he said to himself. 'Yes, I'll trust him for he might well have shown some slight satisfaction. He must have been quite sore over his passing over.' Aloud, he continued, 'You know how puzzling to us—as I said this morning—and interesting, are all mind-body relations—the queer connection between, for instance, the nerve-ends just under the skin and the moods and mental states of the man as a whole. Many, how many we really can't know, are just disturbances caused by just nervousness, you recall my saying that?'

'Yes, yes.' The two further assents showed rising impatience. Though the doctor was nervous himself, for some reason, he now tried to hurry on.

'And others are infections—some again quite slight; one or two, on the other hand, quite grave—for instance, Erysipelas—quite. Well, Mr. Canon, I'm mentioning all this rather confidential and professional matter to you, because it seems to me just possible that the Archdeacon may have picked up some infection.'

'How?' The question had an edge of sharpness on it.

'Oh, in a dozen different ways—using someone else's toilet articles, leaning on a cushion in a railway carriage compartment—once there is a strong strain of infection, well, anyone might pick up such a thing anywhere—for example, one of the choir might, by touching the same towel or something of that sort, pass on the germ. It would probably fail to make a lesion on the hand but who can avoid for long touching their head with their hand. An infection of that sort, of very little virulence in its "host"—if I may use our technical term—invading a system in a condition of some strain—well, we really don't know anything about resistance, really—but once such a toxin gets hold it may suddenly flare up and the condition become, well, baffling.'

He felt he was talking too much but evidently his listener was not impatient yet. He hurried on hastily-apologetically, 'You see I thought I ought to ask—and you are the proper person—that all towels and such things be carefully washed. Of course if there is no further trouble in a week or so, we shall know that whatever the danger was, it has at least spared everyone else.'

He was getting ready to take his leave on the bright note, the well-known exit line of successful doctors, so much more important even than the bright entry. But the Canon actually held with him, 'I shall certainly give orders that what you have suggested shall be done—a very right request—and I share your hope that we shall all escape the contagion. But I would like you, as we are acting in this matter now in something of a joint capacity, to tell me something of the actual condition of the Archdeacon?'

'I'm hopeful, yes, I'm hopeful... for the face is still clear—it is certainly not the usual Erysipeloid syndrome... but, but the top of the head is severely attacked. Of course'—now that he was speaking freely he had begun really to speak to himself. The censored confidence is of all human communications the hardest to achieve—we are either secretive or quite unguarded. 'Of course, you will say why not suspect Herpes? But there again, has one ever known a herpic case which brought about such a swift and complete alopecia?'

Had he not, by then, been looking at the ground, as men do when they are turning over their thoughts, had he thought that the Canon could really help him in his diagnostic doubt, he certainly would not have been helped. On the contrary he would have been considerably distracted. For his really quite considerable psychological knowledge would have found itself faced with quite another question in the face he would have seen. 'Well, well,' he roused himself and raised his eyes looking across the lawn to the house of his patient. 'We are now doing all we can and must wait, wait on the *vis meditatrix Naturae*, always by far the greatest of our allies, the organism's basic will to live.'

He bowed and left. But the Canon himself did not move for a few moments. Then he said to himself in clearer tones each time, three times and slowly with summary earnestness, 'Pure coincidence, absolutely pure coincidence.' Then he turned and began to walk toward his house. But he still found it necessary to say a fourth time, as he had reached the door and was putting the latchkey into the lock: 'Really one of those absurd coincidences—the kind of contingency which makes the ignorant and credulous mind—the uneducated that have never had a grounding in mathematics, still less in the calculus of probabilities—imagine that there is evidence for such fancies as thought-transference. My poor old Sufis, it is true'... He was now in the hall taking off his greatcoat... 'thought such things could happen. But we must defend them so far that even they confined such action to great wizards and great saints. Besides, they had the transmitting or refracting medium in the thickly opalescent atmosphere of faith.'

As he washed his hands—and with something more than his usual careful cleansing—he looked at himself in the mirror that hung over the basin. He scanned the features carefully and then smiled deliberately at the rather grim grey face that was looking out at him.

'You really must polish up your sense of humour,' he remarked to the reflection, 'This is one of those events on which all humour is based. Luck, or as we who have had the advantage of an education at Cambridge know to call it, contingency, working at its great loom of probabilities, spinning its great wheels of causality, brings opposite to each other two completely unrelated events—we are amused, not surprised, still less dismayed. Dermatitis appears in Case A. Shortly after, or really in point of fact quite a number of days after, a purely private and personal psychotherapy is worked by B to humour his own emotional sense of fun. *Post hoc propter hoc*, the commonest diagnostic mistake of half-trained minds. How my medico consultant would laugh at the superstition of the Church, still lurking behind a front of scholarship. I should lose all status in his eyes.'

Then he put the smile a whole wrinkle wider until it was almost a grin. 'And you must confess,' as he turned from his leering reflection, 'that as a joke it is really an uncommonly good one, in that perfect ill-taste that makes retailing for ever impossible and private consumption all the more to be relished. Humour to be good can never be too extravagant and this gets its flavour because it is about an absolute impossibility, pure fantasy, pure farce.'

The last words were said with an emphasis that made the slam of the door come as a fitting close.

CHAPTER SEVEN

The subject, however, followed him into tea. He ought to have suspected that the news of the Archdeacon's involuntary tonsure would already have circled the Close, at least on that inner circuit of the Cathedral ladies. But his sister's rather quickly sympathetic comment and sigh, 'Poor Archdeacon,' roused, like a 'cat's paw' gust on a lake, a sudden resentment.

'A good Verbal Inspirationist such as he ought to see some fulfilment of Prophecy or a return of the Plagues of Egypt because of our infidelity.' He added a chuckle as an alibi against charge of uncharitableness.

Still, her, 'Oh, don't say that,' instead of warning him that he had not succeeded in disguising some malice only made his ill-will break out on her: 'Oh, don't be a fool, Laetitia! Can you really be taking my jest seriously! "Oh, don't say that".' He parodied her tone, 'You would think that this wasn't nineteenth-century England. How thin is the layer of culture! How few set minds compose the rock of reason covering the lava flow of superstition. And then women venture to say they should be given the vote!'

His sister sighed again. Though this time it was more silently it was certainly not less sincerely. She was sorry for the Simpkinses. Her conscience upbraided her for not having understood that the Archdeacon's wife had been *gauche* that day she called because she was already anxious. She, as hostess, should have put her guest at her ease—all the more if she felt herself to be her visitor's social superior. But in any case her brother would not have been likely to maintain the intimacy they had been enjoying. 'After all,' she reflected, 'the fair weather was too good to last,' like their summer climate described with some wit by a French scholar who had visited them the year before—'Three lovely days and then a thunderstorm.' Well, she had had during this spell of mental weather rather more than that, and she could be thankful. Her admiration of her brother was as deep as it was wisely silent and her sympathy was not less. She still suspected that his disappointment over the Archdeaconry had been all the more severe because suppressed, and she was sure that both his past amiability and present outbursts were successive symptoms, though there was something in the whole matter that puzzled her to the verge of constant uneasiness.

He had left the room after his outburst, leaving tea and toast untouched. As he strode along to his study, he muttered, 'Just a small experiment that was really negative—though would seem to the uneducated to be positive. The therapeutic value failed to emerge, through one of those one-in-a-decillion chances. Well, the thing was first to last really a joke. And there's certainly not the slightest need for a sane man to draw false conclusions and see utterly unreal connections. Exceptions prove the rule, and disprove and discredit the fool.'

He had reached his room. The curtains were drawn, the fire well settled, the quiet green-glass shade of his reading-lamp set on his desk inviting to come into port. He could berth himself securely between these two reassuring lights. Here he might enjoy undisturbed that pleasant play with words which the literary are allowed instead of the tedious limitations of 'Patience' with which the unliterary lonely must pass their empty time. The scene was both tempting and soothing.

True, he hesitated a moment by the big bookcase with the built-in drawers under it, but only for a moment. Then he drew up his chair and began his game with the ever-growing index-cards—so much richer than the weary limitations of the playing-card pack.

Dr. Wilkes's faith worked, or his prophecy was sound. It is unlikely that his physic had much to do with it. An astrologer could quite as well have said that the amelioration was due to the change in the moon. Certainly as soon as that sickle, cold and thin as a curved icicle, was seen low in the sky, where the west was still red from a frosty sunset, the Archdeacon was up and about. His hair, however, did not return. Bishop Bendwell, who had been away throughout the little crisis, and was now back at the Palace, tried the joke about the tonsure. It was wise that a Father-in-God chose to be the laughing comforter. His advances were received so stonily that his second card, about God tempering the wind to the shorn lamb and hence we might expect a mild Christmas, was wisely left unplayed. Canon Throcton was wary enough to avoid a meeting. Certainly, whatever the queer coincidence might mean or develop into, his clearly was a waiting game. And in two days the Archdeacon had left on his visitation circuit. Dr. Wilkes, was, of course, not a little pleased at the recovery, but also a little more puzzled than usual. So, as the Canon had evidently been interested by his diagnosis—if it could be so called—when they next passed in the street, he made as if to stop, and the Canon consented to be brought to a standstill. Further, to the doctor's, 'Well, we had an even swifter recovery than we hoped!' the antiphon, 'and no further outbreaks—the plague seems to have been stayed, satisfied with one victim?' showed an obvious agreeability, even a certain lightness of humour. Dr. Wilkes therefore added, 'I let him go on his rounds. He was so anxious not to begin ill—as one might say—the first step, you know, how often it sets the pace, free or halting. But...' But the speed of the rapid reply question, 'But what?' the doctor saw it was safe to add: 'I confess I would like him to go carefully. I am inclined now to think—you will recall it was one of the links in the sequence as I diagnosed it—that there may be a general blood condition—there so often is—and in this case perhaps a potential anaemia of a none too benignant aspect, aggravating, if not causing such a severe and I fear final alopecia—the relationship of the hair to the general vitality—well, the extravagances of folk-lore have frightened off investigation. The fact however remains, there's no better criterion of the curve of vitality than the condition of the hair.'

The doctor pushed back his high black hat and rubbed his temple on which like a sundial his age was well marked by the retreating shadow of his hair line.

'Yes, he must take care. That's my prognosis and prescription, reasonable care. Yes, I believe in the old adage: "After forty a fool or a physician." We are rightly called Medical Advisers—as you are Spiritual Directors.'

Pleased with his reception and that he had been able to close the interview leaving the Canon in no doubt of the precedence that medicine was prepared to grant theology, he did not attempt to hold his honoured guest longer. But when he left, the Canon walked away with no symptom of relief at being set free for his own reflections.

By the time that the Archdeacon returned from his circuit the doctor had ventured to speak in the same tone to the Bishop. Dr. Wilkes had been summoned to the Palace for the humble duty of examining the inflamed throat of the second kitchen-maid. Mrs. Bendwell, ample, kind and shrewd, wisely did not like infected throats bending over food to be served shortly after at the high episcopal board. She asked that the doctor be told to wait on her when he left after his visit to the patient. As he left her *salon* after reassuring her that it was no more than a slight catarrh that had affected the larynx, the lord of the palace entered. Bishop Bendwell was rightly more popular with the laity than with his clergy, for the latter he had to control while the former it was his duty—as well as his taste—to persuade. Sure of his own position with all but the nobility he was kindness itself, affability incarnate to the professional classes. 'They are our problem and our objective,' he used to remark to the Chapter meetings when discussing diocesan strategy. 'Hold them, or at least do not alienate them, and then there is nothing to fear from the masses going Socialist or Catholic. Always, my brethren, you will perceive throughout history it is because the clergy and the aristocracy lost touch with, lost the respect of, the professional classes—that now like to call themselves the intelligentsia, as we once liked to call ourselves the spirituals and still are called divines—always it was that loss of contact that was the first and the irretrievable step toward revolution.'

So finding the doctor in the door leaving conference with his wife, the Bishop took him by the arm bringing him back into the drawing-room. His wife remarked, 'Dr. Wilkes has assured me about Emma's throat—there is no danger of infection.'

'Good, good,' the Bishop replied perfunctorily, and then, thinking how he might leave an impression of friendliness on the summoned visitor, who otherwise of course would not be invited to the palace, he thought of Archdeacon Simpkins.

'Well, Dr. Wilkes, we owe another piece of competent repairing—if I may so phrase it—to your skill. I am glad to hear that our new Archdeacon was on his feet again and hard at his new work so soon after the strange little upset that somewhat inauspiciously marked his initiation into his overseer-office.'

To be held in conference by the Bishop in the Palace was, of course, even a higher pleasure, considerably higher, than to be seen in the street talking at some length to one of his Canons. Besides, there was no reason why he should not, perhaps there was some element of duty in the urge to, tell the Bishop what he thought of the case.

'Yes, My Lord, a very encouraging beginning of convalescence...'
'Beginning? But then was it wise to let him go out so soon?'

'Often, My Lord, to restrain a man who is fretting under a nervous condition brought on by some strain, is a mistake. The balance between the rest of work and the rest of lassitude—I mean, the doctor's task is very difficult when he has to judge whether stimulant or sedative is the right course. It all depends on the diagnosis.'

Bishop Bendwell was listening—he generally did—as human beings really interested him. But now he pricked his inner ear. This little leech was no fool. Perhaps he might not be able to diagnose—who really could—where was spiritual direction in the Church, for that matter—but he could observe. A few moments more would not be wasted. Anyhow he would see some of his alien intimates—as he sometimes called the Chapter, to his wife—from another angle. The appointment of Simpkins to the Archdeaconry, of course it was right. Still he did not enjoy the fact that he was sure of Canon Throcton's resentment and the other fact that Simpkins, though with a perfectly good case, had influenced things in his own favour.

'And the diagnosis in this case? If, of course, you choose to confide in me information that might be taken to be at the professional limit of discretion...?'

'Oh, no, My Lord. In any case are you not the shepherd of all of us in this county and to whom should the veterinary report but to the guide and overseer of the flock? Archdeacon Simpkins is undoubtedly tired and the little trouble is lurking, possibly, still in the system. But change of place, of air, of occupation, these three so often can rouse the organism, as it were turn it on another facet. No, My Lord, you will never find me among the materialists—as long as I observe human beings as they actually behave and respond...'

'Well then?'

'Well, My Lord, I wish you could see our patient on his return. I would value highly your impression. I still stick to my faith that exercise, in this case, is the thing; change and meeting new people and—if I may put it that way—the evidence that he is at work—and,' he hesitated 'is respected... I mean everything that tells against introversion, against moping, and takes his mind off himself. These nervous conditions, and I still think this at base is one, these nerve-ending irritations, they are such delicate adjustments, responses. Often I feel that something, how shall I put it, is being balked in the patient and that this blind invisible force can find expression either in outward activity or in some inward and in the end morbid frustration.'

The Bishop had been increasingly interested. But though he gave quite a handsome share of his attention to anyone who gained his ear, and was giving over-weight in this case, like all born administrators he never became engrossed. He had two perspectives out over which he was looking as he spoke and listened: as a preacher he knew you must never forget the clock, and as a discreet holder of confidence he knew and, as something as little to be lost sight of, the need to remember where you are. While they had talked he had steered Dr. Wilkes out from his wife's presence chamber and down the broad stairs. Both the time-table and the area of private conference were being kept in view and observed.

'Well,'—they had now reached the big hall and were by its massive door,—'you would like me to have a conference with Archdeacon Simpkins as soon as he returns. Yes, I think I can manage it.' And with that the two wary men parted, each pleased with each other, and with what he had gained and given.

Bishop Bendwell kept his word without any reluctance. He postponed a couple of days his going to London and to his fellow Lords Spiritual in order that he might have the promised interview with his new Archdeacon. True, he did not suffer much from intuitions, but in this case he could not help feeling that there was present some element of potential conflict which he himself had yet even to diagnose. His kindliness—which was more composed of a native sense of kinship and insight into human motive than of the theological virtue of pure charity—it, too, was roused when he saw his lieutenant. The man looked undeniably tired. Of course, sudden total calvine baldness does give an effect of rapid ageing. Further, no doubt, to go straight from a sick-bed to a full round of new work, might easily prove severely fatiguing. But the man's colour didn't look right: his lips were a grey only subtinged with red: his skin a curious waxen tint and his teeth—he still had as fine teeth as he once had had hair—were still as even. But they looked more as though made of a dull glass than of ivory.

'Yes, you must take my advice and go quietly, for a little.'

'Hardly possible, My Lord, when you rightly put me in because my predecessor had gone too quietly for too long.'

'Well, better a little now than nothing soon!'

'My Lord, it is not for us to say, as the Scriptures put it, "I shall go softly all my days".'

His wife asked the Bishop how he had found the new Archdeacon. 'Oh, a bit tired, but as I suppose one of your household staff would say, a new broom is bound to lose a few of its hairs at the first attack it makes on what the old one has neglected.' She smiled and seeing that he was not going to tell her more, nor feeling much wish to do more herself than express a casual interest, she changed the subject.

CHAPTER EIGHT

Retiring to work in his study Bishop Bendwell found his chaplain-secretary. 'Just a few papers, Sir, may I run through them with you—for your work in London.'

'Halliday, you serve the unleavened bread of legality and politics made palatable by efficient sympathy!'

The young confidant smiled. The Bishop had picked him as his squire because he saw that he was one of those boys who under a cheerful healthiness disguised uncommon adaptability and method. In the ancient atmosphere of a Close it was good to have one contact with the energy of youth.

The Bishop's mind was still running on his last interview. He was not unnaturally concerned that his sympathy should have been judicious; kind, of course, but stimulating not enervating.

'The main aim of my policy,' he remarked to Chaplain Halliday, 'is to keep the Diocese up to average.'

'Yes, Sir, and the average is rising all over England.'

'It should, of course, it should. Ecclesiastical efficiency has been scandalously low. You can have little idea of the laxity in many parts when I was your age. But we must advance on a balanced front: efficient organisation, sound scholarship, sane devotion—that is the triad the Church should aim at.'

'And the order in which they should be achieved?'

'Well, ours is the great Church of the Middle Way and I've always held that our service and our *forte* is to appeal to the educated through reason. Emotion lies at either end—social reform and its fanatics—and private salvation and the fanatics of the extreme low and the extreme high. Yes, it is a nice problem of balance, of balanced advance.'

'One of the problems, is it not, Sir, is that of the wonderful longevity of Chapters?' Halliday ventured the slight pleasantry and seeing that it was well received, added: 'It sometimes looks, doesn't it, Sir, as though the Church of the *Via Media* was rewarded by Heaven for its faithfulness in avoiding extremes, by being granted an uncommon extension of life in this world?'

'Yes, I suppose that would have been the blessing that the saints of the Old Testament would have asked and as the school of thought we serve does not stress either heaven or hell, magic or mysticism, perhaps you are right. An eminent vital statistician, whom I met at the Athenaeum when last up in London, was certain of it. Maybe we have the reward of longevity granted specifically to us. Beneficed Clerks in Holy Orders he told me enjoyed far the longest of all the expectations of life.'

Their minds were running on the same example.

'I don't think there will be any change in the Dean's condition, while you are away,' the Chaplain remarked.

'His condition is just the same, isn't it?' questioned the Bishop.

'I have a feeling, Sir, that his family is a little more concerned for his health. Of course one has now to judge of his condition almost entirely in the mirror of their looks. I don't know who saw him last.'

'I confess I have not. They have not asked me to call. And you will find when you reach a station like mine that you never find time to make any casual visits. Besides, even when I last called on him, which was some time ago, it was like using that new notion—a speaking tube, you shout something down and then switch your ear round trying to catch an answer incomprehensible to you as your shout was to the distant listener.'

Another couple in the Close were also discussing the Dean and his scarcely measurable decline from decrepitude, through bed-riddenness, to final decease.

'A perfect example of suspended animation,' Canon Throcton was remarking to his sister, 'He has now achieved the pace of that problematical tortoise which swift-footed Achilles himself is supposed to have striven in vain to overtake. Time himself seems now to be unable to gain for good on the Dean.'

But in point of fact the Canon, as had the Chaplain, had been observant—equally so of the minute 'sign of the times'—though not equally communicative of what he believed was to be perceived. He was sure that the Deanery family was not as much at its ease as is the habit of those who fear no disturbance. The replies to the constant convention of inquiry as to the Dean's health had a slight overtone of defensiveness. That tone confirmed the Canon's suspicions, suspicions tinged like the eastern horizon of late night with the first faint hint and hope of dawn.

The only indication that he gave to his sister (a clue which her generosity mistook for an improvement in his own condition) was to remark: 'The Bishop is shrewd, as indeed many men who have no pretence to learning often are. I believe, after all, he may have been right to prefer Simpkins to the Archdeaconry. He certainly is working hard' he nodded—'A plough horse takes kindly to the plough.' He left her with that.

'How fortunate we are,' she reflected with a sigh half of relief, half regret, 'who aren't clever. The able seem to have to feel as insults what we take for granted—the fact that we may be passed over. But surely his wound is healing.'

Had she asked her brother instead of herself, even had he wished, it is very doubtful whether he could have answered. His interest was swinging over from past disappointment to future hope. He hadn't forgiven—it is doubtful whether in the whole of his far from unsuccessful life he had ever forgiven anyone. The few injuries he had suffered he either revenged, and so discharged from his mental system, by holding up the injurer to a quite effective contempt, or he used a method perhaps not less dangerous, of refusing to mention the matter again, repressing the memory by the powerful concentration of attention which as a scholar he had learnt to command.

In his study, though his notes and index cards passed through his fingers, under his eyes and before his mind, his reverie was hardly disturbed. For now he was free to attend to the issue of his ambitions. He need no longer either repress or generate counter-spleen. It would well turn out to have been the best thing for Simpkins to have been shunted in to the Archdeaconry—put out to grass. He felt he had been a little crude, even. For the Bishop may really have meant it, when he made the quite true remark that just having to do administrative work was absurd waste of a true scholar's time. He owned that he had never thought of the Archdeaconry as a post in which he could stay and shine. No, not if it meant that a mitre might be added to crown the apron and gaiters; he could say honestly *Nolo Episcopari*. For him it meant a step to the Deanery—this one or one of the greater—perhaps the 'Peculiar' of Westminster where even the Archbishop of Canterbury—the Primate of all England—had, when he came within those central walls, to walk only alongside the Dean. Yes, the Archdeaconry was not a step but a shelf. And, further, it was now filled by a man who the more he suited it, the more he proved he was unsuited for the higher office of Dean.

'Of course it is a Crown appointment, while the Archdeaconry lies in the direct gift of the Bishop. But Bendwell himself was an appointee, and staunch supporter of the Government—indeed more than once of considerable use to them in The Lords. This time he can make no slip. He must put his best—in fact his only ranking scholar—in the scholar's post and stall. Besides, the very thing that these oafs have brought against me—my Semitic scholarship—would tell with the Prime Minister, himself an Oriental. Yes, it is all opening out into the plainest of plain sailing. 'Pon my soul,' his voice was now quite cheerful, 'I'm amazed at my own pettiness and lack of foresight! But,' he added with that philosophic leniency, that is nearly always extended to our own past extravagances, 'after all, I've probably been able to make this quick and good readjustment to the shock of a very unpleasant insight into a colleague's character—a man never resembling a gentleman but who had been mistaken for being a Christian—by not being ashamed to take the matter seriously.' That was certainly a satisfactory way of putting it. His voice ran on giving him the conviction of another opinion confirming his thought. 'Yes,' he summed up, and began to smile with an even more generous self-leniency, 'and then there came that ridiculous coincidence which I can now see turned the whole thing into a joke, all the better for being all for myself and, indeed, I can maintain wholly against myself and at my expense. Yes, I can own now, I haven't an iota, not a jot of resentment against that poor fellow—whose natural ambition and ignorant prejudice thought the post he now has should be his and not mine. I wish to allow that he's filling the job quite well and I'd add as a parting blessing that his looks are actually improved with the cleaning off of those locks far more suited to the stage than the choir.'

It is possible that certain kinds of hope can transmute themselves into a form of working faith. Whether this was so in this case or whether another cause was in action, there is no doubt that a result much desired by the Canon soon became known to him. He was particularly glad that he had not snubbed but even encouraged Dr. Wilkes when one March day the general practitioner came over to him on the street.

'I am just from the Deanery, hardly more than a routine visit, and of course nothing that might cause misgiving, I agree, should be done—such as requesting prayers. So I have said nothing to the family save to advise a little more quiet and a slightly lower diet. There is a slight congestion at the base of one lung. Puts a strain on the heart. And gout is quite enough for that organ after it's been beating almost a score more years beyond the "three-score-and-ten".'

Then cocking his head on one side, as a sparrow will sometimes glance at a solemn rook, the speaker added, 'I realise how much in big and slow-moving institutions—which are indeed part of the very administration of government—there has always to be much foresight. So many eventualities have to be taken into consideration. Forewarned is, is it not, foreappointed?'

The slight flavour of general compliment and deference, referring to the Church as part of the ruling of the realm, made the really delicate sugar-coating for the otherwise possibly resented assumption of inner confidence almost amounting to intimacy. The Canon was therefore able to take the tip, as his informant might have put it, had he been calling on one of his hunting or racing patients. The two parted with something approaching friendliness based upon private confidence.

For the Canon, no less than the doctor, wished to keep the information of a change for the worse-better, or better-worse, in the Deanery to himself. There should be nothing precipitate this time if he could prevent it—everything as far as he could manage it should be put in the most favourable posture before the final bolt be drawn back and the moribund obstacle be slid out of view and its stall be left vacant. As far as inconvenient rumour was concerned he felt safe in regard to the Dean's family itself. They would keep as quiet as he and the doctor.

The weather was doing its part by proving exacting, at least to lungs whose reactions were getting slow. Looking out of his window at the racing dark clouds Canon Throcton quoted, 'He blew with His winds and they were scattered.' West and East kept up a shuttlecock game across the heavens. For three days the West would send in roaring rain-gales, and then, as February Fill-Dyke's excess must be balanced by March's 'Peck of dust, worth a King's Ransom,' the East, with what seemed staunchless breath, would hiss cold dry gritty air—no doubt necessary for the water-logged land, but 'neither good for man nor beast.'

Miss Throcton with her feet on the fender and her fingers grooming Tissaphernes' fur (that stood electrically on end in the dry wind and became tangled and matted in the wet) thought she should inquire about the most vulnerable of the Cathedral healths. She had heard nothing through the distaff side of Close communications. Her brother, however, seemed without concern or interest. 'It would take more than a whirlwind straight from the mouth of Boreas to budge our leading limpet from his carved rock.'

Then sitting back in his chair, he smiled easily: 'For that matter for all we know his Very Reverence may have already breathed his last but by his imperceptible dying have cheated decay and turned into a fossil, not a cadaver. Is a funeral necessary for a fossil? A nice point for Cathedral casuists to follow up when they have settled the moot question, when is a stall vacant—when the actual stall has been unoccupied for a number of years, when the occupant has lost two and a half out of the five senses (or, to be generous, three) or when the sanitary authorities demand that his residence shall not be used as a sarcophagus!'

Her, 'My dear, should we mock at their grief?' only brought the reply-raillery: 'Why, I'm congratulating the family on their possible luck! The Arabians say of some of their Sufi Sheiks that they don't decay or indeed die when they stop breathing. They pass into a potent state of what I suppose our lively little leech would call Catalepsy Perpetualis. And they are treasured, in the diadems of sanctity, as gems of the first water, though dry, of course, as the dust. What a jest if our Church of England, with its most malleable motto, "All things to all men," should here produce on its own an imperishable Dean—to be shown on pilgrimage days like the head of Sienna's Catherine. I wonder how our Anglo-Catholic wing would take such a queer answer from Heaven to their wish for miracles and relics!'

Again Miss Throcton attempted to check his exuberance. She found the subject macabre, and even more disquieting the jauntiness of his humour. A word taught her by her Irish nurse came back into her mind, 'Fay,' those irrational and unsteady high spirits which attack the mind when it is approaching a crisis in its fate.

He was checked by the slight offence he felt at her mild censure, and retired to his study.

When they met again he was his normal self, neither friendly nor unfriendly but aloof, treating her as another species which shares one's house but not one's thought. They were, it appeared, back at their normally distantly tepid relationship. It seemed, the more she thought of it, that her disquietude had been as groundless as—the other extravagance—had been any hopes of a growing intimacy and confidence.

As it happened everything was favouring the secrecy the Canon desired—even to the point that the Bishop came back into residence and the Archdeacon was away again on his widespread diocesan duties: even to the point that the Bishop asked the Canon over to tea at the Palace to discuss the Easter services. And these ever finer points came to the needle fineness of perfect opportunity—of an opening as natural as it was inviting.

When they had closed their business session and decided what should be yielded to the demands of the Ritualists in way of new vestments and what retained for the Evangelical Laws in regard to postures and attitudes, the Bishop relaxed to a cigar. While drawing on it quietly, he remarked with that easy geniality and apparent frankness that his critics allowed was his chief asset: 'I'd like to say, Canon, that you took that disappointment,' he looked through a fine wreath of blue smoke at his visitor as an intelligent octopus might view, through the skein of sepia, a diver rather uncertain of his ground—'No, don't try to deny it: I felt it in my way as much as you—that disappointment about the Archdeaconry—well, very well. Thank God, I am a father-in-God, as well as just the rather weary administrator of too much patronage. And I did for a moment fear that the—the postponement of preferment might cast a cloud of embitterment over the bright quiet field of pure scholarship. But it didn't, and I am grateful to God that your natural resilience, your pure interest in learning and your religious exercises, have stood you in good stead.'

To this statement both bland and wary, for under its assumptions there was surely a question which he was meant to answer with reassurance, the Canon presented a mien of dutiful acquiescence. He was ready to make his submission. But his mind had ceased following the sermonic flow when it had turned into its peroration. For it had been arrested by the Bishop's hesitation over one word in the easy run of the practised verbiage, the word postponement. All this talk, yes, without a doubt, it was to sound out its hearer as to whether he was suitable to be put forward for the Deanery. If he was still sulking, why then no doubt he would be passed over just to teach him not to flout authority. It was clear that the Bishop would not place any closer to himself any man that would not second that geniality and general adaptability which had brought him his preferment and might raise him still higher. Clearly, everything now turned on his making exactly the right impression at this moment.

He looked up with quite a convincing assumption of frankness. 'Thank you, My Lord, for your counselling. I see that your eye is over your sub-shepherds just as much as over the more general and larger flock. I'll confess—and you have shown that denial would be of no use, confronted with your diagnosis—that I was disappointed, wrongly disappointed. I see now that you were not only wise to the diocese but kind to me—a gracious and statesmanlike blend, if I may say so. I would not have been suited to the duties of maintenance of structure and inspection of parochial administration: that work would have suffered and my own work, which is my vocation, that would have lost, too. May I then, as a dutiful son, thank you for your wisdom and kindliness not only to all of us in this our big family of the diocese, but to me in particular.'

He looked up. The large, kindly face of the Bishop (who, like the ageing Caesar, liked to have men about him 'who are fat, sleek headed men and such as sleep o' nights'—and sometimes even take a nap after lunch) that handsome round of wide brow and large smooth jowl, beamed like a mild September sun. It was a real relief to his soul, which remained honest enough because of its limited objectives and moderate dreams, a real relief that once more he might feel the Precincts were free of malice and envy. Maybe not a high ideal, but alas! harder to achieve, he very well knew, than could be imagined by those who lived far from what seemed the easy sleep of Cathedral Closes.

Indeed he was so pleased that he actually went further than he intended. He, too, had been aware that he hesitated over the word postponement. He could have said 'passing over' or simply 'loss.' But those words had about them a flavour of finality that might depress his hearer. He was a truly kind, if adroit, man. And now that his wishes had been fallen in with by the man who had undoubtedly suffered, now that the matter was closed and at last taken well, surely it would now be safe to give him a little encouragement—in a most general way. Throcton knew as well as himself that the actual gift was in the hands of the Crown. Yes, it was a position where something was to be gained and nothing lost by good wishes that higher authorities in the end could overrule. And now that the quiet, proud man opposite him seemed to have been relaxed by the hope it might be wise to take the opportunity to learn something of his outlook and work. After all, for all one knew, he might very well be the next Dean, the political situation being what it was.

'How goes the work?' was answered by, 'I believe that there is increasing evidence that Arabic studies are being perceived as an essential correlate to Hebrew—indeed, as much as Hebrew is to Greek!' That was modestly said and he could confirm it, 'I expect you are right. Indeed, I had the pleasure of passing the time of day with the Prime Minister when last in London at the Athenaeum. And, of course, I need not remind you that, as he is of a stock which has come within the Fold, he has hopes, that they, if we will strive to understand them better, "Jews, Turks, Infidels and Heretics"—as we shall soon be praying for in the Good Friday Collect—may yet be brought within the one Flock.'

Canon Throcton now felt that he might safely, with advantage (for it might be passed on directly to the real Fount of all Preferment, the Head of the Government), and, indeed, out of courtesy, take the opening that was being offered. He could now be more particular as to his studies and show their relevance to religion. Now with a clear conscience he could remove the least fear from the Bishop's mind that, should he advocate him as Dean, there might be a peril of paganism. An explanation that he would have despised himself for offering to Simpkins and indeed would have denied to the Bishop a few months ago when he felt that Bendwell had betrayed his rightful hopes, now could be offered to aid his prospects and yet not to lower by a jot his *amour propre*.

'The local Fold and the world-wide Flock, yes; my particular studies have often kept that key passage from the Theological Gospel before my mind. Again and again, I am impressed with the extent that Christian thought permeated Islam.' 'I once read that, at an early age, Mohammed himself was instructed by a Nestorian monk?' 'Yes, I believe it to be true. And we must remember that Nestorianism was cast out of the Church because of its Protestant refusal to consent to the new and temerarious title for the Virgin, Mother of God.'

This, too, was well said. The Bishop was having—as most of his colleagues—more trouble given him by his Anglo-Catholic clergy than by any other of those sectional semi-schisms which the Establishment combined and contained more through the power of a common endowment than by the appeal of a common obedience. Bishop Bendwell therefore continued interested, more interested than he had expected, in what he was hearing. 'But, surely, as our German theologians say (and then those Tübingen rascals do the very thing) Mohammed emptied out the baby with the bath?'

'True, My Lord, true. But, to go to true culture for a motto—*Expellas Naturam a furco tamen usque recurret.* The saints of Islam, and such I can't deny many of their Sufis seem in the past to have been, these men appear to have restored many practices which would go far to redeem the religion of the Koran from its original superficiality—or at least aridity.'

'Oh, I thought Sufi was just the accurate name for Dancing Dervish—fanatics like the Holy Rollers of the Commonwealth times and the Revivalistic frenzies of to-day among the Nonconformists?'

'It is a natural mistake. I understand that the many orders or devout Sufis have—as in the Church of Rome, and for that matter, as you have said, in our Protestant sects—fringes of "enthusiasts." But the main bodies deserve attention and, as far I know, respect.'

There was a knock at the door and it was opened by the Chaplain. 'Oh, come in, Halliwell. Canon Throcton is bringing me up to date in his advanced studies.' The Bishop felt it would be no harm that his Secretary should act as a second listener now that there seemed an opportunity of getting the Canon to explain his position unguardedly. If the Deanery should become his, then young Halliwell could answer any such questions about the new incumbent's views on theological matters. It would be better than that the Bishop should have to say anything in his defence.

'Take a chair.' Then, turning to the Canon. 'You won't mind my Chaplain being in on this informal instruction, will you? Remarkable, what you were saying in regard to the Islam devotees and their widening of their rather narrow religion.'

The Canon was certainly not displeased to have an audience, if only of two, if the two were the Bishop and his confidant.

'Yes, remarkable; because, though Islam is so severe, yes, in a way such an obvious religion, these men have added to it a depth which one might suppose to spring from a profounder metaphysic.'

'Have they elaborate rites of their own?'

'To the best of my knowledge, no. Their liturgy, as far as I have read, strictly conforms with the Koran. It is their type or quality of what I suppose would be meditation or contemplation that is said to be the reason for their spiritual prestige.'

'Weren't the greatest Persian poets nearly all mystics?'

It was Halliwell's question, and, pleased that the junior was showing interest of his own, and not merely attention by command, the Canon agreed with some cordiality. 'Yes, I believe it is an exception for any author of the great classic period of Persian verse not to be a Sufi. Indeed, I owe such knowledge of Persian as I have acquired to the fascination of this poetry. Even as an outsider—and I certainly have as little claim or wish to be a mystic as to be a Persian—I do not find it hard to understand the Persian pride in this work. They assert that it is the equal of any poetry in the world.'

Then with a slight hesitation, 'Of course, it is strange to take as the theme of lyric love, devotion to Deity, and to such an unqualified Transcendence as Islam preaches.' He paused again and then added, 'And surely even odder to use the simile of intoxication to describe the state of mind such... such prayer produces!'

He felt that he might have wandered too far into speculation, lured by the wish to make his case, to show the religiosity of his subjects and at the same time his interest informed but restrained. It was awkward even to mention in comparative privacy such emotionalism; even when, as in the case he had been discussing, it gave rise to a literature that for polish and power could compare with the Greek—and surpass the Hebrew—and rose from men who were evidently, apart from the extravagance of their devotion, of the highest respectability, intelligence, and most careful theological severity. Partly to deflect the subject and possibly even to gain support, he turned and asked the appreciative Chaplain, 'How did you happen to hear of these very neglected devotees?'

'Oh, my father was inspired, when at Cambridge, by the example of Henry Martin. After that pioneer in the mission field had died, my father went out over his tracks. And, like Martin before him, he was surprised when he reached Persia to find these strange, but to him really quite sympathetic, people. He used to say to me that he thought they must be more like what the first generation of Quakers seem to have been, and he'd quote Robert Barclay, the early Quaker apologist about there being no true Quakerism without quaking.' Both the elder men looked at the younger who now also felt the need to take refuge in a question.

'Mr. Canon, have you come across—I suppose you must, in your reading—the, the—well, what I suppose we'd call the fairy-tale side of their records?'

'Of course, of course! Spiritual, and indeed scholarly prestige—we see it from our own medieval record—among an uneducated people, always is refracted as thaumaturgy. The white light of Reason, falling on the scored surface of the popular mind, breaks into iridescence. Besides, as I've said, they were themselves often superb poets and the rainbow metaphor of the "lord of language" can only be translated by the vulgar into the materialism, both gross and fantastic, of "the pot of gold".'

'But, my father used to tell me of some very odd things he himself had seen. Once in Fars, an ancient and now largely ruined town—I believe Persia is named after it?' The Canon allowed that. But it was clear that his guard was now mounted. 'Well, three Sufis with whom he used to meet on Fridays for silent prayer... they knew, he was sure, a great deal... He said the atmosphere was very remarkable at such times. One day he had a fever, a troublesome one. It went while he was at the meeting...' 'Such fevers are notoriously undulant.' 'Yes, but they laid their hands on him.' 'The commonest—I had almost said the vulgarest—way of impressing anyone.' The Canon tried a little to soften his sceptical scorn with a smile. The contempt however, only roused his unsuccessful informant to continue.

'But the next Friday, or the one after the next, a beggar came in. They never latched the door of their unfurnished meeting room. He had a horrible sore on his shin. He did not ask for money or food, but settled down quietly behind them as they sat in their little square. As the group broke up, the leader leaned back, quietly and quickly putting out his hand, behind my father who was seated next to him, and my father, glancing, saw the Sufi's first two fingers touch the sore's centre. He was shocked, and then grateful that, as they only bowed when parting, he did not have to touch that hand. Then, next Friday, the same tramp walked in and sat with the group. As he sat cross-legged my father saw the lesion was completely healed.'

'Typical story, if I may say so; I could, from my authors, quote you a score such, and a hundred even more entertainingly impossible.'

'But would that actually prove that Halliwell's father was completely deceived?' It was the Bishop, driven to defend logic, not physical research. Then seeing the Canon bridle and hearing him utter, '*Post hoc propter hoc*—the very gateway of superstition,' he tried to soothe. After all the subject was the Canon's speciality. So, retreating to his home-base, and putting the accommodating flavour of a question into the reference, he remarked, 'After all, as far as we can judge, St. James and his Church apparently believed, didn't they, in the laying on of hands?'

'My Lord,' the Canon suddenly challenged, 'you have had, these last Lenten weeks, to add the round of Confirmation Services to your other heavy duties. May I ask (and I do so for instruction) is the additional labour of the administration of the rite evidentially worth your time and fatigue?' The Bishop felt that with Halliwell present, this small conference, as it had become, demanded that he should answer unequivocally. How could he in honesty sound the Canon unless he himself would be sounded because he was sound? 'The Greek Orthodox Church permits all priests to practise the confirmational laying on of hands. I do not see why we should not. As it is, you are right, it puts a strain on the Diocesan.'

Halliwell rose, evidently aware that his master might soon be put in a difficult position. Loyalty to his father and his present father-in-God moved him to break up the small meeting. 'My Lord, might I—as soon as you and Canon Throcton have finished your business—see you about some small diurnal question?'

He withdrew and, as he did so, the Bishop rose: 'Very well, Canon. Thank you for this interesting discussion. I feel I am now up to date in your researches and can share, in general outlook, your point of view. And thank you for your help. Whatever we may personally think of the physiological aspect of the *charismata*—and I think that we of the Church of England are permitted a certain very considerable latitude of view—we know that the sharp points of ritual are not getting any easier to accommodate. Easter is always a busy time and I own the Lenten Confirmation visits having to be discharged and intercalated with one's presence at Westminster—have taken it out of me considerably. And Easter always gives us a staff depleted by some form of catarrh. Catarrh and choirs have naturally an affinity. And the Dean, really compelling me to put his office into commission, I have to look upon you as a kind of temporary and *de facto* Dean, don't I? I am sorry to encroach on your work...'

'Not at all,' the answer was more than genial, it was said from the heart. 'At any time... at any time.' They were out from the mists of speculation and controversy into the bright sun of actuality and future firm hopes. Canon Throcton dismissed from his mind the silly boy's talk and the bishop's kindly wish to protect his lamb. The Bishop waved genially to him as he left the spacious Carolingian study in which they had met. With real lightness of step he went down the fine carved stairway with its wide shallow steps. As he made his way across the lawn the high cathedral clock chimed, 'Ding, Dong, Bell!' and to his mind set the words '*de facto* Dean!' 'As good as done,' he murmured to himself. 'And all by keeping one's temper, swallowing one's disappointment and waiting cheerfully for the best which is the real substitute for the good.'

Then his mind, now fully at ease, ran back over the past highly-satisfactory conversation. He had made a good case for his studies and his standpoint. Not only was he clearly useful to the Bishop, he had now been able to show that he was sound, soundly within Anglicanism's ample bounds. But—his mind ran back onto the silly subject again—how odd young Halliwell had been fostering his father's folk-tales. The mission field—what a strange and indeed presumptuous vocation. They pick up more tares than they sow our own wheat. And what was it, that used to be said at Cambridge of the three types of ordinands? Yes, that was it—the picked few, who had fine enough intelligence to have succeeded in the lay world, never went to parishes—they were given—like himself—dignities either in the Universities or in the Cathedral closes. The large middle lot became the ordinary parish clergy. The simplest of all that could only get a pass degree—they went out as missionaries—yes, to such places as Persia and China. Unteachable, and so unwaveringly convinced they would teach others. He smiled to himself. Quite apart from reason, common sense proved that there was no need for the compensations of superstition in a world where rational insight, an understanding of men and sound scholarship, made a clear path to preferment. As for health of the body—well there, as science went on increasingly, the medical profession could cover such risks and cancel such distresses. Dr. Wilkes was a lively enough mind. He smiled still further—I wonder whether he is interested in the nice problem of euthanasia? I suppose we 'of the Cloth' would fight him, if he ventured to hint it—but we have much to gain. When one is hale then one should be in office. Does that poor half-corpse in the Deanery really want to be kept living? Anyhow, isn't it clear that my pleasure in the place while I am sound in wind and limb would add more to the sum of happiness than his semi-miserable semi-consciousness?

CHAPTER NINE

The spring weather had now decided definitely to begin—after a number of rather exasperating false starts. The whole Close, therefore, was far more cheerful—almost at its best. Indeed, it was 'A lovely spot, God wot!' Poetry of such a calibre was at this time almost too much quoted by its inhabitants as Crocus took the place of Snowdrops, then Daffodils that of the Crocus, and Hyacinth, Narcissus and the first Tulips completed the cycle of the bulbs.

Miss Throcton felt that happiness, too. She felt, also, that she might have real grounds, based on something more assured than an English spring. Her brother seemed almost purposely trying to make up for his quick and sharp retreat into estrangement. Now with the brighter days their relationship seemed to have reached a degree of ease—if not of intimacy—that she never remembered before. She sometimes felt that he must almost consider her as his friend and companion. Day after day he would come and sit with her. He would stay on over their tea telling her of his work. And now a couple of times he had gone as far as to hint that the political sky being what it was, the Deanery expectation of life being what it was, and therefore it must ultimately be limited, and his work promising to be more widely known and appreciated—well, putting the three trends together you might almost extrapolate the line caused by the parallelogram of forces and see the formation of something that soon would be practically inevitable. And what would that mean for her? Well, in other words this trajectory might move her out of the house she had so beautifully appointed—but not too far. To all this she kept a smiling non-committal unquestioning face, knowing too well to ask him to explain or enlarge. Yes, and feeling for him too deeply to let his hopes take form in actual words. She was really more of a realist than he, and she felt that he was less armed against disappointment than herself.

Certainly, nothing outwardly seemed to point to the issue being decided one way or the other. The Dean seemed once more, with that infinite capacity for shamming death that sometimes characterises nonagenarians, to have stabilised on a new level. Yet this pause on a still lower rung of life's ladder did not discourage the Canon.

The Archdeacon continued zealous in his outlying work—'A true sheep-dog racing over the outlying pastures,' said the Canon to his sister and she noticed that, though satirical, the voice was not ungenial. On his side, since his talk with the Bishop, the Canon gave plenty of attention to the Cathedral. By nature commanding, and able to manage well enough anything that he thought worth while mastering, he had no difficulty in keeping the queer team under him at the pace and in the step he thought right. Everyone looked upon him now as being virtually in command and as most people who are routineers like being managed and only give trouble if not controlled, he was on the whole approved.

'If you know your own mind, people will save themselves the trouble of consulting their own,' he remarked to his sister. 'Well,' she consented, 'I suppose if anywhere a hierarchy should rule it would be in a Close.' Himself he often counselled, 'It may be a little tedious, but detail now mustn't be neglected. With the prize at one's finger-tips it would be criminal carelessness to neglect any precaution. Every small efficiency goes to build up inevitability. The place has not been so well run for fifty years—perhaps never. And when the end comes to this long hiatus, why the transit will hardly be noticed. What has become actual will merely be formalised and the services which I've rendered will merely be given their recognition—after which I in turn will be able to rest in my scholarship and appoint someone else as my vicar!'

Even when the Archdeacon was home he was pleasantly passive and never challenged what was being done. He seemed too tired, or preoccupied, by his extra-mural work to pay attention to what was taking form in the Precincts themselves. Nor could Dr. Wilkes, sounding for impatience, be sure that he detected any increase in congestion of temper. They nearly always stopped and spoke as they passed nowadays. So the physician on being found coming from the Deanery saw an opportunity for taking, as he put it to himself, that pulse of spirit that can be read in the face. He remarked with a humour meant to appear as a disguised condolence, while in reality to provoke a possible reaction, 'I have never known such a staunchless fund of suspended animation! Wherever the Very Reverend soul may now be, the animal vitality now at bay and bed is certainly managing to keep the decanal body still undecomposed.' The Canon was not to be drawn either into theological speculation or human self-pity. His mind, that, when unsettled, had made him give way to that outbreak with his sister, was now certain of itself because so sure of its prospects. With something like supple geniality he then sidestepped the suggested condolence by turning the conversation on himself.

'I believe I am the one resident of these Precincts who consistently keeps you "professionally" at a distance.' The tone might be taken for that of easy friendship and certainly caused the doctor grateful pleasure. But his gratitude did not move him to become unsteadily indiscreet. He was aware that though he had not been rebuffed but rather welcomed, his probe had met resistance under the genial surface. His counter-move was clear. It would still be well and wise to share every detail of the super-slow descent of the Dean to decease. Yes, there was no doubt about that. But it would be wiser not to speak of another's condition which interested and puzzled him far more—that of the Archdeacon. It was a hunch, but of the sort that he had never found at fault. And if the Canon, *au fond*, was not going to trust him, well, it would certainly be wiser to keep this stranger issue to himself. As he went on his way, he, too, indulged in what he would call a piece of social diagnosis. Rooks were already squabbling in the tops of the lime-trees, for favourable nest sites. 'Mr. Darwin is right,' he remarked aloud alone; 'There's not merely the vitality of each individual but there's the struggle between the individuals in the group—the group is a kind of body and generally in poorer shape than its constituents because the members war one with another, as St. Paul, isn't it, says. There's still "an unreduced dislocation" between those two important members of this queer Cathedral Body. I suppose I ought not to have spoken to Canon Throcton first about this. But then I didn't realise this inflammation, and the Bishop was away. Now it would serve no purpose... do harm. You can only give true inside information if you are giving it to a true insider, not to one alienated by ill-will. Yet someone ought to be told. The Bishop is available now.' His steps had taken him out of the Close and by a lane that skirted round the garden walls of the Palace. He had no more patients to see that morning. Why not ask if the Bishop was at home and would be able to see him for ten minutes. He felt a little shy and even clandestine. Well, it would be all the better to get it over. If the Bishop said he could not see him, then he would think over further what should be done.

But the answer came down that he should go up. And the interview turned out well, confirming his hope. Bishop Bendwell was gracious, concerned, thanked him for coming and agreed that they should keep the matter '*entre nous*.' 'And what do you think should be done, Dr. Wilkes?' 'Rest, My Lord, when the body is showing signs of hesitancy in its resilience, then we must give it more time. Every fatality begins with fatigue.'

'But no Archdeaconry can be a rest-post, though men have no doubt turned such mobile commissions into sessile wards and even cubicles, and not been removed. I cannot have it held again by one who is not strong enough to do the work. I don't understand...' he went on, almost to himself... 'I don't understand. I picked him because he was still youngish and seemed a man of outstanding energy—a better choice for the hard work of the office than any—that could have been suitable. Then that curious indisposition as soon as he took office. And now again, according to you, he seems to be ailing?'

'I don't know, My Lord, if I would use quite so strong a term as ailing. But certainly he has not now his full energy... depleted... enervated.'

'Well, what is your diagnosis?' 'I think, My Lord, I would rather not yet define my views to that extent. I am observing, not as yet prescribing. And if I may say so I have come to you not merely as a possible informant but to ask for your insight. Still I might offer a prognostic. You know that there are pre-consumptive conditions, pre-cancerous, pre-anaemic—conditions when a touch may send the organism one way or the other, when some slight shock or strain may suddenly precipitate a manifest morbidity, which rest and peace of mind would have permitted to dissipate. That's the state I hold him to be in. You see it is on the very borders of my field, and, if I may say, where it adjoins that of the Church. Alas! we are usually called in when the enemy has already taken all but the citadel and then are asked to oust him.'

'In brief you mean that prevention is better than cure.' The doctor nodded a trifle crestfallen that the man of the pulpit should have been more succinct than he of the pharmacy. The Bishop was silent. Then he rose. 'Thank you again for coming. Please say nothing of this to anyone. I will see what can be done. It is difficult. Of course...' and now he was again almost talking to himself, 'There are others through the diocese, two or three that might fill the post—but, but...' then turning to the door, and giving the doctor his hand, 'Well, good-bye. We will no doubt have time for another consultation on this matter. There is nothing to be feared at once?' 'Oh, no. We have time, certainly. It was because I wished that you, My Lord, should have the earliest advices that I ventured to call. Thank you for granting me this consultation when we can see ahead.'

But they could not. There was not time. True, the Archdeacon remained much the same. But not the Dean. Without word or warning while one of his great-nieces was reading to him—or to be more exact in the presence of the body on the bed—for the hundredth time Jane Austen's *Emma*, she noticed as she rose quietly at the ending of the usual evening portion that the coverlet was no longer being raised and let fall, however slightly. The Dean was at last undeniably, certifiably, dead.

The Archdeacon was naturally back in the Close for the funeral, and, as at such times the worthies of the city liked to make prophecies as to who would go next, his pale appearance gained him quite a few votes for this ultimate preferment. The Bishop eyed him, too, and solicitously agreed, when asked to give an interview. 'Come over at once,' he replied, as they unrobed in the vestry, and Canon Throcton had gone out to see to those minutiae of routine which everyone now took for granted were his concern.

In the Palace the younger man turned to his superior, 'I should never have taken the post. I have tried to do my duty...' 'You have; you have.' The Bishop was both concerned and embarrassed. Was there going to be a nervous breakdown? As were most of those men who survived to reach the higher levels of Anglicanism, he was bland. Blandness is a curious and rather fine glaze which to the casual eye is assumed to have a base of dullness or indifference. The reverse is the truth. It is generally the patina or ex-precipitation produced by a sensitive and wary nature exposed to situations in which a frank response is impossible. It is their defence against 'the corrosion of the world's dull stain.' A double price is paid—the bright, clear response to events is lost—the unguarded reaction of the innocent: and also, under this crust of circumspect culture, the repressed sensitiveness hurts the man, making him dread any show of emotion. The tougher the nail, the quicker the quick. Perhaps then, the Bishop's only passionate revulsion was for what he called with a monosyllabic emphasis, alien to his pulpit style, 'scenes.' But he was not to be spared. 'I should never have taken it,' the voice rose to that thin whine that in a dog's distress immediately precedes the full howl. 'But you have done well. You've simply strained yourself a little too much—that's all—the willing horse, you know. Just learn to take it in your stride. You'll get the pace...' 'No, no, I must tell you; you are our father-in-God. Do you, My Lord, remember that night last year when I dared to counsel you against making the appointment which you thought might be required of you. I was wrong, very wrong. The office belonged to him by a certain prescriptive right—and you were right...' 'I don't think I can enter into that now.' The Bishop felt that he might and should let his immunity of position be known unmistakably. Health was one thing; policy quite another. 'Besides,' as he saw the poor man's face draw into an even deeper mope—'Besides, I can assure you that the person to whom I presume you are referring, bears not the slightest hard feeling. I cannot, of course, infringe even on the frontiers of confidence, but I must ask you with my authority to believe that.' The appeal for faith was not well received; indeed it led to something like a resumption of the storm. Perhaps the man was going to have a real bout of hysteria, here in his study. It was the incongruousness of the thing that made Bishop Bendwell feel something like gooseflesh under his gaiters. He could meet crises as well as any man provided he felt himself on familiar ground. But Anglicanism has naturally never thought of having an answer to insanity. Its success, and it was not inconsiderable, lay in its power to disregard the abnormal. The voice rose in its thin intensity, 'I beg you, My Lord, I beg you to let him have what I know he desires, this wretched office.' 'But what of you?' The Bishop asked with that kind of kindliness that is at the edge of exasperation. The Canonry that Simpkins had evacuated when he took the Archidiaconal stall was already filled by one of the deserving diocesan clergy. The other man simply hung his head. He looked like a chased animal completely spent, not caring whether it is caught or no. After a pause he did speak but mainly in a mutter and to himself. 'It all started the moment I took office. I had a guilty conscience, I could feel his resentment and had to own I deserved it—a guilty conscience, fatal for any religious work. I am ready to resign.' The Bishop's concern became acute enough to overcome his suppressed fear of emotion. Something must be done. The man couldn't be let drift till he was no use to himself and had gone outside any help that the Bishop would be at liberty to grant. There was one thing that could be done. It was really not out of the question and this crisis made it necessary to break through conventions—after all, David ate the show-bread and the highest authority condoned the breach of ecclesiastical order. He got up and put his hand on the huddled shoulder of the man who was still crouching in his chair. His sympathy grew as he felt the thinness of the muscle and the poor tone of the sinews. 'Believe me, it will come all right and trust me as your father-in-God. I will do all I can to get the matter settled satisfactorily.'

As the Archdeacon had gone into the Palace his wife had called at the Throcton residence. When brother and sister had come in from the funeral the Canon had gone straight to his study saying that he would not be down to tea as he must now settle a number of pressing details. He was already having to give a considerable part of his time to the Cathedral's agenda and the actual death of the Dean had rapidly increased the dependency that the staff now put on the accepted successor. The organist, naturally the last of the crew to be reduced to obedience, had now—as often happens—become a constant asker for interviews. Indeed, Canon Throcton was discovering that it may be less fatiguing to carry on campaigns against rebels than to manage every detail for slaves. Now, however, that it must be a matter of no more than a fortnight before the prize was awarded him, he was determined to finish with finish. Once appointed, once *de jure*, then let who will manage the finicking detail. Till then if the sub-verger couldn't light a candle or mark the right lesson without the match being lit for him or the marker put in the proper page—well, he would be at every underling's shoulder. He would oversee every detail up to the day on which, with the effrontery of Absolute Power, 'The Crown' (whose real name happened to be Benjamin ben Israel) informed the Chapter that it was free to elect the person chosen for them to choose. The organist proved as long winded as his voluntaries. The Canon began to wish quite strongly for his tea. He would not, and by his social station was indeed forbidden to, offer the organist any refreshment. Miss Throcton was, however, on this occasion, relieved that he was detained. She felt determined to remedy the unkindness into which at the last visit she felt she had drifted. Besides, surely Mrs. Simpkins would not have called again in so short a time and after so 'short' a parting, had there not been a sufficiently unusual reason. Perhaps she needed help. The putty-coloured face of the Archdeacon came into her mind—not an attractive impression but not without appeal. In her resolution to do better she was however more than taken at her word. Miss Throcton began to find that she was losing sight of her objective, indeed really losing sight of her guest as she became involved with herself, contemptuous of her own contempt. Why did the poor Archdeaconness (what a dismal title and yet no doubt her guest would like it)—why did the poor woman grate on her? From the moment her ill-shaped button-boots squeaked across the floor to that other equally protracted moment when she had equally noisy trouble with her veil and the tea, those small, wordless contretemps that feed contempt and prepare us for overt acts of ill-will, followed without relief. So when the visitor—the preliminary speech—conventions exhausted—volunteered a remark it was inevitably unhappy. 'What strange tea!—almost like stale pepper. It caught my breath!' 'It's China.' 'I always say to my husband, "If we have been given an Empire and have given India the Gospel, we owe it to them to drink their tea!"' 'I don't quite see the inference?' The sub-acid reply-question led to a succession of ever-widening exchanges. From tea to theology the steps were short and swift. 'My husband has found a shocking state of affairs in the Diocese. It has worn him down. It seems that we who live a sheltered life can't have any notion...' 'Of what?' 'Why, Romanism among the clergy and, in consequence, open infidelity among the laity. That is what we pay, for letting our Protestantism go out of our preaching. Scholarship may have its place, but it can't win souls. What then is it doing in the pulpit!' 'I thought that St. Paul said we were to give a reason for the faith that is in us?' '*If* we have one!' The Archdeaconness ruffled her magenta plumes. Her taste in colour was aniline. Her hostess preferred Pre-Raphaelite tones. Suddenly, however, Miss Throcton's sense of humour won respite from complete breakdown. The nodding purple bonnet—giving a culmination of apoplectic colouring to the flushed face from which it reared—made the poor Archdeaconness look like a cornered hen. A hen with its back to the wall loses a great deal of its normal silliness for it is usually defending its chicks. Humour often rouses interest and interest may warm into charity. 'Yes,' Miss Throcton found herself saying, 'Faith is the crux, isn't it. St. James says faith can heal not only the soul but the body also, doesn't he?' Her surface mind felt that she must have said this to lead her ruffled guest off controversy and to ground on which they could agree. For the Close had lately closed ranks when one of the most troublesome of the ritualistic parish clergy had begun to anoint his sick with consecrated oils. Her deep mind was signalling up to her some stranger significance when she was distracted by a sudden change in the fat homely face confronting her. It wasn't relaxation: it was increased tension. Fuss had been replaced by fear. Through the show of defiance was now emerging the real reason for the visit. 'You don't believe that stuff!' Then, feeling that this Anglo-Saxon brevity was crude, 'I mean—Oh, I don't know!' The fat face went into a third phase and by far the most surprising of the three it had registered. It actually became dignified. Miss Throcton stared. Some basically powerful emotion had risen and, as the tide floods the shore, all the petty confusions were gone. Further, it was evident that the emotional tide was a double one, a blend of the two most powerful feelings—love and fear. Mrs. Simpkins was not going to break down or up. Under some extreme pressure the commonplace carbon of her normal temperament was becoming crystal. 'Can I be of any help?' Mrs. Simpkins's call had been so clear though unspoken that her hostess felt no hesitation. 'Thank you, and forgive my being so upset. I don't know why I came to you. I don't know about healing but I do feel sometimes sure about guidance. I had to come here—as you see against my will. I don't know if you can help, help…, but you could, maybe, help me.'

Miss Throcton went over and put her hand on her guest's shoulder. The other looked up and Miss Throcton was struck by the dignity of the face raised to hers. True, the eyes had tears in them and pouches under them. But the lifting up of the head removed all heaviness from cheek, jaw and chin. It was not beautiful but it was tragic. And the whole cast and turn of feature expressed a real strength—all the more convincing because quite unsuspected. The voice, too, agreed now with the expression. 'I am sure my husband is gravely ill. That is what I came to say last time, but hadn't the courage. And now it's worse. I haven't any doubts about it. His father died—some mysterious condition of the blood—at his age. He won't face it yet, but I know he knows. I love him but I'm frightened, too. I know it's wrong. I mean I'm frightened in the wrong way—about the wrong thing. We're poor. He made his way. His father was a carpenter. I was—I was a small governess, I mean I went to poor families who could pay very little. We have no savings. My mother was ill a long time before she died...' Miss Throcton knelt beside her guest's chair. Mrs. Simpkins now looked down at her own hands in her lap. They were finer, more descriptive and more worn than her face. She had taken off her gloves. The fingers had been well and strongly shaped and also well and heavily used. 'If my husband fails now we have nowhere to go. I am sorry, but it frightens me. The Close has always despised us. My husband, if he is to recover, needs my faith, I know, and it's going. I have no friends.' Miss Throcton put her hand on the hands that lay folded before her. 'You are wondering why I came to you. Perhaps it's harder to tell you than it would be to ask for—for help. Of course, it's an appeal for help but not for the kind of help people usually ask for. I came here because I was sure I had to. I didn't want to. I knew you could help. But, you see, I wasn't sure you would. No, listen to me now and then judge. I've said, my husband's ill—more ill than he dare face. But also more ill—ill in a different way than he knows. He had, you may remember, a very nasty attack in the early winter. He was more ill than the doctor knew. The skin trouble was only a symptom. I know. I slept with him—at least he slept and I was kept awake by his talking in his sleep.' The speaker's voice, too, had become thin, monotonous as though reciting aloud a reverie rather than addressing a listener.

But at this point, Mrs. Simpkins roused herself, withdrew her hands from under the other's and looking sideways at her asked, 'Do you know what he said again and again? "He hates me: he will have his revenge. Skin for skin." Perhaps I'm wrong but I was frightened. For the words, though they sound silly, Oh, they were said with such fear. So I asked him, "What's wrong?" I thought at first he might be awake. But you know sleep-talkers answer if you speak to them. He rambled on, "He hates me. He won't forgive me. He always despised me. I took what he claimed. And now he'll be revenged".'

She stopped. The two women looked at each other. Miss Throcton took again the hands that lay in the other's lap! 'You want my brother to stop disliking your husband.'

She looked steadily into the slightly bloodshot eyes, past their weary commonplaceness to their profound anxiety. 'I will be frank. My brother was—was upset by the appointment. But please believe me, he has now quite overcome the feeling. I can give you my word for it. He has in fact told me that he considers your husband as the man for the Archdeaconry, and not himself.' The other looked at her first with doubt—but doubt in which relief began to struggle with growing success. Miss Throcton was a person hard to mistrust for long. 'Then, after all, it may clear?' 'I am sure you may reassure him completely on that score.' Mrs. Simpkins gave her hostess's face a last searching look, then turned her hands to hold the one that rested on them and rose. 'I am deeply grateful.' For the first time the voice was unsteady. Miss Throcton took the two hands in hers. They went to the door together.

Returning to her seat after the maid had let her visitor out into the street she sat doing nothing, until round the door her domestic's face appeared at what physiognomists call the angle of inquiry, 'Oh, yes,

Mary, you may take the tea things. The Canon is detained by a caller.' Then her mind went back to consider her other matters. Well, she had wished—yes, to be frank, she had asked—and to be frank again, she had asked out of wounded self-love at her own failure in what she prided, her courtesy—she had asked that she might have an opportunity to remedy this *faux pas*. And her wish, her rather perfunctory prayer, had been answered? She smiled, recalling the Scotch story of the Minister who prayed for rain and, a cloudburst following, was heard adding, 'But moderately, dear Lord, moderately.' She could not deny that it was an opportunity. But she doubted whether she would have asked for one so considerable. What an odd and really rather unpleasant incident had emerged. How her brother would laugh with more force than pleasantness at what to him would be an utterly farcical story. She was glad that he would never know this new evidence of the uneducated vulgarity, the uncultured weakness toward superstition that still vitiated minds such as the Simpkinses. But the poor woman was in real enough distress and had needed reassurance. She was glad she had been available: particularly glad, yes, thankful, that she had been able to reassure the poor thing—in fact, had been able to quote her brother. It proved beyond a doubt, even to the frightened woman, that the morbid fear of, obviously, a highly nervous man—with some constitutional weakness—had been quite groundless. She had heard that such reassurances, when they can be given with complete sincerity, often prove the decisive factor in dispelling quite grave states of mind. She was resigned that now she must show something more than conventional courtesy to Mrs. Simpkins. Poor things, she thought, with all their nervous reactions and anxieties: so uncertain of themselves and their future! One isn't grateful enough for the security that birth, health, education and position give. One takes too many good things for granted. Well, I can show some gratitude by being kinder to them. I did fear at one time that Charles might show his disappointment by brusquerie of some sort. But, thank heaven, that's all past now. And it's an odd little finish that I should be let put the matter right and close it. We women are thought to be touchy, taking to the vapours and hysteria when offered marriage or any distinct attention and to our beds and consumption when we're not. But men seem just as emotional.

The Bishop would not have disagreed with her had she stood beside him as he watched the drooping figure of the Archdeacon pass across the Palace garden and go out of its gate. He, too, suspected with the doctor that there might be quite as much emotion as infection in the Archdeacon's debility. Well, all the more reason for putting his plan into action. Practical sympathy, doing something for them that showed your consideration, could often do more for the ailing than most of the pharmacopoeia. What he had planned was no doubt difficult but would serve very neatly if it could be effected. He certainly wasn't a timid man and he knew that once you had made up your mind about a plan, the sooner it was put into effect the better. He would make the whole approach as gracious as possible—an appeal for co-operative assistance, not an instruction. He wouldn't, therefore, send for his colleague in this negotiation. He would himself call.

Ten minutes after his decision he was in Canon Throcton's study. The organist was still with him as the Bishop was shown in. The Canon was pleased. He could rid himself of his too dutiful captive: the captive would see the Bishop coming to consult him; the Bishop would see the '*de facto*' Dean indefatigably in action, unwearyingly attentive to Cathedral detail. He waved the musician out of the door and led the master of the Precincts to a chair. The Bishop also saw, in the little scene, an opportune opening: 'Ah, Canon, I see I've come on one more item of fresh evidence of your gift and care for administration. Everything in the Cathedral is now overseen, and everyone feels they have a real rector to keep them in line.' The Canon smiled. 'Do you know,' the Bishop sat back in his chair and gave his voice that tone with which we convey that we may have been wrong and our listener the better judge, 'Do you know, I think I must have been mistaken. After all, organisation may be your *forte*. Several of my colleagues on the Bench seemed to be headed for high scholarship. Then the call, "friend, go up higher" came... and I can say that few men who have the gift, the vocation, for administration, would exchange it for mere scholarship. The scholar is a looker-on and at an irrevocable past. The man who manages makes the present.' Canon Throcton's easy mood felt a slight chill of incomprehension. Could there be some new device, one of those modern things, to make him a Suffragan Bishop? He who did not want to be a Diocesan, why, just for the sake of lawn sleeves, to have to rush about as a kind of kite's tail to Bendwell's energetic peregrinations! 'I am well content to "let my due feet never fail, to tread the studious cloister's pale".' 'But if natural aptitude and native generosity both should indicate a wider field, I am sure you would accept.' Then, seeing that the Canon's first agreeability was now obviously becoming over-clouded with a startled puzzlement, Bishop Bendwell judged the time had come to be definite, concise. 'I am sure you are not unaware of the general state of the Archdeacon's health—puzzling, mysterious indeed, and possibly grave.' The Canon did know it. 'I am sure you sympathise with such a state.' The Canon did not, and, as his assent had been slight to the first proposition it was slighter to the second. Besides, what he had now heard showed him that he had grounds for further irritation. Could he trust no one? He had taken for granted that his unbending to Dr. Wilkes (he naturally overlooked that it had always been to his advantage) had bound that source of information never to be so disloyal as to give news to the others before the latest bulletin was first offered to the first dignitary who had ever treated him with any sign of intimacy. He felt the resentment which a Civil servant feels when some wretched member of the public dares to write, over his head, to the Chief of the Department. The climate of friendliness now fell rapidly until it sank almost to freezing point. The Bishop felt he had tried to the point of weakness to make his subordinate offer cheerfully what he must accept once it was issued as a command. His authority was being challenged. Evidently this arrogant scholar had once more decided as to what he felt he had a right to be given. The needs of the diocese, let alone those of a sick colleague, weighed with him not at all. Sympathy and self-respect both urged him to act now as the disciplinarian. Yet he was a good-tempered man and competently sure of himself and his dignity. He had never blustered or scolded in his life. But he had often spoken with unsmiling and effective decision. He would put the matter quite plainly. 'You see, I am sure, the situation. And I surely may still feel that I can and must rely on your loyalty to cooperate. Your care with the Cathedral has shown that you have the gift of administration. You have put it in order...' 'That a fresh invalid may let it relapse?' 'It is a restricted field. What you have done will last. The Archdeaconry offers work I need to have done. The Deanery will offer quiet occupation...' 'But not only is he now a semi-invalid, he is no scholar.' 'Please let us attend to you and your gifts. You are an administrator. I must think first of the diocese. Do for me there what you have done for the Close here.' It was the last gleam of persuasion before coercion. Though exasperated and feeling that he was trapped, the Canon had also throughout his life never openly let fall his outward caution. He must gain time. He saw that he could refuse and get nothing. The offer was a kind of sorry compensation for having been given the Deanery in all but word and then having it filched away. What a fool he had been not to have disguised better that he had desired the Archdeaconry and had resented it going to that other. Yes, he must think out this sudden and most unpleasing capsize of a plan that had seemed sailing straight into port. He bowed, to the still seated bishop, as he rose—a kind of ceremonious dismissal. 'I am—please, My Lord, be assured—deeply aware of your consideration for us your ailing flock. I am sure you will give me a little time to consider in silence, in prayer, this offer prompted by generosity, but, as you see, so unexpected that it has slightly left me at a loss.' Then, seeing that he could with safety go a little further in relief of his feelings. 'My need for an hour or two's reflection—if you will grant me as much—is due to the fact that I had come so completely round to the view you did express to me—that I was temperamentally unsuited for rural administrative work.' The Bishop had risen, too. 'We used to say at College that any of the Fellows could take any of the administrative posts if he really wished to do so.' He turned to the door saying with quiet authority that had in it more than a touch of moral force, 'I believe in this case you will find this to be so and I know you will be doing a kindness to everyone concerned.'

However, to be told that you could be kind when normal selfishness has been inflamed to keen resentment is to talk of the joys of exercise to a victim of the gout. It was too late for tea—and anyhow he did not want his sister's company. Nor when he had seen his weighty guest to the door did he feel he could go back to his desk. The early evenings were drawing out and the air was mild. He would take a walk. He might relieve the mood of severe congestion caused by all the prospects of the future appearing equally unattractive. He was striding along, his mind turned inward on this problem. It was not, then, till he was accosted that he saw the doctor standing in his path. Evidently, Dr. Wilkes did not suspect that he had fallen from his place of almost-confidant to almost-suspect. But he had judged that the time had come when it would be wiser to speak to the Canon about the Archdeacon's health, or lack of it—for anyhow the Archdeacon had reached that state of debility when self-pity makes the patient a constant publisher of his condition.

'I'm now uneasy about Archdeacon Simpkins—more, considerably more, than earlier. Indeed some step may have to be taken—in regard to his work and rest—if he is to be saved from a serious breakdown and maybe permanent invalidism, indeed from something, something even more final. A little while ago I felt that he was falling so rapidly into a despondency which makes the physician's task almost impossible, that as I had had medical reasons for going to the Palace, I ventured to raise the problem of his health to the Bishop. I'm sure you, too, will realise that here we have a condition that can be tackled with most hope of success if we can spare the sufferer all exertion and worry, and yet not in any wise alarm him: as he might well be if he thought of himself as being consigned definitely to the "sick-wing".'

'The Deanery has now a well-matured reputation as an environment wherein suspended animation easily becomes a second and enduring nature.' The remark was neither witty nor wise but it gave the Canon's companion an insight he needed. And the Canon himself, feeling that he had gone too far in show of his resentment and reflecting that the doctor had, after all, cleared himself to a great extent by making a clean breast of his Palace conference, relented into friendliness. 'You think it is vital that we have rest and yet just sufficient interest?' 'Well, let me be frank. Several times I have ventured to give you my medical confidence, and you have been good enough to help me with your advice. I am now inclined to think that here we have a further and grave step in what had been maturing for some time. I would not be at all surprised if the whole thing started with that strange small trouble when he was first appointed, you remember. These circulatory cases can show such symptoms. And he is of the age—just over forty—when one of the most pervasive of diseases—I mean one that can have the most widely diversified symptoms—does appear. We know little of it and can do somewhat less. Common anaemia, for that we have a number of well-tried helps, and, maybe, cures. But with the pernicious form or forms—we can do little. But I have a feeling that there is a stage when, say, the common form of one of them turns into a deadly type. But the whole matter is very mysterious. Pernicious anaemia, you probably know, pervades the whole system—it attacks the marrow of the bones, the digestion is out of order, though the patient may grow fat, the spinal cord very often becomes involved—the victim may die of exhaustion in a state of protracted unconsciousness, the mind seeming to fade away, or he may be ended by a rapid paralysis spreading up the body—it is certainly very confusing.'

He paused, lost in the no-man's-land where the general state of that unknown necessity we call health meets specific attacks from a masked enemy. He was roused by the Canon's voice, 'Your prognosis, in this case?' 'Well, I have told you,' he spoke now with the authoritative voice of the explorer who has at least penetrated into the dark far further than he who questions: 'we must give him every chance. Exhaustion must be highly dangerous for him. For the body's total resources are now engaged on some internal front fighting for life. But, frankly, I am uneasy. Maybe what we should aim at, if we are not to raise false hopes in our hearts, is prolonging life, not...' Then he smiled. 'Well, of course, that is all any of us can have—a reprieve, not a permanent recovery. In a way, just by the process of the calendar, we are all losing ground!'

The Canon had however heard enough. It was the particular news he desired—not a homily on humanity but the life-expectation of one man. He said good-bye quite graciously but definitely: he wanted at once to be by himself. He walked for some considerable time till it was fully dark and then came in, pleasantly tired and not uncontent. There would be just time before changing for dinner to write that note. After five minutes at his desk he rang the bell. While it was being answered he read over what he had written: 'My dear Lord Bishop, you will, I know, forgive me if this afternoon I was too surprised at the generous offer you made me to accept it instantly. Nor do I think you wished me to act with anything that might be called precipitation. I am aware—as I know you are—that I am no administrator. And, though my own desire (natural in a scholar) to avoid the feeling that he has, as the phrase goes, been "put on the shelf," made me wish to be of use and to be tried in diocesan employ, and I was therefore left with a sense of disappointment when you, with greater wisdom, passed me over for another, time has removed all shadow of doubt as to your perfect rightness. It is to that judgment that I am again trusting when you would now offer what then you had to deny. I have sought the guidance...' The reader paused in his delivery and said in another tone of voice as though speaking to and answering some person quite other than the Bishop, 'Well, I have certainly gained an answer.' He resumed, 'The guidance which you had already won before you came to see me. And I realise that, as your authority is greater than mine so has been your insight. In these circumstances I am prepared—as you justly said—to attempt to fulfil those unfamiliar duties, which so often yield with profit, to those who have the humility to accept that which has been laid upon them by no choice of their own. Believe me, My Lord, your obedient son in God, Charles A. Throcton.' The knock came at the door just as he had repeated his own name. He sealed the letter and as the door opened to his 'Come in,' he held out the envelope. 'Mary, see that the boy takes this over to the Palace at once and asks that it be taken up to the Bishop.'

CHAPTER TEN

At dinner his sister was further reassured, though he granted her no information. The present was not in his view. But he was in doubt how far he should look into the future. He felt he must make an effort to settle that doubt. He could certainly add to his general information enlarging his interests as a whole. And certainly there were grounds for a hope. His sister as clearly felt his cheerfulness. She even felt that he was sufficiently at ease with himself, sufficiently satisfied, that he might have some spare interest for the misfortunes of others. 'I had another call from Mrs. Simpkins this afternoon.' Not even his 'Then, though I knew it not, I was granted the better part with the organist and no tea' discouraged her. 'I own I have wished to avoid her as much as courtesy would allow!' 'Certainly you two have nothing in common. You may not have inherited the Throcton brains, Laetitia, not that they would be much help to a woman. But you have undoubtedly been given the good taste which seems to be even more strongly a matter of heredity, of breeding. So we complement each other—if you will forgive me for what I suppose if we were not brother and sister would be called a left-handed compliment.' She began to answer, but he ran on in that tone of irony that was the surest symptom of his spirits being 'good,' 'and the Simpkinses match each other, too. Perhaps there is a particular place where there are made—those matches that can only be called happy in their odd mutual aptitude. It certainly wouldn't be heaven but some kind of limbo where a demiurge, with a prettier sense of humour than of beauty, works out his entertaining designs. The Elder Church would allow you to keep house for me even if you were not my sister because you have attained to what is called Canonical age. I think that Mrs. Simpkins might be called one of those women who are born with Canonical looks. From adolescence she must have been qualified by an appearance that suited her to being a housekeeper and nothing else.' 'But she's very unhappy, very frightened,' she broke in, his note of mockery, after this afternoon's visit, jarring her into interruption. 'She fears her husband is really ill.' He seemed about to say something more, but suddenly his mind must have changed. 'Well, I suppose every hen lives in a panic for fear her chick has picked up something unhealthy. As they have no children, naturally she has nothing to do but to fuss over him.'

Miss Throcton felt it was wise to be content that her brother allowed the poor woman some virtue and to her husband no greater health-risk than the over-solicitude of his wife. Evidently the Canon had noticed nothing in the Archdeacon except perhaps such fatigue as might be expected—and mean no harm—in one who had thrown himself perhaps too eagerly into a task made desirous by former protracted neglect. She steered the conversation then into the safer waters of the weather. Her brother followed her out onto these harmless reaches of human ignorance and speculation. For his mind was fully occupied with further particular questioning.

The problem as to how far he must look into the future, he tried to settle next morning. To some extent he was able to do so by a visit to the Cathedral library. He recalled, from visits made when he was first appointed to a Stall, that this strange lodgment of folio and quarto flotsam contained the books of one of his predecessors, books which might aid his inquiry—an inquiry which he would prefer to make without having to mention it to any—as he would have to did he apply to any more official library. This predecessor had been—before he took Holy Orders and his Doctorship of Divinity, a Doctor of Medicine. His care for the soul had not lessened his interest in the body and the cure granted him had brought with it both an amount of leisure and of stipend that permitted him to pursue as a student what he had ceased to practise as a profession. This association resulted in a fine private library of pharmacy and pathology. So when death forbade him any longer so to study and to accumulate, he left to the Cathedral the fruits of the income it had granted him. It was to this collection that Canon Throcton went. And in the quiet of the unfrequented room, into which he had let himself with a rusted key, he did find the oracle for which he was seeking. There was quite a good deal of information here about diseases of the blood, of the anaemias and, of course, of the pernicious form or forms. Yes, it struck usually between forty and sixty: there was no known cure—at least to date: it was multiform in its attack: the mind became comatose: the digestion was certainly affected: indeed, some fault in assimilation might be one of the causes of the entire condition: the spinal cord might gradually go out of action—creeping paralysis, 'scissor walk,'—and of course the blood itself showed degenerative changes, etc. Yes, yes, all very interesting... But... Ah, here it was—the attack could be mitigated, and brief ameliorations often achieved, by giving arsenic. But the patient, once the condition had become unmistakably evident to his medical adviser, generally died within the year.

He closed the large quarto—already itself smelling of decay, put it back in its place with some little caution to see it fitted to its exact dust-marked frontiers and left the library. As he crossed the Close lawn, he thought, one year? Not enough time for me to lose the thread of my own work, not to get into too much boredom-cum-confusion over my archidiaconal duties. I shall have shown my good will and have gained for good that of the powers that be. Yes, Fabius Maximus must be my master of strategy. I will wait. Maybe all these delays and apparent thwartings have only been, as it were, traverses to make my approach to the quiet citadel more securely inevitable.

As he intended so he did. Nor had the Bishop been wrong. As an able man the Canon could turn his attention to the not too difficult routine of the countryside administrative duties, provided that a twelve-month was the length of the sentence, and the reward a return on a higher level to the precental amenities.

Neither did the first six months go badly. He did not even have to meet the new Dean who, almost as soon as he was installed, followed his predecessor's example, taking to his bed. With a not-uncheerful malice, he remarked to Dr. Wilkes, 'We might call the Dean's stall not a stall but a bed!'

He forgot that he had said that suspended animation brooded over the deanery—not death. He had also overlooked the fact that the doctor might take his Hippocratic Oath more seriously than a scholar felt that he must take his to the Thirty-Nine Articles. Dr. Wilkes was certainly not less interested in this particular case. There had been much that had puzzled him in it. And now that Pernicious Anaemia seemed to be the enemy who was to give the *coup de grace*, the doctor was determined to fight the battle out to a finish. He was a bit of an original, too; enjoying his liberty as a general practitioner to attack his enemies, the diseases, on any part of their lines.

'Discipline, diet, drugs,' he remarked to his wife, 'Those are the three sectors of our front. Why confine ourselves, as it were, to the last ditch!' 'Yes,' she replied, for she was well above the average of the Cathedral wives, let alone those of the small settlement that called itself a city because of the monster church that sat on it, 'You're certainly not that every third doctor who's said to be an atheist.'

'Well, I take man as a whole—have to. And what a piece of work is man. And who but a Creator could ever have made him… That's plumb, physiological sense to my mind. When they can make one cell, then I'll begin to attend to their quack that the body is a machine and the brain secretes thought as the liver bile!'

'What's on your mind?' She asked shrewdly. For when one day he told her that if a woman made a generality she always had some one person in her mind's eye, she had replied smilingly that any human being was like that, unless they had abstracted themselves from living too much theory and too little observation. She was a companion of his head as well of his board and bed. So he replied without hesitation:

'The new Dean lately Archdeacon, and, as an accompaniment, the new Archdeacon lately Canon. The first ought never to have become ill,' he paused a moment, then added, 'The second is not ill but maybe will be—or perhaps I'd be more cautious if I said, maybe he ought to be. But of course that's not my business, only my diagnostic curiosity practising itself for the love of the thing. Throcton hasn't called me in—seems to have what we used to call an iron constitution…' 'Built up on the base of an iron heart, do you mean?' she questioned. 'Let's go back to my duty. What I have to do is to fight for my patient. He certainly seems to have fallen into what hereabouts we might name Decanal decay.'

'No, tell me what he's really contracted?' 'Oh, I don't think there's any doubt about it. Of course, it's not the senility of his predecessor. I'm pretty certain, indeed, haven't a doubt in my own mind, it's Pernicious Anaemia.'

'What's it look like?'

'Oh, pretty obvious when it's got you, skin like parchment, teeth like old glass, walk like a centenarian, mind like a mist...'

'You didn't see Mr. Longman's, the greengrocer's child, did you? Of course you didn't. He doesn't hold with doctors, he's often volunteered to me. He says greenstuff is the food for everyone and that Genesis declares it. I was sorry that the joke seemed against him at the expense of his child. For she became a complete shadow. I did what I could. But good advice—well, you are always giving it without bringing down the death-rate. I was certain she was going. Then one day—it can't be more than a month ago—I saw her wonderfully better, actually gay and bright and with colour. The recovery seemed to have been far more rapid than the decline. I congratulated the mother. She seemed ashamed. At last, though (her husband was out), she evidently felt she must tell someone and that I might prove sympathetic. The child had been in at a neighbour's. She liked to crawl in there for she was let sit in a sunny window. There happened to be a large dish of broiled liver on the table. The child asked for some; the people gave it. The next day she came back asking for more. They didn't like the father. And to defy him, as much as to humour the child, they kept on giving what she asked and they knew he'd detest. They would order liver for her. Within a week neither they nor the mother could doubt it was having an effect—they told the mother then, and...'

Dr. Wilkes cut his wife short. 'Well, I must be setting out on my rounds again.' She looked up at the clock; yes, it was time. But the doctor's first visit was not to one of his patients. He went down a small street that opened into the market square. Looking rather more like an inquiring and cautious bird he glanced ahead of him and then went on with more assurance. Yes, Longman the greengrocer was out, his wife and a boy keeping the shop, for the afternoon was a slack period after people had done their morning shopping and the proprietor had gone out to see his market gardens for to-morrow's supplies. Fortune favoured him further for, as he passed the front of cabbages, potatoes and other ranked vegetables, a small girl ran out. Adroitly patting her and turning to Mrs. Longman who stood guardian over the greenstuffs, he remarked how well she looked and without pause asked for a bunch of watercress and two bundles of radishes. As this small traffic was being negotiated Mrs. Longman, out of a certain nervousness that always has to 'pass the time of day' with a customer, naturally seized on the conversational bait he had offered her. Yes, Mimmie really looked a wonder now, didn't she—and it was a wonder and no mistake. And a bit of a mystery, too, if one might so put it. For there she'd been so that you'd have thought—even if you didn't see much of doctors—that she was straight set for a decline. And here she was now really a positive tomboy as you might put it.

Half a dozen exchanges and Dr. Wilkes had the story in all the detail, and with some cross-checking, that he needed. A sixpence to the daughter, a smile to the mother, and he left with far more than a handful of tea-time vegetables. With the sudden dart of a true diagnostician he was sure he had now something which he might use. 'Through the greengrocer I glance and find my real instrument at the butcher's,' he smiled to himself. 'Well, it's certainly simple to try, and no harm done if it's no more than coincidence. *Post hoc, propter hoc*? Well, who really knows about causality. The germ or the general resistance: the bottle or the bedside manner? Thank heaven

I am a G.P. and don't have to explain how things work—or take too much blame when they don't.'

The liver treatment of course worked. Dr. Wilkes was wise enough not to draw attention to what he was doing, still less to talk about making a remarkable cure. After all, the condition was not acute, and many conditions, even cancer itself, do, on occasion, remedy themselves. All that the Cathedral public knew was that the Dean had rallied. And rallied he remained as the year went on upon its course. The Bishop was pleased and attributed the improvement to his sagacious swapping of the posts. The Archdeacon tried to disguise his impatience. On meeting the doctor he could not however prevent himself asking for a forecast: was the improvement due to temporary alleviating measures? He had heard that sometimes such conditions, when there was present some anaemia, were benefited, for a time, by arsenic. He trusted the Dean was finding some relief through such alleviants? Dr. Wilkes, though a far more tolerant man than Archdeacon Throcton, shared the ecclesiastic's objection to trespass on his own ground. Besides, his natural prejudice was amply supported by a quite rightful wish not to share any more confidences with one of whose goodwill he felt less and less sure. He therefore replied with perfect honesty and equal discretion that he now had considerable hopes and would venture to think that grave worsening of the condition might long be postponed. The reaction this almost non-committal statement awoke in his listener's mind was however so strong that even the doctor, who sensed that this general good news might here be a little less than welcome, would have been surprised. Nevertheless, though not surprised, he was quite a little shocked when the rather grim face that he was looking at suddenly showed something like a sneer: 'Are we to endure another living corpse at the centre of our corporate life here!' That rhetorical question he had met with the rightly discreet answer that his task was to preserve life; to the Church belonged to say what were its uses. 'Besides,' he added, 'with a little caution there is no reason not to hope that the recovery might prove so extensive and sustained that the patient might well undertake all the specific Cathedral duties.' Faced with that possible prospect the face opposite him began to show an even grimmer aspect. But the anger that was becoming evident to the onlooker had evidently risen to such internal force and with such speed that the cautious brain overlooking the undisciplined will, threw its considerable weight against any further expression. Here then, too, a respite was gained. Archdeacon Throcton realised now that he had shocked the doctor that he had let his impatience render him unguarded—and for no purpose. But the sheer force of the thing that had twisted within him, almost unseating his power of judgment! As he found his heart beating and his breathing shallow, he was almost more shocked at himself. The spasm of frustrated violent anger gave him real alarm. He loathed all passion, as the coldly selfish do. He had never thought that he was capable of such black rage, any more than of lechery.

'You are right, of course, quite right. We must hope for the best.' The voice was gruff but the words were conventionally suitable and with them discharged—a dust of decency over the larva-leakage—he turned on his heel. The other stood looking after him.

'If only we knew the connection between anger, greed and fear and the organs of the body we'd know more about illness than the chemist will ever be able to tell us.'

He repeated the remark to his wife when he got home, giving her the occasion that had made the generalisation form in his mind.

But Archdeacon Throcton had no confidant. He would not have trusted himself with his sister had not years of domineering distance made any real intimacy, any freedom of communication, as difficult as the movement of an arthritic finger. He knew that she watched him and, though lacking definite and sharp lines of information to draw round the vague intuitions of misgiving, she was aware of his moods and in general knew their sources. It made no difference that she had a deep affection for him. What he dreaded was that she should—however sympathetic—see that he was not the man he had masked himself to appear. Her very loyalty, the fact that he knew she would endure seeing him as he now himself sometimes feared he might be becoming, only added to his sense of frustration and inner fear. That evening he sat in his study before the empty fireplace. He could neither work at his routine duties—there were plenty of letters to be written—for a 'faculty' to be granted to put up a hideous painted glass window with a mendacious inscription in the church of Pugton Regis; for an inquiry whether the incumbent of Melcombe Porcorum should or should not be let have a reredos with a Nativity in high relief, etc., *ad nauseam*. Nor could he turn to his Arabian studies. As he turned over the increasingly irritating letters, which as letters do, grew the more exasperating the more he neglected them, he muttered to himself:

'So now he won't die and here am I caught again. You'd think I was being played with... by what, whom? I'm getting the feeling of being trapped. Those attacks of anger, too. I used not to get them. A bad sign. They can't be good for the heart. They must come, I suppose from the digestion. Perhaps I ought to see a doctor—and turn myself into a hypochondriac and join the choir of croaking incurables that this place seems to produce as its sour vintage. And give a clue to that shrewd-eyed little leech. No, that would put the fat in the fire. But I don't feel rational when that bile rises in me. I suppose old Hippocrates was right. We are creatures whose moods are the fume given off by our organs' secretions. What a fool I was to show my impatience in front of a suspicious physician. Of course he dislikes me and the Dean hates me and the Bishop despises me. What a fool I was to fall into seeing omens in the burning of that nauseous garbage and thinking that such a piece of foolery might help get the gall out of my system. The fact that the silly thing, even on its own ridiculous level, failed to work, obviously affected my mind. I suppose if you take omens and they go wrong you have to pay the silly forfeit. If you appeal to the witch-doctor you will find yourself bound to pay if the fool decides against you. Perhaps I've appealed to a caesar of the underworld and unto Caesar I must go.'

He got up and began to pace the floor. Finally, he came to a halt not at his chair but at the bookcase. After a moment he reached behind a big row of volumes on the last shelf that, breast-high, stood on the base made of built-in drawers. He groped for a moment. When he straightened up, he had between thumb and finger a key. He fitted it into the keyhole of the top drawer, turned it, drew on the knob and looked in. After a pause, he remarked, 'I expect it's acting like a red rag to a bull. If I'm not rational then it's only rational to act as though I weren't!' He smiled wryly. 'But I *must* get rid of these rage attacks. Perhaps hoarding this rubbish somehow inflames the back of my mind. If we are really chemical machines, well, chemical mixtures outside the body may affect us, just as much as those within. Dr. Pasteur certainly seems to have proved that invisible microbes can attack and kill us over very considerable distances. Perhaps our medical science will find that there's something in the fairy-tale view of things. So I'd better follow that sort of logic, at least with myself.'

Once he had decided to act, he was again methodical and deft. What was to be destroyed was to be given swift and proper dispatch. He lifted out the old, soiled handkerchief, now discoloured and musty, and the little glass bottle become opaquely iridescent with the dried scum of the hair-oil. The mixed odour of mould and stale scent made him wince. 'Smells like a tomb,' he muttered, taking the noisome handful and depositing it by the fender. Recrossing the room, he locked the door. The weather now was held to be too mild for fires and so a fan of blue fluted paper attempted to relieve the gaping blackness of the hearth. 'Our social magic,' he sneered looking at it. 'We put azure decorations in the place of winter warmth, to encourage summer skies and so again heat from Heaven.' He flicked out the fan and picking up the refuse threw it into the empty grate. The contents of his wastepaper basket and a packet of squills he added, remarking, 'I can say that I had to burn a few confidential papers, matters of administrative discretion.' He added, to aid combustibility, some pieces of sealing-wax from his desk and the contents of a sticking-gum bottle. He lit the little pyre cautiously, perhaps afraid that there might be the sudden outburst that had followed his first *auto-de-fé*. On the contrary, however, the ignition was slow! but once started was persistent. Hardly any flame showed—only masses of smoke poured out. The hearth was cold, there was little or no up-draught. The opaque fumes, therefore, instead of going up the chimney, crawled down out over the hearth toward the fender and hearth-rug. One heavy skein slowly rose toward the ceiling. A whiff of it touched his face. It felt like a greasy feather smeared across the nostrils and the smell and taste were nauseous. It was the smell of carrion being slowly charred. He raised himself, for he had been half crouched watching his experiment. On the table by his desk stood a carafe of water. He snatched it and poured it over the smouldering heap. There was a hiss and steam mixing with the smoke began to fill the room. Once again, he was driven to the window. As he opened it, the fumes poured up past him, into the still clear air. As before, he noticed the calm outside—a quiet evening sky, and, on its lapis background, like a cameo, a moon that might be taken for a mask held before the face of an invisible watcher.

He turned back to the room—his seemly study as squalid as a pot-house. The smoke however continued to pour out past him: the reading lamp on his desk shone with its tranquillising green glow. He went over to the hearth and taking the poker rummaged in the charred paper. The fire had done its work better than he had thought. The handkerchief was gone and such paper as was left untouched showed clearly it was merely routine correspondence. He changed weapons, taking the tongs. With these he recovered the small bottle, black but unbroken. After cooling it a moment by the fender he bent down and took it in his hand, went over to the window again and then, bending sideways, he flung it out with all his strength. The curve of its fall carried it till it bounded and rolled on the Cathedral lawn.

'The Close gardener will put it in his basket to-morrow morning,' he remarked. Then, half-way turned from the window, he stopped. A large slinking cat had come out of the shadow of the low Close wall and was approaching the bottle. He could just see that faint gleam of it lying on the grass. When the beast reached the object it snuffed at it for a moment, then turned and looked up at the house.

Archdeacon Throcton was sure of that, because the light in the room behind him caught the animal's eyes and made them gleam bright green. Somehow the creature seemed considerably bigger than Tissaphernes or any of his tribe. But, of course, dusk always makes objects larger. We add to their actual bulk their shadow. He was just waiting to see whether, when it made off—on discovering the inedibility of the bottle—he would be able to observe it better, when he was startled by a knock on the door behind him. He wheeled round. 'Who's there!' 'Oh, Sir,' piped a mahogany-muted voice, 'Oh, Sir, you're there. I thought, Sir, you just mightn't be and it might be your fire was smoking bad—p'rh'ps a coal'd jumped and caught the carpet?'

'Everything is all right!' he boomed a dismissal.

'Certainly, Sir, very sorry to disturb you... only thought...' The voice died away carrying its thought beyond earshot. Archdeacon Throcton listened, however, carefully, till far away he heard a dull but specific bump. That was given by the spring-hinged baize door, that, like the veil in the Jewish Temple, kept the profane from the reverend side of the house. Cautiously, even then, he unlocked the door and let a draught blow through the room. Fortunately, the wind was now from the back of the house. Yet after ten minutes the room still had not lost its unpleasant smell while it had been stripped of its pleasant warmth. Leaving the door open he went down to visit his sister. On her lap dozed Tissaphernes. 'Not much use for mice,' he remarked, taking a chair, 'Has he been drowsing like that for long?'

'Well, his working "day" is polar to ours, is only beginning. He's taking his last nap before going on watch.'

Gradually their conversation became easy, almost unguarded, and as earlier she felt her feeling-tone of hopefulness spread over her mind—the quiet though long-postponed day-dreams that some day they would be intimate, with full confidence in each other. But again, as low clouds skirt the far horizon shown by a clear evening, she felt, as though from a greater distance (while she watched the spread of hope) there rose a vaster, vaguer misgiving. Why should she be so queerly pessimistic, always trying to find justifying fears to explain surely not too irrational hopes. She knew that her nature was neither cowardly nor gloomy. Was it wrong to hope that, though she had had great blessings, things might turn out a little better, especially as the improvement would be for the sake of one who she knew was not happy? Why must she suspect that he was showing and indeed feeling such pleasure in her company because... because, well, not because of any enjoyable element in that, but because he who so often had shown he preferred his own company to any others', now did not, now disliked, feared even, being alone? She felt an additional overtone of uneasiness that she should be entertaining such thoughts—entertainment, what an unhappy word for this involuntary harbourage, almost invasion—while keeping up the appearance of being at ease, in the complete calm that this room and this company seemed outwardly to guarantee. Surely, she reflected, as she looked round and listened to the purr of cat and kettle, the sound seeming the very echo of the visible peace, surely it was absurd to suspect her brother of uneasiness, still more of nervousness. Even had he been a nervous type, this place, these sounds, would soon allay such a state of tension. Her mind then began to wonder whether he suspected her divided attention, felt he must, and then a further flash of uneasiness shot into her mind as she reflected that surely if he did not his mind must be obsessed with some secret concern or suspiciously determined not to disturb the appearance of peace.

Neither did the fact that he kept up the habit of spending with her quite a large part of every evening for the next couple of weeks by its regularity do anything to reassure her. That his evening visit should have become almost customary should have gone to prove what she so much wished to believe—that this lonely, sardonic man, at heart disappointed and tending to become embittered, was at last willing to be human, drop his pride, abandon the hope of that recognised ascendancy which is ambition's prize, and find in simple association with his oldest of friends the quiet and lasting pleasure of elderliness, the sharing of lifelong memories and experience. Her doubts insisted on transmuting all this possible and indeed probable promise of calm happiness into misgiving. Surely if something were wrong, how deep and persistent, how watchful and minatory it must be so to keep this wilful, proud solitary so persistently—she used the nursery phrase to herself—'on his good behaviour.'

One evening, however, when he entered, his amiability had about it an additional gleam, almost a glow. She could not doubt it. It was in fact an unique reversal of a mood she had too often endured not to recognise that here it was present in counterpart. She was all too used to him when he would preserve an outward show of bantering courtesy and ironic pleasure while inwardly savage with arrogant impatience. Now he was behaving with what she could only call, in spite of the word's inappositeness to the subject—demureness. He must be pleased by something, deeply, doubly deeply pleased with an odd suppressed elation. She had never seen him in such a state and indeed would have been at a loss to diagnose it, had she not recognised that somehow his favourite role of the disabused cynic had been reversed. He looks, she found herself saying under her breath, like someone who has had a very big surprise, a shock, but one that is only startling because it's too good to be true. He might, she added with a sense that the very inappositeness made it necessary for her to think it out almost to the limit of aloudness, he might be repressing a wish to share some sort of joke! Again in spite of anything she might gather from such signs to encourage her, her spirits sank. Once or twice he rallied her for falling into a 'brown study' and not paying attention to what he was saying. But he kept her with no explanation of his mood until he rose to bid her goodnight. Then she realised she had the truth and her distress closed on her like a trap-door.

'It's really a happy release—spared lingering. I received the intimation just after dinner...' She recalled he had been handed a note and had told her he must go out but would be back before long—'yes, the actual end came with merciful suddenness. Yes, the Dean has died.' There was no doubt he was pleased, elated. It was natural, she tried to argue to herself. There had been no friendship and he had repressed a sense of wrong. The reaction was inevitable. After all, most grief expressed by comparative strangers is, as far as true feeling goes, completely insincere—it is courtesy and he had no need and very little capacity for courtesy in her presence. But she felt not only shocked, she recognised that she was dismayed, alarmed. The very force of her feelings warned her to say nothing and he passed out of the door telling her perfunctorily to sleep well.

He certainly was now uninclined to notice her moods or indeed those of any round him. His mind was fully taken up reviewing the prospect that now seemed clear and open. He was a trifle surprised and so amused at the happiness of the situation, 'A certain simple inevitability' he said to himself as he reached his study, 'I see, I see.' He stood with his back to the empty grate reviewing the events before going to his bedroom. He was, after all, to come into his rights. A series of absurd obstacles, very varied, though pivoting round one unimportant figure, had quietly and naturally melted away.

It was he who the next morning, in the Close, called out a cordial good-day to Dr. Wilkes, who obeying what was clearly a cheerful summons, came alongside.

'You look not too bright this fair morning!'

'You know of the Dean's death last night?'

'I am going over to the Palace now to make arrangements. Surely between ourselves, it is a relief! It was pernicious anaemia, wasn't it? And no one, with the patient's best interests at stake—let alone those of the Cathedral—could desire a useless protracted dispute with inevitability.'

'Still, I had had some hopes of prolonging the condition, I mean sustaining the remission and maybe to some extent improving it!'

'Of course, of course; that's your rightful duty and interest. But you'll as naturally see our professional point of view. With the world in its present state, questioning all pure scholarship and divinity, well, sinecures are proving too expensive. The Establishment just cannot afford to carry too persistent a quota of permanent invalids.'

'But there had been a distinct rally, you know. He was beginning to respond most promisingly to a rather empiric, rather unorthodox idea of mine... and then...'

'Then?' the other encouraged him.

'Oh, complications. Of course one shouldn't be surprised at them in any case of severe debility. His general resistance never seems properly to have recovered from that first attack of alopecia. There was a herpes condition again at the end. About ten days ago I was sent for in the evening. There had been a sudden rise of temperature. Not to be unexpected. But it was sharp. And at the same time an eczemic inflammation was evident. That yielded to treatment, but the fever stayed. Soon he began to wander. Of course, he was a devout man, of the older school, I judge. He kept on quoting fragments of Scripture, mainly from the Old Testament—Job—that would be natural enough, wouldn't it?'

'Yes, yes,' the Archdeacon answered perfunctorily. Did the doctor really think that he was interested in the last wandering words of a Fundamentalist! 'And Samson I remember came up more than once and then he quoted several times, "The little foxes that spoil the vines." That's in the Bible, too, isn't it?'

'Certainly, certainly. "The Song of Songs".'

'A strange book to quote from!'

Archdeacon Throcton cut the interview short, 'Well, doctor, I must be getting on to the Bishop.'

'Of course you must. He was very kind to the Dean. Calling on him nearly every day. Good-bye.' The Archdeacon waved a dismissing hand and turned to the Palace. The queer well-known line went, however, with him. Foxes, how they figured in all folk-lore. Foxes—he ran through Reynard's name in half a dozen ancient tongues. Reaching last, he repeated, 'Alopex'—then paused. What was the association in his mind? Of course: What odd names the medicos did give to ailments! The Physician's name for baldness really meant Fox's Mange!

He had reached the Palace grounds—quite large with high shrubberies, almost coppices—a delightful spot on such a day. The Bishop's gardener and his boy were clearing out undergrowth and dead branches. But as he approached they had paused and were looking down at something. The old man touched his hat and then remarked, just as Archdeacon Throcton was about to pass by, 'Here'a a queer thing, Sir, to find in a garden like this. It must have crawled in to die. Don't touch it, boy. Turn it over with the rake. We've just found it.' The gardener drew aside a sweeping bough that made a wall of foliage to the path. Just underneath it lay a large black fox. It wasn't a pleasant sight for the hair had fallen off large parts of the body owing to very extensive mange.

The Established Church is a complex social device to cushion the shocks of actual experience. The attraction of the sexes, reproduction, parturition, disease and death, the main successive events in the life of every one, the hard facts which Gautama cited as manifest proofs that existence in the body is a baited trap, Anglicanism has now been able to treat as occasions for the delivery of prose and poetry recitations. That the poetry—called hymns and chants—is sometimes banal, the prose, on the contrary, generally magnificent—is of course of purely secondary interest. The real anthropological importance of the whole process is that it has the peculiar, unperceived and perhaps inexplicable power of turning, by the magic of words, shock into boredom. Every rich arrested society, from Confucianism onwards, and probably far before, has discovered this secret of survival and has had the sense to practise it and not to preach it.

A dead Dean—dead of alopecia-cum-herpes-cum-erysipelas-cum... every Greek word whereby, on their side, the doctors had (with the aid of the desiccated contents of the Greek Lexicon) powdered over the discharging details of human decomposition—such a decent cadaver could be the occasion for quite a tasteful exhibition of Jacobean threnody. It could be pacifying, uplifting and provocative—if that were not too strong a word—of quiet thankfulness: for the sufferer's release to higher realms—unspecified, and also for his relinquishing a material benefice the worth of which could be stated to a penny and which when totted up came, per annum, to some twelve hundred pounds sterling.

But, somehow, a dead fox, dead of fox-mange, alopex, the fox coming in like some silly sinister folk-tale figure to die in its tracks right by the Archdeacon's path as he was going to the Bishop to arrange for the Dean's funeral...? The Archdeacon's thought was interrupted and at the same time unpleasantly completed by the gardener quite unnecessarily adding, 'Why, in all my life—and I've been thirty years man and boy round the Palace—I've never seen such a thing. Shy beasts and cunning they be and scarce about here—the farmers liking their hens more than the hunt, and turkey rearing coming on now and doing well on this dry soil. And to come in to die here by this very path, and see, a big black one. That's rare in itself. For reynard they're called and that, our schoolmaster said, means the red or rusty one, as they nearly all are. They die by themselves, as do all the wild ones. No friends round and funerals after, for them. But this one, you'd almost fancy, he was trying to find someone, doctor or parson, so sick was he of his mange. Queer...' Without waiting the Archdeacon strode off.

The incident was slight, one of those small odd 'natural history' happenings that people who have not the capacity for ordered studies and not enough necessary work to do, collect and improve into unconvincing, silly stories. Still, it not only buzzed in his mind like a fly (like one of those blow-flies already settling on the suppurated fox-flesh). It attacked him at a lower emotional level. For a moment he felt almost as though he might be sick.

A step away from the somewhat dank shrubberies; a step into the quiet, polish-smelling hall, clean and spacious under the quiet inspection of the morning sunbeams; a score of steps up the thickly carpeted stairway, flanked all the way by an unbroken succession of painted bishops; at the foot of the sweep Bishop Bendwell's high-stocked predecessor; at the curve by the oriel a bevy of 'full-bottomed' peruked Lords Spiritual; at the top Laudian ruffs, square caps and small, white, pointed beards. The whole ascending progression was an effective exercise in psychotherapy. As you rose, easily, almost effortlessly, up these broad-shallow sweeping 'treads,' your eye carried you on simultaneously up the stream of time and showed you under the change of fashion the power of continuity, proved to you the calm assurance of the centuries that had raised and sustained the present. The 'Come in' with which the Bishop's voice summoned him, set final assurance on his rapidly re-established sense of complete security. He was sure in its ring of welcome he could hear as an overtone, 'friend come up higher.' Nor was he mistaken.

They agreed about each detail of the funeral: they went on and agreed about the death being 'a merciful release': further, they agreed that all that had been done and all that had befallen, had been done and had befallen rightly. 'Have a cigar, Throcton.' The Bishop reached out his box—as clear a sign of friendly intimacy as the offer of snuff by an eighteenth-century gentleman to one he wished to indicate as his almost equal. And the use of the un-prefixed vocative, the intimacy of the plain surname. That, too, argued well. He refused the weed, but waited without impatience as the Bishop persuaded the roll of leaves to smoulder and then, the little bonfire drawing well, sat back enjoying the first pulls. As he looked at the big aproned body cradled in its big easy chair, the round face raised to the ceiling and with the succulent wad plugging its pursed lips—a picture of one relapsed into unweened content, the ridiculous pseudo-classical line floated through his mind: 'Hera, All-Mothering Air, feeding with vaporous nectar her favourite child!' The joke, with the sense of superiority that it gave him to this sucking overseer, made him because of his pleasant expectations feel a real liking for the old boy. 'At heart,' he thought, 'he's as broad of mind as I, though of course his poorer brain doesn't let him see it. Well, no harm!' He began to lecture that unfailingly appreciative audience himself, 'Do not despise what you call our duller dupes. It is profoundly, anaesthetically soothing to the lingering and still painful remnants of an ecclesiastical conscience that there should be those who can yet subscribe to thirty-nine impertinently inquisitive Articles with neither a smile nor a sigh.' That was really quite a neat sentence. What a pity he could never use it over his own name. Perhaps it could be brought in, in some posthumous memoirs. His mind threw back to the present. Those Thirty-Nine Articles—yes, he'd have to swear to them and his belief in them again when he took the next step up. He turned again and looked at the chief shepherd who could bar or open the next and larger pen in the fold. The Bishop was looking at him through a comforting coil of smoke and after letting a cloud rise upward, which it did in the most auspicious way, floating right on into the lap of a painted angel on the ceiling, he volunteered that he could now say that he had foreseen this eventuality. This re-opening was too promising for Throcton even in his mind to question the Bishop's claim to the gift of even deductive prophecy. Finally the Lord of the Diocese spoke to the Close point. He went so far as to convey that the Prime Minister would, he believed, prove 'gracious to his supplication'—he used the liturgically flavoured phrase almost with a smile. And that now he felt the issue might be left with that exalted quarter with some assurance as to the outcome. The thought under the Mitre—he passed a hand over his forehead—he was prepared to foretell would be found to agree with that under the Crown.

When Throcton went back through the shrubbery the laurels had once more become ornamental foliage. All suggestion of the dank and the sepulchral had gone from them. They were the proper background for dignified buildings and for the dignitaries that dwell in them, suggesting, too, a classical overtone of flavour of that literary recognition which laurel and bay naturally propose. The Bishop, his cigar finished, had strolled to his big bay window. His eye was caught by the retreating figure down below. 'He's not an easy man—proud as the devil. But a good scholar. And considering his pride, he showed some strength in swallowing it. Yes, for him, he took his disappointment well. Of course he thinks I'm a fool. That's the weakness of the scholar—no power to recognise knowledge unless it comes out of a book. He thinks we "prelatic preachers" are simply big tongues that have free play because pivoted upon narrow brains. But there's more in good administration—yes, and in a good sermon than can be put in a book or a series of textbook propositions. What did "Anglican's big loss" say'—He strolled over and found the volume of J. H. Newman that was lying on his desk; 'yes, that's it—"We are not saved by a smart syllogism" still less by an impeccable style.' He shut the book and drew his chair to his work-table. 'Yes, I'm glad the P.M. will pretty certainly give it him. He was never cut out to be a reporter on country church structural repairs. Well, I must find someone who is.' As he turned over his files his mind, however, still lingered on the metaphysical problem,

'I wonder what he believes? Well, we are in a state of transition, and, after all, Anglicanism has always been more a transit than a stasis—perhaps that is why it lasts, because it can always compromise with the present and at the same time is never quite happy in it. The perfectly successful is the perfectly finished, isn't it?' Then seeing that his private speculations were tending to sound deep enough to be in danger of fouling with submerged theological rocks, the Bishop coiled up the line of his unravelled thought and turned his mind to its real business—finding and fitting men that were fit, good middle men, into posts that required a double duty, spiritual and temporal.

CHAPTER ELEVEN

The P.S.—as he was always called by the other Secretaries, that rose above him to the towering Secretaries of State—the P.S., they said, deserved his name because everyone in the know knew one of the P.M's ways of ending certain of his political letters—'P.S. the following piece of Church Preferment is now available: suggest someone sound.' For the P.S. was, of course, the Patronage Secretary. But the P.S. did not share the contempt for his office nearly all his colleagues showed. Nor for that matter did the P.M. Both of them had a sense of humour and also a sense of romance, an uncommon blend that made a common bond.

This was the P.S's. morning. Once a fortnight—if the political sky was not too lowering, he had his hour, or at least thirty minutes, alone with the Magician. And to-day the Wizard, as he did when in high expansive humour, dressed for the part. The Patronage Secretary in the Whitehall uniform of black frock-coat, rose, as there entered a flowered silk dressing gown and a scarlet fez. Between these two splashes of oriental colour looked out the half-mummified features of the most powerful face in Europe. But it looked no more formidable than the fez that crowned it. Besides, even the eyes, that could not hide their penetration, were now wrinkled round with humour.

'Her Majesty's Chief Minister...' he swept a bow to the standing secretary and the fez nearly fell off, 'Soon may be saluted as Grand Vizier by far more subjects than have ever hailed him under the dubious title of First Lord of the Treasury. The Royal Titles Bill is now assured of its passage into Law, when, May the Queen Live for Ever! [the fez bobbed its tassel again] the long, thin line seen by Macbeth extending down the centuries will suddenly "conglobulate" (as the Great Lexicographer has phrased it) and produce—if I may be forgiven under the stress of emotion for mixing my metaphors—and produce, as a crowning pendant, an Oriental Empress!' The fez was whipped off, revealing for a moment a skull so bare and wrinkled that it seemed more like a fossilised brain than an ordinary head. Then the scarlet cone resumed its uneasy seat at an even jauntier angle. 'That, my young friend, is neither rhetoric nor irrelevance but a very pertinent introduction to our business. Let us be seated. What fare have you for me to-day?'

Before, however, the P.S. could settle on the chair he drew up beside the couch on which the tired garish figure had sunk, the voice crowed again, 'The Imponderables—as my "opposite number," the Kurfurst Kanzler, calls them—they decide; he knows—not arms nor battles but, as he's finding, Kultur-kampfs. So, young sir, to the Church, to the Church. "No Bishop, No King" as the "British Solomon" so wisely remarked. But, as he and his son didn't know, if the monarch should become an oriental empress, then the *episcopus* must become equally spacious, equally latitudinarian to embrace East as well as West, now that a mightier Venice once again holds "the Gorgeous East in Fee"! Now to business. The See of... That's a bishopric though a small one. What peer who could give us trouble in the Lords, might want a minimal mitre for one of his wife's poorer but scholarly relatives? Yes, that must wait. Give me something simpler to start on. "The Deanery of Norminster?" Yes, that will do. Yes, surely I recall something about Norminster—an Arabic scholar there? That's it—one of the Canons?'

'Yes, and he's "in line of succession," too, Sir. I mean he's conservative and people would expect it.' 'He's not a Ritualist? I and the Empress Designate, '*Ego et Regina Mea*,' won't stand for that, "man millinery," church costuming! Naturally, a Lady doesn't like men competing in the choir with flounces and trains. Sunday bonnets and shawls put out of countenance by mitres and copes! And, mark my words, neither do I, young man. The British like theatricals but they like them in Parliament, not in the pulpit nor at the altar. "Mr. G." Cotton-and-Phrase Spinning Bright and your humble servant, we give them their variety show. They go to church, as I do, for peace, seemliness, to hear and see what their fathers have always heard and seen. There's more than a little in the Poet Laureate's vernacular summing-up of a proper service, "The parson said what he oughta said, and then I coomed awa"! These posturing young papalists will break up the Establishment and I won't have it!'

'Oh, Archdeacon Throcton is certainly a weight on the other side.'

'Anything against him?' 'Innocence itself, Sir. You know the Epitaph (I understand he may himself earn a repetition of it)—"Sacred to the Memory of the Very Reverend Dean... of this Cathedral, who in this place pursued the cure of souls for forty years without the least trace of enthusiasm"?'

A loud, appreciative cackle came from the horizontal master of the Empire. 'You've read your Talleyrand, my boy, "pas de zêle, pas de zêle." No danger of this Arabian flirting with Mr. G's penchant for Greek Orthodoxy or finding affinities and unions of hearts with the Balkan bishoprics and archimandrites?' 'None, Sir, I'll wager.' 'He's our man. Let him have it.'

A small clock tinkled discreetly but peremptorily from the mantelpiece. 'Allah, be merciful! Why cannot The Eternal extend Time when it is pleasant. Here, give me a hand.'

As he was raised to his tottering feet he snatched the fez from his head. 'In that wardrobe, there, get me out my frock-coat. Here, take this dressing-gown. Help me into my prison garb.'

He turned to a large mirror and touched carefully a strand of hair, dead black and coiled, like a withered root over a rock, that snaked along his skull till it just reached his forehead. He pulled at the black coat as he trod stiffly to the door. His squire had it opened. 'The disguise is convincing?' He asked, as he passed through, 'I look the part, do I?' The P.S. felt all the enthusiasm that his loyal 'dresser' feels for the grand old master of 'the boards' about to face one of his last performances. 'You're grand' he dared smile. The old mask, already facing the stairs, was fixed; only the eye that his attendant was watching, drooped for a moment. 'You can write that Deanery note' was the final instruction. The P.S. went back into the room. In five minutes the little letter—a life warrant—was written and put out for dispatch.

CHAPTER TWELVE

Miss Throcton always distributed the mail. Every morning she was down first; winnowed the weighty letters from the chaff—bills, advertisements, etc.; then gave to the cook for the servants' hall any missives they might have received. The grain she placed on the left-hand side of her brother's plate.

The morning came when she found among the usual deposits in the mail-box a neat envelope, unstamped, but having across the top of it four letters, then, and for a further couple of generations, more powerful, and over a wider field than even the other famous four—A.D.M.G. To its initial assertion of an almost world-wide right-of-way—through its superscription O.H.M.S.—this particular envelope had added to its top-left-hand corner a couple of words as to its origin—'Patronage Office.'

Miss Throcton's cheek had turned quickly pale while the envelope turned slowly in her hands. There were perhaps half a dozen other letters—no doubt archdeaconry business. 'Well,' she sighed, 'it would save him from work which is really distasteful and really for such a mind wasteful. Perhaps it is all right—but I wish I felt sure.' After a slight hesitation she gave the O.H.M.S. its rightful place of precedence at the top of the others.

On his entering her brother glanced at the little pile but she looked away. He had said 'Good morning' before reaching the table. She listened during 'Prayers' for the tone of his voice. Yes, a certain resonance told her that he was trying by a slight increase of vocal emphasis, if not to attend to the words, to keep his mind off what in a few minutes he would be reading. And when they rose from their knees and took their places at table he continued to show self-control. Not till she had handed him his coffee did he open his letters—all of them, carefully with a knife, then de-enveloping them, and putting aside their husks, the actual letters were spread one on another. He read each of them in silence while he ate and drank. Then holding out his cup for it to be refilled he looked at her steadily.

'Well, you can move into the Deanery as soon as you wish.'

'But surely you would seek guidance?'

'But surely,' he replied, using exactly the same question-tone, 'you would not have me a hypocrite? You must know the vulgar story—I have heard the Bishop tell it—of preferment; "Is your father going to accept?" "Dunno. Father's in his study praying for guidance. Mother's upstairs, packing!".'

Her sense of humour came to her aid. 'The story must be apocryphal. No appointment, however important, would require a flight!' He smiled at her refusal to be shocked and she pointed her persistence with:

'Besides, in this case it is the woman who is asking guidance.' His smile became almost genial. It vanished again, however, when she continued:

'If guidance isn't to be sought, because there is no doubt as to the step to be taken, then doesn't one give thanks?'

'Laetitia,' his voice was as sharp as when he had chided her for what he held to be superstitious apprehension. 'I have told you already that I will not be a hypocrite. I have had to wait through a series of frustrations as absurd as they were highly inconvenient for all concerned, that tardily, at an almost unbelievable length, the natural and right thing might happen. What is due to me and to the Chapter has at last eventuated. If I am to thank God for this obvious, inevitable, unavoidable solution then I have to blame Him for hesitations and confusions, muddles, of which I myself, or indeed any rational creature, would be incapable. To have such a view of Deity would be to degrade one's intelligence and conscience to a level at which one would find oneself believing in the Devil!' His tone and uncharacteristic volubility showed that she had fully roused his resentment. Even had she felt her theology equal to his, her practical anthropology, which was certainly superior, had long taught her that once anger is roused, intelligence, far from aiding understanding, actually invents arguments to show why no reasonableness can be allowed in the case that is being resented.

She did not speak to him on the matter again, nor he to her till he remarked with careful casualness three days after at lunch—'The Bishop is pleased. He also tells me Mrs. Simpkins wishes to leave as soon as possible and not to avail herself of the six weeks she could legally remain. A wise solution in the circumstances. Naturally a woman of her modest station could never have been comfortable in what is almost a mansion. She is to live, I gather, with her brother, a retired accountant, I believe in Cheltenham. It would be wise if you could manage to make the move in ten days or so.'

She said nothing, only signalling with a nod that she assented. Her mind was upbraiding her. She had delayed calling on the bereaved woman—only writing a brief note and that, she felt, had been stilted, stilted for the same reason that had made her hesitate to call. Her excuse was of course that she must not yet intrude upon grief at its height, that she would have time to offer real condolence and sympathy when the time for Mrs. Simpkins to leave drew near. But she knew that she was shrinking from and shirking going to the Deanery to face the woman who was being ejected that she and her brother might take her place. And now if she delayed... She was surprised, shocked to find that the alternative course to calling at once entered her mind and refused for a moment to yield. If she waited a couple of days then it would be impossible, and she was very busy, and her going over would be misunderstood by the other woman who, no doubt, would attack her brother. Surely it would be wiser to wait, kinder to write a long letter when the widow had settled in to her new life at Cheltenham, without the obvious painful associations that this place must rouse—and make bitter. As soon, however, as she had heard the inner voice out she recognised its source.

She went to her room, dressed and walked over to the Deanery.

'I know I ought to have come over before, but...'

'But you feared being misunderstood.'

For a moment as her effort at frankness seemed over-met she almost gave way to formality. She probably would have, had she met the other woman's eyes. But her wisdom in shrinking from that possible additional provocation was rewarded. As she looked past the defensive figure that stood watching her, she caught sight of a small pile of worn books, cheap ornaments, rubbish scraps that this proud house seemed shaking from its stately panels and mantelpieces. And she herself was the living form of that assured, arrogant good-taste.

'Yes, I feared to be misunderstood, I'm ashamed to say. I was shrinking from coming here because I felt that you might well resent it. So many of us who like to feel we look self-assured are really cowards.'

She waited. The other, however, was evidently waiting, too. But brave enough to own herself a coward, Miss Throcton now had the courage to go on. It didn't matter if after all she was going to fail. All she had to do was not to run away.

'I hoped you'd let me come and have a talk with you. Those who face great sorrow always can help us who have been spared—help us, prepare us.'

Her voice had become steady, detached, convincing. She was no longer talking to put the other at her ease. She was treating the bereaved woman, who had lost her meaning and place in life, as an equal, and an equal who had won a temporary elevation through loss and pain. She felt Mrs. Simpkins's hand on her shoulder. It wasn't the gesture of a woman to a woman, still less of one slightly but of distinctly lower social station toward one higher. It was one mortal signalling to another, over the low fog of conventions and words. They sat down, silently, for some time. It was Mrs. Simpkins who spoke first. Nor did she speak of herself, at least of her disaster. 'At moments I almost understand,' her voice was low but definite, even more objective than Miss Throcton's had been, 'and then it's all submerged under another... another wave.' Miss Throcton did not look at her but took her hand. The grasp was returned gratefully but tonicly. 'So,' the voice was quite steady again, 'So, you see, when I'm in the clear I can't find words for it. And when I have words they only spring from, from feelings.'

They were silent again and gradually Miss Throcton found herself recognising the calm, feeling relief because of it, wonder at it and finally conscious thankfulness for it. 'You'll understand, then,' Mrs. Simpkins continued as though giving directions about finding an address, 'I can only put it, as it were, back-side front. I know that's clumsy but there doesn't seem any other way of saying it. Wilkins'—she spoke her husband's rather ridiculous Christian name without hesitation or sentimentality—'Wilkins is safe. I see he did make a mistake, a very grave one, out of pride, ambition, the wish for us to succeed. I suppose we who are religious'—the tone had not the slightest smugness in it. It was reflective, speculative—'I suppose we aren't allowed to make the mistakes that those who are worldly can make with apparent safety. So he exposed himself to retaliation. He paid for it. That is over. He's safe,' she repeated as though closing an episode. She turned and put her hand again on the other's shoulder, 'You've been good to me and brave. But for you, I think I would have been caught. I'd have given way to hate—my wrong would have...'

Miss Throcton put her hand on the hand on her shoulder. 'So I can tell you what I couldn't have otherwise. I didn't know I could till you said I could help. In my feeble way I was trying to see, to test if you could take it, when you came in. Like you, I'd decided if you didn't call—and I thought you mightn't, mightn't feel it was worth the risk—then all real attempt between us to help each other would be over. But you came and stood my clumsy questioning...' She stopped again, this time for longer. 'But you know what I'm going to say. I know you love your brother. You know...' Miss Throcton stiffened her spine—not for withdrawal. It was the body responding to her summons to maintain contact not to shrink into social stiffness.

'Yes, I see,' she replied in exactly the same tone as the other's, 'I wasn't honest when I told you that my brother didn't feel any bitterness. Your husband, he felt, had wronged him. I know you will agree that the amount of wrong or right doesn't concern us now. He did resent it.'

'There, my dear,' the endearment awoke no sense of patronage, 'that's what I wanted, needed to say: You will take care, won't you? Because Wilkins managed to get past it, because it was so bad, had in it, we know now, such power to do harm... Do you think your brother could really forgive Wilkins? Believe me, and please don't think I'm being ridiculous,' then she smiled. 'Of course I fear being misunderstood far more than you. But you see I do know now how very dangerous it is to hate—perhaps even more when it's disguised as contempt.'

The conversation had taken on a quality of detached intimacy that Miss Throcton never recalled having had with anyone before—as though two experts—or at least keen amateurs, not knowing each other's names, were met before an enigmatic piece of work. The subjectivity of the personal point of view, the fact that the problem happened to be their own private concern, seemed for the time being to have disappeared. So when she inquired about help, as they went to the door together, the offer was accepted as easily, as detachedly as the question had been asked. She did, however, find herself flushing a little as, when they actually parted, she held on to her courage as she owned: 'Of course you know how little I can influence him. He has always taken for granted that his class—and a scholar as well—could not be petty, still less base. So he can't allow he could be resentful, still less'—she insisted on the word coming out, though it did strain her tone in uttering it—'vindictive.' She looked up. The other face was now far more flushed than hers. For a moment she felt her feelings getting ready after their period of anaesthesia to rush back and cramp her into offence. The woman was losing her self-control, her temper. Her basic vindictiveness was coming out now that she, Miss Throcton, the true lady, had granted her confidence and completely let fall her guard! A moment later a keener stab of self-recrimination than any she had yet felt struck her, as Mrs. Simpkins, her hand on her side, said hastily, 'Quite a catch in my breath. Do forgive me. I suddenly go all flushed like this. Dr. Wilkes says it's the strain and all. But it's nothing, nothing at all. And I'll never forget what you've done for me.'

Miss Throcton walked home hurriedly. Her brother, herself and that poor gallant woman—what a plait of three different strands for Providence to interweave! The interview, however, though it did not seem to give her any light as to how she might help her brother to take the smallest step toward altering his character, did help her immediately in her dealing with him and give her a certain further restraint. On coming in to tea, he remarked, with a brightness that just now grated on her more than gloom, 'Glad you have been so prompt in seeing what would need to be done at the Deanery.' 'Not much,' she replied guardedly. 'The poor things had few things.' Then feeling that she need not or should not be either a coward or a liar, 'They had the good taste to alter things hardly at all.' His, 'H'm! That's a lady-like damn of faint praise!' nettled her but under her vigilance only drew her into a sudden neatness of speech. 'I don't know why,' she smiled, 'that painstaking product of charitable honesty should be christened with the clumsy name of a left-handed compliment!' He laughed, surprised and indeed slightly startled at her almost epigrammatic repartee. He even felt it was perhaps due for him to make some conversational dismissal of those who were now going out of his life for good, fate having at last made them make room for him. 'Many women, I have noticed, are happiest in widowhood. They have then secured to them an assured part and a fossilised romance. The Simpkins marriage might well have proved increasingly difficult. Marriage,'—he felt he should show he could match her phrase-making—'if it is not to fray should be woven of three strands, Romance, Finance and Prestige. The first could never have been present; the second only the Church supplied—that house calls for more than its stipend. And as for prestige...' he waved his hand dismissorily. They were, she felt, back again on dangerous ground. 'I think we can be moved in fairly soon,' appeared as a safe way out. 'Good,' he said and was gone. Miss Throcton's efficiency foresaw that if she was to move at the pace which her brother had designated as wise she would have to begin without delay. Well, it might permit her to speed two voyages with one breeze. She would go over and see if Mrs. Simpkins would let her help her move. She felt now fairly sure her offer would not only be accepted but appreciated, and so looked forward to this opportunity for a last kindness. Leaving, therefore, as soon as her household round permitted, she had nearly arrived at her future residence when she heard:

'Excuse me, Miss Throcton. I was just about to call on the Dean.'

'I have just left him, Dr. Wilkes, at home. I'm going now over to the Deanery.'

'You have heard then?' 'What?' 'I am just coming from the Deanery. I feared there was cardiac strain. She had been through a great deal, of course. They were a devoted couple. Mrs. Simpkins died early this morning. Yes, I have called in a nurse.'

'May I...?' 'Of course. May I accompany you.' She thanked him. They did not break their silence until they were out again in the Close.

'I have telegraphed her brother.' Dr. Wilkes paused. 'He has replied that he wishes the burial to be at Cheltenham, and gave me instructions which I have handed on to the undertaker who will arrange everything very nicely.'

Miss Throcton thanked him for his company. As she went to the florist to order a wreath the face of the dead woman stayed in her mind. Yes, she, like her husband, was now, as she had put it, safe. The serenity of the dead should make us at least less hurried.

At lunch her brother asked her how her plans had shaped and when given reason for a few days' delay only remarked, 'Her brother's behaviour shows some sense of the situation. It will certainly save much more time being wasted.' His tone showed that he felt he was behaving, seemlily, generously, with a final finical hesitation on the part of Providence—or Fate. Miss Throcton worked with a will that he might have no further frustration, though she often felt that his urgency, far from deserving the word 'wise,' showed that rush which marks the fool's pace rather than the angel's.

But she comforted herself by remembering what she had once heard the Bishop say—and surely he should know—that he had often found men who had been quite difficult as long as they were denied recognition, become open and generous once their capacity had been honoured. Her brother seemed to be responding to this kindly treatment. That he had greatly desired to be 'in'—as movers say—was very clear. The jar that had shaken the growing intimacy of their relations before his 'elevation'—as he once or twice referred to the change of status—that strain now seemed removed and forgotten. And she herself was, she felt, free to accept this new offer of a closer relationship at its face value. Before she had feared—all the more because she repressed the fear as baseless and irrational—that he could have no positive reason for pleasure in her company—there must therefore be some latent, negative cause. But now—the sequence was not in strict logic but served her wishful purpose—now that he was safe, was arrived, surely it was safe for her to enjoy their present assured state without further irrational misgivings. As she glanced at his face, listened to his voice's timbre, watched his carriage, no shadow of further suspicion rose behind her. 'Of course,' she concluded to herself, 'he was always hypersensitive, and so hardened himself to save himself pain. The persistent disappointments deeply wounded him. Yes, characters which are at base good, are often helped by rightful success.'

She was sitting in the Deanery parlour. It was a beautiful room built as the whole house had been by Gibbs in the mid-eighteenth century, looking west, with large stately windows reaching down almost to the polished oak floor. The sun's western light poured in; the slanting rays seemed almost as solid as the great carved gilt 'Glory' which, before the Tractarian-cum-Gothic counter-attack, had stood over the Cathedral altar and now had been placed as a chandelier-pivot on this room's ceiling. She was waiting for her brother to come in from evensong and watched idly the steady drift of motes—moving specks of brighter gold passing across the belt of deeper unmoving gold. As he came in she saw the motes swirl as though wheeling to salute his passage. His remark, too, kept the tone of the place and hour. 'Well, this is peace at last.' He sat down and looked about him, 'I feel'—he was speaking with almost as much unguarded ease as if he were by himself—'as though I had arrived, after a stiff and tiresome pull, where one can sit and take in the view. And it is a fine prospect, a fine prospect.' His eye ranged round from the great window set in the south wall and through which the north-west tower of the Cathedral could be seen, and then down the three stately west windows. Their upper panes were flooded with the oncoming sunset. The lower showed the red and white of the brick and Portland stone walls of the lovely formal garden and the tops of the topiary-trained yew hedges that a century of shaping had made into green walls and towers. 'I shall work well here,' he added. And then his pleasure making him wish to show graciousness, 'This place suits you, too. It is a house worthy of that care which you have a remarkable ability to yield. That such a spot should have so long housed a living corpse—I mean a suspended animate, and then...' 'Dear,' she interrupted, 'Don't... It's all turned out well, hasn't it? Why...?' He was not vexed with her check. His attention had strayed for a moment and when he did look back to her he was smiling: 'I thought your domestic drill had produced a staff so armed and agile with mop and turk's head that no cobweb however high could escape, no ball of fluff however close-clinging to the nether wainscot avoid the sweep of their brooms!' As he spoke with facetious eloquence, she glanced again to where his eye had again gone. He was watching with a half-amused, half-puzzled look, where the panel which was under the furthest of the west window-seats met the floor. The sunlight, pouring down diagonally onto the polished floor-boards, made here an angle of shadow into which one had to look through a haze of golden shifting motes.

'I think,' he continued, 'I perceive that a witness against your cleaners has stolen out to disprove their thoroughness. There is a small gossamer ball of "sweepings" at this moment availing itself of a favourable ground draught to coast along the wainscot, seeking, no doubt, to gather to itself contributors.'

'The light,' she remarked, getting up, 'I can't see through it into that shadow.' He rose, too, came beside her and then said, 'Oh, it was only a trick of the cross-lighting. Queer!' he added, taking again his chair, 'my eyes, in spite of Arabic and forty years of study, seldom give a mistaken diagnosis.'

However, twice again in the following ten days, variations of the little incident occurred. First he asked to see that his study—also a stately room with polished floor—should be floor-polished every day. She consented and just in time prevented herself adding—'Has Mary's cleaning been perfunctory?' She knew it had not. For not only did she herself inspect and praise each room as it was tidied; she had trained her maids in her own concern. Besides, some sub-twinge of anxiety checked her. Her brother, though something of a martinet, had never been of the fussy, meticulous, 'house-proud' type. Indeed, like most thorough scholars he did not like his room too ordered, saying that a good maid's sense of order and a good mind's were each good but different. This fussiness was, then, out of character. It began far down in her heart to re-stir her misgivings... The second incident made more restless the roused uneasiness, but offered them no explanation. It was a repetition of the first incident—when they had been together in the parlour toward sunset. This time, however, they were dining. Candles had been lit. But as the evening was very still and warm the curtains had not been drawn. The last sign of a clear sunset remained in the west, a quiet lake of cloudless green, into which, from above, the deep blue of full night was percolating. She had been resting her eyes on that vast tranquil distance when glancing back she noticed that he was, as before, looking in a slightly puzzled way at the floor by the wainscot. All he said, however, was, 'I haven't seen Tissaphernes for some while?' 'I'm afraid,' she answered, 'he didn't like the move. Cats are like that. Houses and not their human hosts seem their real friends. He wandered away, going back to his old haunt twice. And now I've had to send him to the veterinary. Cook thinks that's the real cause of his restlessness and when he comes back he'll be all right.' 'Can a veterinary "minister to a mind diseased," or even distressed, and cure a cat's nostalgia!'

'Oh, I thought I'd said—she says she found that he had mange coming on.'

'I must say then that I'm glad he had the considerateness to cease using you as a cushion.' He laughed. Then again his eye wandered and he glanced at the floor, before continuing. 'If the Veterinary cannot cure him, as we lack an Elisha nowadays, we had better get another mouse-warden.' 'Oh, we must give him every chance, don't let's be heartless.' 'Oh, don't be sentimental!' A sudden flaw of irritation sounded in his voice. 'Besides,' she added conciliatorily, 'Cook would perhaps be unsettled. She says she's not seen a mouse in the place. And she'd certainly complain if she did. She says the smell of a cat, just in itself, will keep mice away for weeks.'

'Well, perhaps they respect the quarters where he dined and slept, but not elsewhere.'

'Have you seen any?' 'If my eyes haven't deceived me, I saw one not two minutes ago, there!' He pointed to the wainscot under the central window seat. She was only just in time to stop herself saying, 'But that's the spot where you thought you saw the ball of sweepings.' All she actually said was to ask him to tell her if he saw a mouse again. He did not. Indeed, the next uneasiness she experienced was provoked by something that happened, or she thought happened—she could not be sure which, and she had no one to ask, for it befell herself. She had not told her brother that some days before cook had uttered the banishing word 'mange,' she had found Tissaphernes unpleasant olfactorily. Indeed, it was because she had found that she could, by this crude sense alone, be aware of his presence in the room, that she had asked cook to diagnose. Now about a week after her brother's suspicion of a mouse, it was her turn to suspect. But she suspected cat.

She was coming back from the cook's quarters, through the passage that led to the front of the house. The passage was dark—darker really in the day, when a distant fanlight gave its lighting, than at night, when it had its own lamp. The passage, for the same reason, that it had no window of its own, did not ventilate very well. But it was not the standard ground of complaint between dining-room and kitchen, cabbage water, that offended her. She drew a guarded breath through her nostrils, enough to be sure; but not enough, she hoped, to prove unhealthy. Yes, there could be no doubt. Tissaphernes had come back and returned uncured. She re-entered the kitchen. Cook, however, was clear. Tissaphernes was still at 'the vet's, if you'll forgive me Ma'am for shortening that long word. I never could get all those letters spoken. And the people I was last with always just called the horse-doctor the vet and they certainly always had him around the place.' Then from the light airs of reminiscence Cook modulated to news, 'I myself, having the greengrocer to take too; the vegs not being what they be and it being high summer still; I took my way home by the vet's—I ask pardon—and he told me I might see him. Poor fellow—why I didn't dare even give him a pat, and he mewing for it as for milk. There's no doubt about it, he's worse. The vet's a real kind man, but he fears the worse...' Cook's voice took on a quaver. Miss Throcton regretted loosing the floods of foreboded bereavement, so retired toward her own quarters. Still, passing through the close passage she once again felt she had undeniable sensory proof of the cat or a cat—in any case a very uncured cat.

The unpleasant smell however only lasted a day more. Her brother made no complaint. She was determined not to ask him if he noticed anything. And the day the smell completely faded, so that she herself could no longer detect a hint of it, cook's tears came on in earnest. Tissaphernes had had to be helped out of his body, which, once his glory, had become his shame. Again she said nothing to her brother and he did not inquire.

The second experience was also olfactory. But here she was surprised into action that did involve her brother. She was sitting with a book by her reading lamp when she felt sure it must have begun to smoke. Hardly looking up she turned the flame a fraction down. The smell did not lessen, rather increased. She looked, and saw the wick was well trimmed. No fume was going up the glass chimney. The smell, now unpleasantly strong, was, she realised, more like a candle-end left smouldering. Could one of the servants...? She went to the door. It did come from the passage. But not from that part of it that led to the back of the house. It was floating down from the front of the house, from the direction of her brother's study. Quite a sharp attack of alarm took her. He might have fallen into a doze among his papers and his lamp. She went along the passage. The smell was not very strong. She had never dared to interrupt him; this, however, might be a matter of life and death. She did listen for a moment at the door. There was no sound of any movement the other side of it. She took hold of the handle. The latch had caught or the door was locked. She twisted at the handle with both hands. Suddenly she heard a movement, a quick stride, 'Who's there!' In spite of the thickness of the door-panels the voice sounded strained, more strained than she had ever heard her brother's. As she hesitated the handle turned of itself in her loosening fingers and they were face to face. 'Well!' he called—that strange protean word for challenge, dismissal, protest... 'Well?' 'I thought,' she began. 'Please never come unless I should call for you.' He said it quietly, looking at her carefully all the while. Then the door was closed in her face. The smell of burning followed her however back to her room. It, too, as had the cat aroma, hung about for a couple of days. Then it was gone. No one else seemed to have perceived it. She thought—with what grounds she was never sure—that she ceased any longer to be able to perceive the taint of singeing when once more her brother drew her attention to a minute domestic incident. She had expected him to be distant after her intrusion, and he had not disappointed her. In fact, he held her at arm's length and without any courtesy conversations until he needed her services. It was a little criticism of her province. She was glad of it, though, for it served to establish, if only on a single-plank bridge, their friendliness.

'Have you been changing the laundress?' She told him No, and asked Why?

'Oh, a small thing but a sign of carelessness. I have found one of my handkerchiefs stained and then, I suppose in some effort to redeem the first blunder, scorched.' Naturally, no laundress is immaculate. But she saw that such a remark would not fit the case. She was correct, but the evidence of her correctitude gave her no reassurance. On the contrary.

CHAPTER THIRTEEN

It was from that day that they seemed to enter another epoch or zone, leaving behind the security of routine commonplace living. It was as though till then—as on the Cathedral clock a tune was first picked out and, after that, all the bells came clashing in making variations on the theme—an outline had been dotted in and now all the same incidents—which could be interpreted as normal, came back together making further explaining away useless. She had longed that her brother would become intimate and give his confidence. They were, it was now clear, to be driven together into a closer relationship than she had ever expected by a force more alien than ever she had suspected. The onset was made without further warning. Nature was so calm that she seemed to desire to soothe 'her creature man.' The moon was over the garden in the early night. 'It is so still out-of-doors,' he remarked as they stood looking out after dinner. 'We might take a turn on the lawn.' 'Yes, it is perfectly dry, too,' she replied as they stepped through the end window which an early nineteenth-century Dean, caring more for garden convenience than architectural correctitude, had cut down through the window-seat, making a two-leaf glazed door. The moon lit the hedge-enclosed place perfectly, beautifully, so that it looked far larger than by day—with almost a sombre dignity. The night-smelling stocks and pinks sent out a perfume so dense that the skeins of vapour seemed almost palpable. Almost palpable, too, in that still heavy air was the purr of the ghostly night-moths flitting from one heavy flower to another. The whirr of their furred wings gave a muted note, hushed and low, the ear felt that it was actually touched, rather than the ear-drum vibrated by an air-wave.

'Scent and sound, the world seems composed of them now, with sight only as a dim adjunct,' she remarked. His more practical mind, glancing about for a reply-comment that might not too stiffly challenge hers, remarked. 'The moon—look at it. It's clear enough!' 'But it, too,' she countered, 'looks now as though it were a mask held in front of an invisible face.' 'Do you know what is the proper name for it,' he asked a little hurriedly, 'when it is in this phase?' And then not waiting—he told her, 'gibbous,' adding, 'But I see you are not interested in seeing or in instruction, only in feeling and intuition no doubt.' True, she was not looking at the sky. She was drawing in deep breaths of the almost anaesthetic scent, and her reply was irrelevant, 'Those night-smelling flowers are really too strong, aren't they. Their scent is hardly any longer that of blossoms, fresh and gay. They remind one more of the aroma of...' 'I was remarking to you about the moon,' he answered. His tone had sharpened and in his impatience he put his hand on her shoulder to make her attend. As he did so he glanced at her face. The moonlight, no doubt, would make it pale. Her attention, however, it was clear, was not wandering. Her expression was fixed, rigid. She said nothing to his reproof, but actually took his fingers in hers—an intimacy that now startled him. She must be frightened. With her other hand she was pointing at the foot of the hedge. He saw what had caught her attention. He felt also the tremor of her fear run through him like a current. For the sight, at least at first glance, should not have shaken them so severely. Two small green-silver spots, almost like small fragments of reflected moonlight, shone up at them from almost ground-level, not more than three yards away, the other side of the wide herbaceous border which, beginning at their feet, there reached the base of the towering yew-hedge. They stood still, trying to make out what in the yew-hedge's shadow could so catch the moonlight. Then, as they watched, the two points moved, trailing after them a smear of black. It was as though the shadow of the hedge at this point began to protrude until passing across the cultivated earth of the flower-bed the black wedge touched the ghostly green of the mown grass path on which they were standing. As it moved towards them the dense scent of the stocks seemed to clot until it was rancid. No flower was ever so rank—it was animal ammonia at its sourest, the odour of an ill-kept civet's cage. The shadow, now having touched the lawn a couple of yards from their feet—it had passed obliquely across the flower-bed—ceased to move further. Instead it began to sink down until the oblong black area, that in outline had looked like a slinking animal, was resting flat on the ground. The ammoniac odour now took on the nauseating stench of decay. The ground, however, seemed to be sopping up this blot of corruption. At the same time the stifling gas of rotting flesh became again the strong animal ammonia that has in it the tang of burning hair and of scorched linen. Then as the grey-green of the lawn absorbed the last stain of black, the ammonia modulated and was lost once more in the heavy scent of the stocks.

The Dean found that he was clinging to his sister's arm as convulsively as she to his. Without a word they turned to the house. But, just as they were about to gain the threshold his arm gave hers a wrench painful enough to rouse her from her numb fear. With his free arm he was striking at something. As she was twisted round by his grip she glanced at his face. He was looking up at the ceiling corner of the high window through which they were just going to pass. He snatched and tore with his free hand at what for a moment she couldn't see. Then he broke out, 'Can't the house be kept free of pests! Every corner has something weaving or spinning in it.' Against the upper cornice of the french window, the light striking out and down from the chandelier within showed her, as she took one more step forward, the outer anchor-strands of a big night-spider's web. One of the lowest of these threads her brother's face had brushed against and torn as he stepped over the threshold. And some of the remainder of the web had wound round his forehead. He stumbled across the step, called out to her to close the leaves of the window, continuing himself to wipe his face and head with his handkerchief. 'Filthy,' he muttered and she saw him shuddering. 'Shut all the windows,' he told her, and himself sat down by the empty hearth with his back to the garden. She obeyed, then turned and looked at him. He was huddled in a big chair with his head in his hands. Every now and then he picked with his fingers at face and scalp. She glanced out at the garden. It looked as calm and inviting as it had seemed when only so few minutes previously they had stepped out into it. She was a sane woman of considerable objectivity. She noticed, then, this fact, the present appearance of things, which was certainly the common-sense impression, and compared it with the nauseating panic she had felt when out there with her brother. She turned back and looked at him. Certainly, however much she wished to dismiss the whole thing as a small inexplicable anomaly best dealt with by disregard, she could not call the whole thing a private fancy. Subjective it might be, but he had been as much aware—of what she had experienced—as had she—perhaps more. 'Hadn't you better go to bed?' 'I suppose so, I suppose so.' His voice was uncertain, as uncertain as hers had been. But her uncertainty was polar to his. Her doubt as she phrased the question arose because she felt that what she said was less of a request than an order. She realised in a dim way that the curious 'attack'—that was the word she picked under which to catalogue the anomaly—the attack that he had just had in the garden had like a capsize—reversed their situations—if only for a moment. What that might mean in the future, still less what actually had in the past caused this present situation, she did not ask herself—did not wish to do so, indeed felt that for the time being she must not. She however sounded her feelings and resolution carefully though she still shunned sorting her thoughts or memories. She found that if her head was muddled her heart was clear; high and steady enough so that she could view it plainly, quickly. She found that she knew two things. The curious foreboding that she had felt when he began to be amiable, that had gone. The crisis, whatever it might be, that she had dreaded, had arrived. And, like most brave but unanalytic people, she was glad—not happy but content that whatever it was that she felt was in cover and had been dogging them, was now come into the open, now could be faced. The time for waiting, wondering whether one was not becoming tense and theatrical over nothing, doubting one's judgment, that phase was over. She preferred this sense of the rising storm to being fog-bound. She might have to go through a good deal, an ordeal perhaps, if that were not too histrionic a word for a test, but she would be going ahead, making headway, yes (she found she was ailing incongruously for into her mind floated the incongruous picture of Tissaphernes on her lap swelled to twice his size by the challenging smell of the fox) yes, give battle.

As her mind—or heart—made these dispositions she watched her brother. After repeating to himself once again, 'I suppose so,' he drew himself to his feet. Once he was standing up his resolution seemed somewhat recovered. Two silver bedroom candles stood on a small table by the door with matches beside them. He lit his, at the second effort and, half turning to say Goodnight, passed through the door. She stood listening. In the stillness of the house—it was the younger servant's night out and cook was an early retirer—she could hear his tread go along the passage, up the staircase and into his bedroom which was above the parlour. He was moving about methodically. At last all was quiet. She lit her own candle and turned off the small tap that extinguished the gas-fed chandelier, then went back to the window for a last look at the garden. The moon was now actually touching the top of the yew-hedge. The effect of a white-masked watcher peering over a wall was ridiculously convincing. The rest of the place was therefore in dense shadow. 'How strange,' she said quietly but aloud. 'We fear the calm and the rest of the night and think the day, in which our passions and resentments are unleashed at each other, the safe and normal time, cheerful and fresh.' She turned back from looking at the almost level light of the moon. The cold beam passed over her shoulder into the *salon*. The room had now no other light in it. Her candle had gone out. She could see the tiny point of red which showed the still smouldering wick and could smell the rank incense of its smoke. For a moment a spasm of panic, as keen as that she felt in the garden, took her. Then she understood. Something was attacking, but it had no real certainty of success. It had no purchase on her. If she refused to admit the fear, if she demanded why, on what grounds rational or moral, she should be frightened, then it would have to show itself or retire. She stood still with her back to the window. The tiny glow of the candle-wick, the other side of the room, died down. The rank smell of smoulder died also. She walked over, lit the candle again—it hesitated a moment before kindling—perhaps there was some moisture hidden in the wick—then as the flame established itself, she opened the door and went up to her bedroom. The sense of being no longer mentally in the dark—at least as far as action was concerned—grew in her as she rose up the dark wide steps, 'wide enough' (she repeated to herself the old saying) 'to bring a coffin down.' She was now facing something that, no doubt, had power to inflict defeat and dissolution, if you were weak, if you were infected and had no right resistance. But only able to scare you, only able to threaten and howl, if you stood your ground.

Certainly she was no longer attacked from within by further misgivings and the distressing feeling that she was at a loss. That did not mean however that she was unaware that she was confronted by something very dark or that she had no fears. Indeed, her grounds for these rapidly increased. Her brother's behaviour became steadily more strange. Now that he had been able to show or had been forced to uncover his real state of mind, a great part of his long-acquired, carefully built-up ashlar of impassivity was flaking away. It was hardly a week after the walk in the garden. He had not referred to that scene. But she noticed that he had not gone into the garden again though she had most days walked in it, hoping thereby to encourage him to come out. The new confidence was naturally a complaint. Again it was about the servants. Family prayers were just completed and the domestic staff, led out by cook, had just trooped from the room. But he remained standing, looking after them. Then he turned to her and evidently was going to speak, but, after a couple of hesitations, sat down. She noticed that he ate little. Indeed, it was not till the afternoon that he managed to say what was on his mind. They were just going into the parlour for tea as they had come in from evensong, when, as his hand was on the door he turned and asked, 'Now, don't you notice anything?' Then, as she did not at once reply, he continued, 'I am sorry to seem excessively fastidious and I wish to say that it is not a complaint. Perhaps if you notice nothing... But then,' he smiled wryly, 'Clement of Alexandria does warn the women on this point, that their olfactory sense is not as keen as man's...' He paused. 'What is it,' she encouraged him. 'I can't help it,' he brought up his trouble, 'I can't help it. It makes me feel quite ill. It's one of the servants, I know. That dreadfully coarse vulgar scent. They really must be told not to use it. I suppose it is some cheap hair-oil.'

She breathed in quietly and deeply. She could smell the cedar-wood oil with which the mahogany door by which they stood was polished, the faint scent of the pot-pourri in the big bowl in the bay window at the other end of the passage and farthest away the toast which must now have reached the kitchen table ready to advance and be offered with their tea. She replied quietly, 'I am sure that none of the maids use hair-oil.' Then seeing his distress increase, she added, 'I must ask them if they are using any of those rather strong-scented furniture polishes.' She saw the relief on his face as he said, 'Yes, yes, that quite possibly might be it. I confess I had not thought of such a, a natural explanation. And you will see that we go back to whatever the unscented variety may have been that was in use previously?' She assured him that she would.

He did not raise this matter of protest again, but his complaints were now frequent. He went back to his concern with dusting and would ask whether she was really keeping the maids up to their old standards in this new, and, of course somewhat larger and so more exacting house. Then one day he actually asked her to come into his study. 'You know,' he remarked over his shoulder as they went rather hurriedly along the passage, 'I'm not complaining. I certainly do not want my study turned upside down. But if they do tidy my desk...' By that time they had entered the room and he took her up to the big desk-table where he worked... 'then,' he continued, 'they should not actually leave my writing pad in that state. To quote scripture—the last state is worse than the first.'

A folio sheet of blotting paper, perfectly fresh, and, on that, some quarto sheets of plain paper also innocent of any blot, mark or stroke of pen or pencil—she scanned the site at which he was pointing, going closer both to assure him and reassure herself. 'I don't quite understand?' she asked him turning round. 'You don't see!' She did see the expression in his eyes and that was enough to show that at least she must say something at once that was positive. 'I'll look into the matter myself,' she remarked, in a cheerful routine tone. And, suiting action to word, she picked up the paper, rolled it together and went toward the door. There she turned round. He was looking after her with an expression half of relief, half of puzzlement. Then as she added, 'I'll be back in a moment with clean paper,' he smiled at her. 'Very kind of you, very kind.' There was real gratitude in his voice. As she went down the passage, though it was broad day and the sun hot outside, she felt the darkest wave of black fear rise up in her that she had so far had to face. She knew, however, she could endure it. For, deeper than any fear at what might be approaching, she knew there was mounting so strong a pity in her that about the courage she would need she did not have to question. She did look over the sheets of paper in her room. 'Of course there is nothing' she remarked quietly to herself as though checking over an item in household expenses. She went back with them, then, to her brother's room. He was waiting, standing by his desk as she had left him, 'These sheets are clean ones,' she remarked, and spread them on the table. He looked at them and then without a word, but granting a small nod, he sat down, and, taking up his pen, drew a small sheaf of notes toward him.

For three days he seemed to be working quietly. Still, she was not surprised when he asked her to come with him again, though her heart, she noticed, did sink a little further when instead of going along to his study they mounted the stair and reached his bedroom. It was clear, too, he was in a more nervous state than before. As they entered the room he no longer led but actually gave her a gentle push forward. 'Look at the pillow!' he commanded, 'You see, I was right. Whoever makes the bed is really so grossly careless, untidy, disgustingly untidy,' his voice was straining, 'squalid, that it is unhygienic. You must speak...' She had approached the bed and was looking at the pillow. It was Monday. New linen had been put on the bed perhaps an hour before. She saw it was spotless. 'You can't see the state the pillow-slip is in! Your sight must be going. I saw it the moment I came back to this room after breakfast this morning. It must be the maid. I saw her leaving with the old sheets.' Talking rapidly he had come up behind her. She could hear his shallow quick breath. Suddenly he put his hand on her shoulder, gripping it. His grasp was hard, but trembling. He was pinching with all his strength. But to the startling discomfort she made no response because of what her eyes now saw. The pillow-slip had something on it, a stain, as of oil, and in the stain she could surely see a number of tangled coarse black hairs. She drew her breath sharply. He left hold of her shoulder. 'You see it!' he said, 'You see it now!' But now she only saw the smooth plump white pillow in its new cover. She bent over it, moving close to the bed so that he could not reach her, for he held back, evidently afraid to come closer. She scented, as a cat will nose over the carpet. Then she turned round: 'I think cook has been a little careless. I always have the laundry as soon as it comes in from the wash dried in front of the kitchen range—a precautionary measure, but damp sheets are dangerous. Over-zealous, she has singed this pillow-slip ever so slightly.' She picked up the pillow. He gave way to her. As she left him at his study door—for he had followed her keeping to her heels—she added quietly, 'Cook is white-haired and the other two maids are light.'

Whether her action checked in some way his psychosis—at least in that district where she could make response and give him replies and support, certainly the attack, when it was resumed, was from a quarter out of her province. He told her some ten days later that he was not going to evensong. And, on her asking what would be detaining him, he replied, almost with a smile, that this was not a matter wherein she could assist. 'The verger is too old,' he complained. 'Always did make mistakes in so many little details. But now he cannot get his staff to carry out even the most rudimentary cleaning. It puts my teeth on edge. The reading desk in my stall is filthy; dust, cobwebbing, wisps of hair. The fluff is always getting on my sleeves. I'm no maker of trouble, though. I don't want the poor old creature turned out. I have decided what to do. I'll wait. When others complain, as soon they must, well, then it won't seem as though the new broom were tyrannously officious and determined to make the old mop feel ashamed and only fit for the bonfire.' He actually chuckled or rather gave a kind of titter—a sound she had never heard him make before—and looked at her sidelongly.

The last phase was entered before he made any reference to it. The information came, in fact, from one of the maids.

'I'm sorry, Ma'am, if I'm saying what is not in my place to say, but please, the Master is not using his bed now. It seems that he sleeps, if sleep he does, in the big wing-chair drawn up near the fireplace in the bedroom.'

So far no sign had better shown how far his old self-reliance had broken down than when, the evening after she had been given the above information, she suddenly said to him as they sat in her room: 'Wouldn't you prefer to lie on the couch here, and then I could keep a small fire going all night,' all he replied was, 'Can you sleep in the day?' She had to: none was to be gained at night under this arrangement. That did not mean that he did not. Indeed, she it was who used to rouse him. He would begin to doze almost as soon as she had wrapped some rugs round him—for though the evenings were still warm, once the sun set his skin was cold, and on the occasions on which she touched his hand she felt it was clammy. Rugs and some cushions were, however, all the covers that he would permit. Sheets and pillow-cases she could see were repugnant to him, stirring some deep terror—a terror he fought so long as he was fully conscious, but which showed itself as a panic that flung them from him as soon as he began to dream. Then as his sleep deepened his distress grew. She would go over and wake him. Once he was fully roused he could still quite quickly regain his composure. It was clear, however, that this could not go on. In spite of all she could do, he was losing ground. The shadow-life was advancing to engulf his day-time consciousness, as at sunset the livid mist of oncoming night mounts up from the east to take over the empty sky. And her own strength would not stand it. Alone with him in the small hours as he struggled with his phantoms, it was now taking all her strength to keep clear her own conviction—that the atmosphere in the still room was subjective not objective, that it was only sympathy, yes, and a relic of her old admiration for him, that made her feel that a positive presence had invaded the place.

Yet to whom could she go? To the doctor, and have him wish to commit her brother to an asylum! The thought of the Bishop and his advice was if anything less helpful, for his recommendations would be even less practical—rest? 'Canst thou not minister to a mind diseased.' The dawn, with the cold alien look it has for all those who have passed through a night of wakeful misery, showed the vast fretted mass of the Cathedral emerging from the low-lying mist. The moulded Gothic design looked like some splintered reef left by a retreating tide. 'Once it was a fortress of faith,' she whispered to herself as she glanced through the curtains, for with the returning light her brother was gaining the few minutes of sleep without nightmare that he could snatch at such an hour. 'The poor Bishop, always haunted, always dogged by senility or premature breakdown, like one who struggles to keep a lamp trimmed but the wicks are either too old or the oil has water in it.' She pulled herself together, went over silently and stood looking down at her brother. After all, he looked so calm now, so much master of his situation and his mind, that surely nature itself would work a cure. Even should she question the doctor, what could she ask? As yet she had no real clue—no adequate set of symptoms that she could describe, and he deduce from.

A few nights after she had begun to wish that even his knowledge might be granted her, it was given. He had been awake while she was beside him and she had only turned to attend the fire when she heard him breathing heavily and muttering to himself. She paused—listening. He was saying over one phrase, a name surely, yes, Ibn Barnuna, Ibn Barnuna. She knew enough of his books to recall that name printed in gold letters on the back of one, perhaps more than one, of his big handsomely bound quartos—those massive volumes, more like furniture than books. She remembered calling forth his humorous contempt when once remarking that they made the handsomest wall-paper that any man's study could have. The voice had grown urgent. She went back to the couch and touched him on the shoulder. He woke but his eyes did not turn to hers. They looked across the room. She followed them, her hand still on his arm. For a moment she heard nothing but the quiet lapping of the flame in the grate, lapping and licking the new small log she had put on. Then the sound seemed no longer to be coming from the grate but from a dark corner of the room. Her brother put his hand over hers. Before he said, 'You see!' she had caught sight of a dark body, a darker shadow in the corner's dusk. It looked like a black animal lying on its side. Every now and then the wavering light of the fire—for she had turned the gas to a pin-point—made it seem that the creature twisted round and licked its flank. Her brother started up, pulling himself out of her touch. She saw that the corner had only shadow in it. The sound it was clear came from the flames. When the sunrise came—for the days were yet long—she left him for a moment. He was awake but did not mind being left, it seemed, if it was light. She did not, however, go to her bedroom. Instead she entered his study. Yes, there stood the volumes as she recalled them. She could read from the door the fine gilt lettering on their backs. His book treasures, his bound 'letters-patent' of the nobility of learning, of the high sanity of scholarship, stood ranged in the fine mahogany bookcases he had had made especially for them. '"Embalmed minds" as Milton calls them,' he had remarked (it was a comfort now to recall an intellectual assurance that then sounded arrogant) 'have surely as much right to their carved stalls as our present Minister minds, most of whom have waited too long for their embalming.' She went across and took out one marked Ibn Barnuna: Travels. Her long years as forewoman of a staff of cleaners made her, in spite of the few weeks they had been in this their new residence, glance automatically at the gap and into the fissure left by the heavy volume she had lifted away. With her free hand she then reached into the gap. She had noticed something that must have been left there by mistake. Her fingers brought out a key. She looked at it for a moment with doubt; then recognised, with her orderly memory, where it belonged. She slipped it into the lock of the drawer just below the shelf on which the big volumes stood. Yes, that was it, it fitted; it was the key, for it turned freely in the lock and the drawer opened. There was nothing in the drawer but a strange smell seemed to float out—strange because incongruous to rise here—stale linen, familiar enough, but not in such a place. And what could be exhaling it? And with it, surely, now she could detect a cheap scent—that, too, was a very unlikely odour. And further, this, too, had, it seemed, no source. Of course it was a little thing but, though small, to her completely incomprehensible. She stood for a moment, therefore, looking into the empty drawer and recognising how offensive the smell, though weak, appeared to her. Then she shut the drawer, putting the key in her pocket. She turned her attention to the big volume cradled on her left forearm. With her fingers she began to turn the pages until, with what seemed a movement of its own, the volume spread itself open. It had been strained at this page—it was clear that the binding had been partly broken. She read for a while in the passage that had been presented to her eyes. Then she closed the book, put it in its place and left the room. She went to the Cathedral that morning before matins and stayed there till lunch. Returning, she brought a tray to her brother who was lying on the couch in her room. He ate hardly anything. She had eaten nothing, but he did not inquire. All the afternoon she sat with him. Then when the sun's beams had spread across the floor till they touched the wainscot he suddenly said, 'I can't face another night now: I can't.' She knew now that the time had come. And she knew so clearly also what she had to do, that she found herself quite calm. Laetitia Throcton was to her for the moment a character in a novel she was writing. She saw what her heroine—far too well known by her authoress to be seen as heroic—must now perform. But she found she had no idea as to what the performance would effect. She could hear her low voice, low, gentle, definite. 'If you were well you would laugh it away. But you are more right now than you would be then. There is something now present with you; something which is highly dangerous to you and which you cannot drive away.' She paused and looked at him. He was watching her with something almost like relief. She continued, 'But which you called on yourself.' 'It's a lie,' he shouted. 'You're a fool, a scheming wretch, you have a plot to drive me out of my mind, you're a witch, it's all a filthy, hellish lie!' She looked at him quietly. He had become very small now, she was four years his senior. She remembered him like that—one of her first reflective memories—when their nurse had frightened him with ghost stories. Then she had been able to be his friend. And, though she herself had been considerably frightened, she remembered, the fear had gone when she felt how helpless he was. The same mood had now returned to her. She did not know if she could win. But she knew she could refuse to yield an inch to that which had him so largely in its power.

She was aware of much pain. But not of the slightest fear—that was gone for good, transmuted into the pain through her profound understanding. She knew, too, what further she must say though she noted as the words came how odd they sounded addressed to the learned Dean of a great Cathedral. 'You drove Simpkins out. I took your side at first. I was keenly disappointed for you. And he must have made some grave slip so as to fall into the power of your rage. But it is clear that he was in no way a bad man. So you could not get rid of him, through his mind. That fate is now yours. What you sent out could only strike at his body. But, returning to you, and armed with your intention, it is striking at your mind.'

He looked at her, his mouth fallen open, the lower lids of his eyes sagging. His head swung slowly from side to side as if he were trying to see her in a difficult light. She knew now she must wait. His mind was being slowly percolated by what she had said. It was trying to keep the knowledge out. But his will was being worn down as a man is, step by step, forced back by one stronger. It took a couple of minutes before he collapsed. He tumbled forward on the couch burying his face. She heard him, as she took him in her arms, whining. 'There's no hope, none. That's my doom. I mocked at senility. I with my first-rate brain—a slobbering, cringing idiot. I'll be degraded to the lunatic asylum to live there in hell while still in the body and then...' He began in a thin childish voice to howl. She held him for some five minutes. Then began slowly to repeat a collect. It began, inevitably, 'Almighty God...' 'Don't,' he whimpered, 'Don't. There's no hope. For He exists. He's just.' She completed the prayer silently.

That night—somewhat to her surprise, though a deeper level of her mind felt it was natural, all part of the process—he slept. She remembered reading in some grim Protestant Church History, that did not spare you 'telling' facts about the other side, that those given their first racking nearly always slept deeply after it. She was tired, too, very tired. Her anxiety had nearly drugged her. Time and again she dozed only to drag herself awake to find him still fast asleep—his face as blank as though made of wax.

The next morning she took his mail. For some days he had refused to deal with it. So she had answered those letters which she could, leaving the others until she could have some idea as to what was to happen. This morning there was one in an unfamiliar hand from Cambridge. She opened it. It was from a colleague in Arabic, of whom she was pretty sure she had heard him speak, a Dr. McPhail. He was inviting her brother to a small conference which he and some fellow scholars found that they could bring together at Cambridge. 'It is quite informal,' the letter ran. 'That accounts for my giving such brief notice. Indeed, it may well be impossible for you to be present at so short indication. I hope, however, that you may be able to make an effort to attend for I am sure that you would find it worth your while. It was because I did not wish our few outstanding Arabianists to miss an unusual opportunity that I am writing to you. The presence of some foreign scholars in this country is an occasion which I was loath that you should miss. And I am sure their visit here would be enriched if they could have a few days of discussion with you. Indeed our small group will feel incomplete without your presence.'

She looked in at her brother. He was still sunk in a sleep of such stillness that she was sure to disturb it would only harm. When he woke she was certain he would—as happens when the mind has so long been unaware and perhaps absent from the body—need some time to recollect himself. After her small breakfast she found he was still sleeping. Then finding the house breathless she took a few turns up and down the pavement outside. She was just thinking of going in again, when she heard 'Good morning' and Dr. Wilkes was beside her. He looked at her with kindly shrewdness. Then, without hesitation, remarked, 'I wish you could help me to understand the health of the Precincts a little better. We seem to have been going through some kind of cyclic depression for quite a while. That seems clear. But for the cause I am at a complete loss. I used to be a great believer in water infections. Sometimes there are slow epidemics, with low fevers and the general decline. Certainly we lie too low here to be sure that our water supply is above any level of possible contamination. But,' he paused, 'I'm not satisfied that the basic trouble is enteric.' He looked quickly at her masking his inquiry with a smile: 'You would be surprised, Miss Throcton, at the extent I have strayed from orthodox diagnosis in trying to account for the indispositions'—he chose the word without satisfaction—'that have lately attacked us.' Then, his face frankly serious and in his voice something that was almost an appeal for help, he asked 'The Dean? When he has spoken with me,' he added, 'about the health of the Close he himself has rightly boasted that he kept me professionally at bay.' She realised that this was the next step. She herself, she felt sure, had done what she had to do and now some one else perhaps could and would carry the issue further.

'I think, Dr. Wilkes, you may be right. But I am as much in the dark as you as to his condition. My brother is gravely indisposed, of that there can be little doubt, more gravely,' her voice was low and without accent, 'than was his, his predecessor...'

'I gather you think it would be little use my seeing him.'

'He has not suggested it,' she answered, 'and I am sure you understand that without his leave I would prefer not to do so.'

'Yes,' he allowed with quiet frankness. 'In many cases if the patient himself has not called in aid, for us to offer it but alarms. Besides, can a profession which depends so much on chemistry and now increasingly on sheer carving, can we minister to a mind...' he stopped leaving out the following adjective. She felt she could reward that friendliness that could be so frank by asking his advice. She felt absolutely alone. And the actual details of her brother's state she could not imagine sharing with even a close friend or relative, not with their parents had they been alive—they had so admired this their successful son. 'My brother,' she heard herself saying, 'has had an invitation to attend a conference...' 'Do you know I was going to suggest that,' Dr. Wilkes gave her his full support. 'Get him away, yes, even if he seems quite sick. One thing I do feel sure of. This place has somehow dragged him down.' 'It's to a quiet conference of some scholars at Cambridge.' 'Couldn't be better,' he agreed. 'Couldn't be better. No physical exertion; the favourite interests of his mind will be entertained; and the place will bear for him pleasant memories of his youth and academic successes. I wish you a happy return,' he said, bowing and leaving her. Dr. Wilkes seemed to have been a reliable prescriptionist even without seeing the patient. For, when Miss Throcton went in to see her patient, it was hard to disbelieve that some slight sign of cure was already apparent. Her brother was awake, sitting up, calm and self-possessed, able indeed not merely to mask things but to say quietly to her—'The one chance I now see is that I get away, put some distance between myself and this involvement. Then even if I still remain incapable of sustained thought, I may be able to comprehend what has befallen me.' She showed him the letter. He read it slowly, then looking up without a smile or any relief of the gravity of his face, remarked, 'Yes, this is clearly the next step.'

There were three days before they should leave. They passed without incident; at least within the house. He still slept in her sitting-room, but he did sleep. And she was learning to enter at least a half-state during the quieter hours of the day. She told her servants that he was suffering from a slight non-infectious attack which would yield to quiet and some little nursing. He spent almost the whole day, as well, in her sitting-room. He evidently felt safest there. Apparently, too, the prospect of getting away had in some manner sufficiently strengthened his mind that he seemed less open—perhaps, for the moment, immune—to molestation. The only event that befell her during these three days of waiting took place when she had one early afternoon gone out to sit for a quarter of an hour under the limes in the Close. It was clear that he was uneasy lest she should go into their garden. The place she had chosen was a quiet spot as it was a corner of the Precincts which led only to the Palace. There was no danger that any of the inmates passing by would engage her in talk and inquisitive inquiries. And not only quiet, it was now cool and fragrant, some of the lime-blossom being still scattered on the ground, and a little remaining in the trees themselves. Bees were busy with it. Scent, sound and light, the three memory senses, seemed blended into a chord recalling all peaceful scenes and episodes. Here was the true, quiet atmosphere of things; this was the climate of reality; bright, unhurried, serene, even when late summer and early autumn had begun to recall it to repose. The shadow and storm, they were simply wavering grotesque darkness projected by our mischievous, greedy, posturing ill-wills.

She started, though, when a voice near her said, 'Oh, excuse me, Miss Throcton, I was just on my way across to the Deanery to see whether I might talk with you for a few minutes?' Looking up, she saw the Bishop's Chaplain. 'The Bishop was intending to call himself when he was summoned away to London earlier than he had expected...'

Young Halliwell paused. He was evidently a little nervous. 'Won't you sit down?' She made room for him on the green bench. She looked at him. He certainly had good eyes, not yet narrowed by too much judging of men and lit with the humour that can play because it still laughs with people, not at them. But now the corners of his mouth, which also had to acquire the narrowed diplomatic line, showed his lack of ease. His unguardedness, the fact that he made no attempt to raise a mask of defensive discretion, appealed to her.

'You are calling to inquire about my brother's health?' And as he nodded frankly to her half-question, she went on, 'It would also seem to appear, would it not, as though preferment might cause a species of vertigo.' There was almost a smile in her voice if not on her lips, but she was grave and sad as she added, 'Perhaps few can climb up and look down from even the lowest pinnacle of the Temple without risking this giddiness.'

'My father,' he was answering her, she noticed gratefully, with the same detached frankness with which she had found it possible to speak, 'My father often used to say that the wisest men he had ever known used to tell him, "The full truth may never shine in your heart so long as you have any power over another!" They thought, it seems, that power itself was bad, or at least must also inevitably blind you.'

'Who were these wise men?' She smiled. 'Surely they must have been "Wise men from the East"?' He glanced at her. 'They certainly were no kings with golden gifts. Indeed, they were, I believe, as afraid of money as of power!' 'That sounds even more Eastern,' she replied, 'I suppose not since the Middle Ages—and then perhaps not ever consistently, I gather from reading our Cathedral's history—have we shunned rank and salary, provided they came from recognised sources. How much simpler life would be if we did!' She paused. 'But you want news of my brother. I am hoping a few days' absence—he is to attend a conference on Arabic studies in Cambridge—will permit him to throw off this indisposition.' She was aware that he was watching her, not impertinently, to read more in her looks than her voice might be willing to tell, but with a real question, an honest concern, 'Yes,' she replied looking at him, 'I have had a word with Dr. Wilkes. He is sure that a brief change of scene would be the best thing.' She saw that he had noticed precisely what she had said—that Dr. Wilkes had in fact only given a general consent and not been asked for specific medical advice. She saw further that her questioner was beginning to blush. He was charged, it was clear, to obtain information and he had the intelligence to judge what he was being given but he certainly had no liking for any task that might be construed as prying. The sympathy which the gentle elderly must always feel for the young as the juveniles begin to enter upon mankind's constant task of keeping charity and truth linked, was suddenly doubled in Miss Throcton by the sense that this boy, young enough to be her son, somehow sympathised by intuition with her.

'Yes,' she said again, 'it is baffling by any medical standards. It is nothing physical. It is nervous strain.' Of course that was such understatement as to be almost *suppressio veri*. But even if she was sure in her own mind, how could this young modern mind understand that a nightmare might be real and what must be his judgment of an elderly woman who told him so. After a moment in which he had looked at the ground he turned again and faced her. 'Please don't think I'm absurd...' he hesitated, 'but the Bishop is uneasy, too, you see.' She nodded. 'I know,' he continued with more definiteness, 'it's what the world calls "just a run of bad luck." But don't you think that religious people really have no right to talk about chance? Whatever happens must be God's Will for us? It's to teach us something, surely? After all, we would never have learnt any Natural Laws if we had said of every run of similar events—"They are simply contingencies, coincidences—*Post hoc* is never *propter hoc*".'

'And sometimes,' she added her question to his, 'sometimes we can see the hidden causes which have set in motion the very evident, but superficially inexplicable, results?'

He nodded. She was silent, too, for a moment. But he evidently had followed her thought when she continued, 'We are free, of course. We can initiate—I mean we ourselves must often be the cause of the things that befall us. I know that sounds trite, self-evident, I mean...' He continued for her, 'We can become involved in certain, certain moods...' He stumbled, then went on, 'What I am trying to get clear in my mind is, I think, a question. I heard Dr. Wilkes make a remark at a conference to which the Bishop took me, where a number of professional men met together for discussion of social trends—Dr. Wilkes's point as far as I recall, was that infection, physical infection, seems to be a thing we must view increasingly as pervasive, general, almost a climate. I know what he said interested me because then our bodily health would depend less on disinfectants than on keeping up our general resistance. He meant it, I believe, to point to a link between his work and ours. If so, then at times we might, by worry, by resentment, by any negative mood, let our mental resistance become lowered.' 'And then,' she concluded, 'the ill infection breaks in, inundates.' 'We do need soul-physicians', was his conclusion. She smiled frankly at him. 'Thank you for being so confidential with me. You are treating me as an associate of the Faculty!' He did not, however, smile back at her. Indeed, his face was now more clouded. But though overcast his expression was more open than before. He had from his first days in the Close felt an intuitive liking for this quiet woman, of his mother's generation, with no children of her own, taking care of that forbidding brother, ready to let him completely eclipse her and ready it seemed with the same silent charity, to let Close gossip and its small petty competitions apparently go by. Naturally he had taken her quietude as serenity. Even the most informative of the Cathedral wives left Miss Throcton's character alone. He had been told, as soon as he came into residence that, whereas Miss So-and-So was lively and Mrs. So-and-So very conservative, of Miss Throcton it was only said with uncommon agreement and a certain finality that she was 'remote.'

'Sometimes, Miss Throcton, I am sorry to say, I get discouraged. I know it is wrong of me. I know I have been blessed, favoured. But somehow I thought it was going to be different...' 'What?' She knew but knew also that he needed encouragement. 'I have been fortunate, as the world says and as it counts. I am sure you know my loyalty to the Bishop. He is a wonderful man under whom to work, learn about administration and the understanding of men. And this lovely spot to work in...' He looked at the perfect blend of cultured comfort and antiquarian picturesqueness which a well-kept Cathedral Close then achieved, all the charm of the past distilled and all its inconveniences strained away. 'But sometimes—of course it is probably impatience disguising itself as zeal—I wonder whether, just because we have achieved such finish, we are not now entirely on the rich surface?' 'Floating in the rich cream?' she asked, 'But with no depth in us?' She had not smiled but he did, 'Yes, this week the Bishop asked me to attend a picture expert from London who is to look over our fine series of Bishops' portraits. This expert thinks it is an unique series. It was extraordinary the things he showed me that he could do with cleaning fluids, etc., to keep and indeed bring back into good condition the faces of those dead worthies. He told me this kind of antiquarian preservation has progressed wonderfully, and then remarked, "And a good thing, too. It will help us preserve the great Italian masters. We need all the preservatives we can lay hold on, for once they are gone we shall never have such treasures again, we shall never be able again to paint as they painted." He added, "Maybe, when you can no longer create, as a compensation you are given the power to preserve".' Young Halliwell glanced again unhappily at the great fretted West Front, mellow in the western light, and the wide lawn spread like a green velvet cloth, on which this precious antique had been put out to sun.

'What do you think we lack?' she asked. 'Oh, I don't know! I know I oughtn't to complain. But you see I'd hoped, I'd hoped the Church to-day might be what it was when it began.' 'That's what the Methodists claim,' she smiled now, 'or at least used to.' 'It's what my father believed could and should be,' he went on. 'It certainly didn't bring him preferment. But then, for years, he was a missionary. And that not only puts you out of the running; it brings you up against experiences not met with and not believed in here.' He waved his hand at the large enclosed calm of garden and architecture in which they sat. 'But a thing may exist, may it not, even when it is not believed?' She asked the question so quietly, so much to herself, that he did not seem to notice it but ran on, 'Yes, certainly he was out of the running. You see he said he sometimes believed God sent him to Persia to learn rather than to teach.' 'What did he learn?' This time her question was definite enough to turn his attention. 'He used to tell me that he was sure of one thing—our supreme need of what he called spiritual mastery.' 'Did he ever tell you how it might be found?' 'He thought it required a very considerable attention to one's way of life. I mean he was sure that it would take time, skill and instruction—perhaps years of training.' 'That is asking a great deal?' 'Certainly the theological students I have seen and the theological studies I myself have been put through are, I must own, superficial. After all, Dr. Wilkes had a longer and more thorough training before it was thought safe to permit him to handle our bodies—are our souls any less valuable or complex.' 'Could your father give you any examples of men who he thought proficient?' 'Yes, he said he had seen wonderful things, things like the therapy described in the Gospels, done by those who had suffered themselves to become adepts.' 'In Persia?' 'Yes, but he said he had been assured that it could be done just as well here—if we cared as much to be trained.' 'But have any of us? Is there anyone known to you that can do—that kind of thing—here and now?' As her questions followed one another her voice had taken on a tone of urgency. Intuitively, however, he seemed to understand the naturalness, the inevitability, of their return to personal matters, now on a level of increased intimacy. 'I wish with all my heart,' he said impetuously, 'I knew of someone who could teach me. My father didn't. Indeed just before he died he actually thought of going back to Persia—I know it sounds almost grotesque. But, as he said, just keeping out of the running, just avoiding ambition, just going the small round, of which this,' again he pointed to the vast front that loomed on their right, like the walls of an abandoned prehistoric fortress, 'this is only the big round, just difference in quantity doesn't alter quality. And we need a new quality, a new species of force. I'd give up all my work here, however promising, approved and pleasant it may be, if only I could find out that—but what's the use giving up one's place on the flywheel though one be but a fly, to become only a miniature crank!' He smiled ashamedly, then added, 'Please forgive me. What led to this, this outbreak, is that, as you know, the Bishop himself is now apprehensive and I believe suspects that we may perhaps be in need of insight which if we cannot command...' The young lieutenant paused, then went on, 'He is wise, you know, as he is shrewd. Indeed, I am sure he does always much more than he says and indeed may be more than he can say.' 'A woman's predicament,' she put in to encourage him. 'I've seldom seen him show anything that might be construed as misgiving, still less apprehension. Certainly he has never before asked me, as on this occasion, to inquire what, if anything, can or could be done.'

'It is kind of him,' she answered in a low, steady voice. 'But haven't you, with your kind frankness, been telling me that nothing can be done, that our Established Church was not established to deal with any who might climb over or fall down from its *Via Media*?' 'You mean that a diplomatic scholar or a nice-mannered, well-informed young gentleman has really no power and maybe no insight. And that the latter is the only bud, the former the one fruit, that this ornamental tree'—again he nodded at the Cathedral—'can now yield.' Her voice as she answered was very grave but not weak, 'I don't want to sound despairing: but I do feel that I should not hide from you that my hopes now depend on a very fine constitution, on Nature's inherent power of recovery and, immediately, on what change may yield.' She paused, 'And on what I feel you will not mind my mentioning, our prayers.'

She had not embarrassed him, or even disturbed the run of his thoughts. 'How I wish you could meet with one of those doctors of the soul my father came across. Of course the ordinary person would be able to get little—they would only see all the little surface differences. Can any good thing come out of Galilee—or, indeed, be in anything but the dress we know? But I think you might find then what might help.' Suddenly his self-assurance seemed to go, his successfully acquired conventionality to return, 'Please forgive me. I expect I don't know what I'm talking about. All I was commissioned to do was to ask how the Dean was and whether there was anything that might be done for him. Please forgive me!' 'Please don't apologise. It has been a relief to talk with you and to hear of those who at least understand the reality of spiritual problems. Thank you for coming. I or my brother will keep the Bishop informed. As I said, the absence now will be brief. Forgive me,' she concluded, rising and giving him her hand, 'I must be getting back.' He thanked her with a clumsiness that helped her more than a finished phrase. 'I have been helped by our talk,' she repeated as she left him, 'and you will continue I know to help us in the one way we know.'

He watched her as she went across the great lawn to the stately house. Its fine nineteenth-century façade seemed the crystallisation of the scholarly self-assurance that had smiled away all the dark fancies of an earlier ignorance.

CHAPTER FOURTEEN

When she re-entered the house it was to find that his improvement—if such it could be called—had been sustained. And as far as his will was concerned it might be said to have been increased. As the light failed he seemed to have full mastery of himself and even to wish to test his power. He still was willing to sleep in her sitting-room. But he insisted on her going to her bedroom. 'You will not be fit to travel,' he said—and though his voice was without interest it was clear he was determined to prevent himself becoming totally unaware of another's health, 'You must get some proper sleep.' And when she went to him in the morning, before she inquired, he told her quietly, 'Yes, it passed and I shall be able to travel.'

The group at Cambridge proved to be one that at any other time would have been for Dean Throcton most congenial. Even now it was clear that the distraction was so apt that he was able to give his whole attention to their discussions. Indeed he had seemed to gain perceptibly in self-detachment each mile that Norminster was left behind. And, while they were driving down the long dreary road, which the University had insisted should keep the railway station at its proper distance, he remarked to her with something that sounded almost like a quiet defiance, 'The master passion strong in death! Well, anyhow it's stronger, I believe, than a doleful delirium! I remember when our father was failing, he would wander hopelessly if I tried to talk any business with him. But if I quoted scripture, time and again he'd cap the quotation. Arabic, I suspect, is my brain-cordial!' She wished that his support was more fundamental but was certainly grateful for anything which permitted time to be gained.

Dr. McPhail, the conference's convener, was one of those thorough scholars who feel that they can have no true linguistic knowledge unless they have lived in the country whose literature they desire to understand. He had spent time in Egypt, Syria, Mesopotamia and Persia. Hence he was able with some pride to introduce as his foreign visitors two men who had been his hosts in his Near East travels. One was a Persian, the other an Egyptian. Both were outstanding scholars. And both proved to possess the intelligence that is so informed that it finds the views of others the more interesting the more alien they are. The Persian had the vivacity of his nation. He was also a poet of considerable standing in a language that is second to none in its poetry. He gave a very welcome finish to his accomplishments by perfect use of English. The Egyptian was however the more remarkable. Experts are, when with the public, generally aloof and taciturn. There is nothing to their taste in the common market, and their special fare they expect the ordinary purchaser to find as unpalatable. When, however, they are brought together with their peers their common humanity emerges. The volume of sound-waves emitted by a group of experts clearing their minds is seldom less in force and range than the noise caused by the clearing of an equal number of common throats. This conference might certainly have been heard some distance outside the massive doors of the large hall wherein they met. Perhaps one voice alone would not have carried beyond the ears for which it was intended. Though the Egyptian spoke English as fluently as the Persian, he spoke far less often. On those occasions, however, the very quietness of his tone, the lack of any nervous advocacy, always gave him the attention of the entire group. Dr. McPhail, pleased with the dawning success of his congress, remarked smiling to Dean Throcton, 'I think he obtains so readily the loan of our ears because he does not seem anxious to inform us, still less to correct us.' 'And, conversely, he appears to have no doubts as to his information,' the Dean allowed with gruff appreciation; 'and I must own that always is an aid to listening when evidently one is listening to any authority.' 'Yes,' Dr. McPhail's voice modulated to a whisper as another speaker began to address them, 'Yes, on his own grounds, few, very few, may be greater.'

The speaker who 'had the floor' had apparently not this power of commanding more than polite silence and as courtesy censored the circulation of further biographic detail, Dean Throcton let his eyes entertain him by studying his host's face. It, too, showed that the ear was failing to hold the eye. 'He looks like a hen anxiously proud because she has just a few more chicks than she can count.' The Dean smiled not unkindly to himself as he watched the man beside him bobbing his head to and fro as his eye ran over the faces around. He had hardly seen McPhail since they were undergraduates. They had kept in that highly insulated touch which can be sustained by a common study, rising at times—say, perhaps twice a year—to the exchange of technical letters on points of scholarship. Now the Dean was amusing himself in fitting these elderly features onto the student face he could recall as clearly as he saw the present man beside him. The lower lid was puckered with a cheerfully defensive vigilance. The corners of the mouth drawn up with a ready criticism. The lips pursed to add construction. 'A lively mind and a sound sense also,' the Dean summed up. 'Of course he's never gained any position in the academic world. But then he never seemed ambitious. Perhaps to some men, if not virtue, then scholarship can be its own reward. Just to know may be enough? No,' he answered himself. 'No. Learning is only an anodyne to those who have never felt any keener distress than gentle boredom.' He shook himself slightly, a shrug to shake off a shudder, looked round him quickly, not at the faces but at the floor, seemed to be reassured but turned his attention now deliberately to the speaker.

Yet every day when he returned, Miss Throcton noticed that her brother was not tired from these long sessions. On the contrary, he seemed actually refreshed. The past he seemed able now to keep at bay. As far as she could judge from those less than hints that can be picked up by an anxious watcher, his anxiety seemed to have set itself a range and the one thing he now was awaiting with foreboding was the break up of the conference. On the penultimate day she was informed that Dr. McPhail had leave from his College to give a small party on the last afternoon in the College garden and to invite the wives of those who had been Conference members. Miss Throcton, was, of course, invited. She naturally expected that. She was, however, surprised that the small and courteously expressed note in which Dr. McPhail invited her should have added to it a postscript. 'I thought women only confined their real intentions to the P.S.' she remarked aloud to herself smiling. She would have made the little joke to her brother had he been in the room; as women, almost by habit, try and cheer the vanity-despondency of their menfolk taking every opportunity to point out the superiority of the male. A moment after she was glad with all her heart that she had not, though perhaps relief had been a juster word then gladness. The postscript ran: 'I trust you will pardon the eccentricity of my request, but it would be—I ask you to believe—of the utmost service to us'—'a few of' had been added above the line and then scratched out—'if you could manage to-morrow morning to be in Sheriton's bookshop at 10.30 precisely. I will be there myself. I need not be at the beginning of the Conference session—your brother will be taking the chair for me. It would be highly advisable that this should not be mentioned to him.'

She realised how difficult it would be for a University Don to write such a note. Her lips, against her will, again curled, as she thought of the outward absurdity of an assignation in a famous bookshop made with her, an elderly maiden lady, by a man whom she had only once met, for the first time this week, and then only bowed to, and, the final touch of the grotesque, that he should not only warn her to be secret but that he had plotted that her chaperon should be kept out of the way. Then the involuntary humour released its gall as she realised that if this was a note from a man not off his head then only one other alternative was open. What other interpretation could the words hold? What but a matter, if not yet of life or death, at least of sanity or madness could make a learned fellow of an ancient college of a famous university write to a spinster, who he really hardly knew by sight, urging such an odd request?

However, the first confirmation came true enough when her brother coming into the sitting-room they were sharing, just after she had put the note in the pocket of her gown, volunteered that the Conference had done him the honour of asking him to preside at the first part of the final session. 'Anyhow,' he added, 'McPhail tells me it will be a kindness to him as unavoidably he finds he has an engagement that might make him slightly late.'

The next morning she walked with him to the hall where the meetings were being held and after leaving him retraced her steps quickly—it was but some five minutes away to the big book-store. Famous bookshops succeed in blending something of the atmosphere of an antique market with that of the quietest of universities. They are what libraries would like to be but too often fail, falling off the fine edge, either into a dusty neglect where the silverfishes play or into a harried dog-eared traffic. Sheriton's has long achieved its balance. The books lie out on tables, spacious tables with thick, green baize cloths. The books stand on black oak bookcases that rise till, like Atlas, they shoulder the ceilings, up to which you might send learned Mercurys scaling to fetch you down some tractate that you and some man in Valparaiso alone want but want enough to make it precious. The bookcases protrude and quarter and octave the floor space, making the floor-plan like the wards of a key, with these wooden inner walls running out and enclosing small bays wherein you may stand encased in books, and, at the opposite end from the defile through which you entered, may gain light from a window again framed and encroached upon by books that seem jealous even of the very light needed to read them. As soon, however, as Miss Throcton entered she caught sight of Dr. McPhail. He had, too, that look of the conspirator that marks and gives away the innocent the moment they deviate, even for the noblest causes, from disingenuousness. He was peeping round the side of one of the outstanding bookcases and, on catching her eye, though he blushed miserably, he felt he must signal her. If any of the assistants saw this slightly odd gesture no doubt they assumed that he was filled with that secret glee that rises when you have found a tract that no one else wants, or will, till you have written your paper on it and its incomprehensible neglect. No doubt she was his favourite student, or rather (for she was certainly his age) one of those athenaphoebes, lady scholars who, denied the recognition of a degree, have to convey their contributions to learning through an accredited male. No doubt they were about to share the joy of a co-operative triumph. When, however, she had followed him into the depths of his chosen cove his confusion grew. Clearly, now that the moment had come, he could not bring himself to say what he had so prepared himself to tell her. She saw that she must now make the opening.

'It is kind of you to have noted that my brother has been overtired of late. Indeed he felt all the more free to accept your kind invitation to this conference because it was clear he needed a change. For an active mind,' she went on, for her listener showed no inclination to interrupt her, 'the best rest is a change of interest. We both know how his Arabic studies have been the joy of his life. And I would like to tell you how much this meeting has pleased him, yes, and refreshed him.' She paused, surely this should reassure Dr. McPhail, at least to the point of making it possible for him to say what he had planned and plotted. To put him more at his ease she had avoided looking at him as she spoke and now glancing up, she found that he had turned his back on her. But after peering at the window for a moment or two he evidently had succeeded in composing a sentence that was at least utterable with the aid of a number of throat clearances.

'I know *oratia recta* is said to be the sign of a bore. But, if accurate, which of course is seldom...'—his nervousness made him titter—'it is more informative. I am therefore asking only that you would listen to my report, every detail of which is certainly impressed on my memory. Then if you judge that I have been wholly inept in this matter I trust you will leave without questioning my wish to be of use.'

The stilted opening seemed to give him self-assurance. For after that he succeeded in acting up to his word as to the style of his narrative. 'We have the honour of Sheik Reshad Ibn Khaldun's presence with us. The fact that he was able to visit England was the chief reason for my so hastily summoning all the lovers of Arabic on whom I could lay hands. As I believed he would be, he has proved a star on our voyages. I so preface my report because otherwise I could not have listened to what I am now about to repeat. It would have been wholly impossible for me to retail it to you. He and I were together as yesterday our noon conference closed. He had been taking the chair for us and I had been seated on the rostrum beside him acting as secretary and reporter. As the members were adjourning he turned and touched me as I was completing an entry. He said almost in my ear, "Do you see that man?" I looked up. I saw unmistakably at whom he was looking. I replied, "He has been introduced to you and has spoken several times. You recall he is..." He cut me short, "That man is followed." "Followed?" I asked, a little absent-mindedly, I fear, for I was writing at the time and, believe me, had not an idea as to what he could mean. "That man is closely followed" he went on, "I saw the dark jackal in his shadow." "I don't understand," I said with complete frankness. I wish he had not felt he must,' Dr. McPhail paused at the word, 'enlighten me further.' (Miss Throcton put out her hand and held on to one of the bookshelves.) 'I could hardly believe my ears. "He has put evil on another," the Sheik continued. "And" he continued quite quietly, "It is now following him until it come up with him." "My dear Sheik," I exclaimed, for we are very close to one another, and he knows the—well, I may as well say it—the more than regard, the reverence in which I hold him, "My dear Sheik, really, that is, I can assure you, nonsense. It's just one of those things that can't be true. You must remember he is a Dean—it is a position of great prestige!" I even attempted, for I was so at a loss, a small weak jest. "You may not need to be told that we seldom seem to produce sanctity but the reason for that, many have thought, is because we so heartily pursue respectability. And a Deanery is, I repeat, a station which only the most highly respectable can ambition or retain." "How did he come to it?" "By preferment," I answered at once. "It, like all the Deaneries, is a gift of the Crown. And I must say that whereas in our time a scandalous appointment can hardly be made, though holiness may be passed over, scholarship may not only apply, but may expect to be called. In this case pre-eminently, as in many others, a scholar of high excellence has been chosen for recognition." "I am not questioning—and would not—his intellectual power. Be assured I have judged of that. Further, I have not only found it powerful. I have detected in it a quality that might have suggested to me the very diagnosis which now my inner sight has confirmed. It is his wish for recognition that gave his present place. Ambition, and the power which it has to raise us high in this world, can always and with equal power drive us to the brink of the unseen precipice of the world unseen."

'"But even if there could be the slightest truth in this," I asked him, for by now I was alarmed (after all, he knows more than we of books and words can ever learn), "even then we could do nothing about it." "There is still a little time," he answered, and then asked, "Is there no one in this world who still cares for him, has a real devotion to him. Of course, he may not have kept any such contacts. It is the danger of the lonely arrogant soul. In its crisis it finds itself without allies, without sureties. It is through such selfless loving-kindness and through that alone that there is a hope of making a passage to deliver his beleaguered soul".'

The reporter had evidently come to the end of his narrative. Miss Throcton heard him sigh deeply, that sigh which is half exhaustion brought on by bewilderment and half relief at the discharge of a repugnant task. 'That is why I ventured to send for you.' Dr. McPhail's colophon obviously called on her to reply. 'What do you want me to do?' she asked distressedly. What was the use of this poor little man pouring out all this to her? Granted it was true, and of course in some horrible irrational way it was, it must be, what could he or she do about it? It was, then, with something that was more surprise, but had in it a species of relief, that she heard him reply promptly. 'The Sheik says that he will speak with you in the garden at the party to-morrow.' The reply, however, with its tone of superior arrangement, the moment she reflected on it, increased her surprise and lessened the small element of relief. 'But I don't know that I want to speak with him,' she said defensively. And as the horrible absurdity of the situation grew clearer to her, she added, 'I mean how, how can a complete stranger, a foreigner...' Her exhaustion coming on her long fear made it condense into a sudden uncontrollable irritability... 'I mean how dare he have such suspicions!' The moment she had permitted herself the irrational relief of trying to put out of countenance her informant, who had told her more truth than she could bear, she felt ashamed. He was watching her now. The fact that he had discharged his task had given him courage. And so he was able to judge hers. 'I realise, Miss Throcton, I realise how utterly painful this must be to you. And,' he turned aside for a moment to put a broad calf-bound folio on its back, 'may I be permitted to say how much the thought of your courage heartened me in my attempt to be of use and my determination—in which I had the Sheik's strong counsel—not to shirk, as I would have wished, the discharge of this duty. I would, therefore, beg you to consider the two things which finally decided me to take this unprecedented step—of sending for you: Firstly, I have never known the Sheik to be mistaken in his diagnoses—yes, that is the word—and, secondly, I have known his advice neglected—neglected with the gravest consequences.'

The offer was still one she would have given much to be able to refuse. But now she saw that choice was no longer offered her. Here, however painful it might be, lay an offer of help. To try and disregard it would be to show that she, like her brother, no longer had the power to face facts but in their determination not to recognise the change in their world, the successful intrusion from another, were taking refuge in a fantasy of common sense. The kindly common-sense world of 'average sensible people,' the quiet highly diluted piety of the Close, these things she and her brother might regain. But to-day they were as banished from it as Adam and Eve from Paradise. She must face the fact—call it madness, molestation, possession. Words didn't matter. Only the price of the return, the redemptive price, had now to be asked. 'Thank you very much,' she said. 'Please understand I realise what this must have cost you to perform. I will certainly and gladly consult with the Sheik.' As they parted in the main room of the great shop, Dr. McPhail said, 'I will see that a couple of chairs are put under some trees that are at the border of the further lawn. You will be able to be quiet there.'

It was a lovely afternoon, the year having reached that turn in its tide when summer's salience and autumn's recoil are balanced, a day when it seems possible to believe that the climate has settled down and might give up having seasons and changes, give up growth and decay and stabilise in a quiet perpetuation of unhurried beauty. Miss Throcton had found the two chairs, had been found, served and left supplied by a tea-distributing waiter. She was glad the main group was still round the long table-clothed benches on which silver cake-dishes and tea and coffee urns rose like miniature spires and domes. Her eye had just wandered, climbing up the creeper-covered walls, to the still sky, when she heard beside her, 'These days, when Nature seems to pause, are of course far more significant than winter's storms or the splendour of spring. It is not really the climate of the land "where it was always afternoon." It is that the veil between that which does not move and our periodic selves is now thin.' The voice spoke English with that perfection of accent hardly ever achieved either by those who have learnt it after they have ceased to be children or those who have carelessly mis-spoken it from infancy. She turned to see looking down at her a man dressed in a dark robe that passed in this group where a number of the residents were wearing their gowns. What could not be passed over were his eyes. Indeed she was held by them so that afterwards she found she was unable to recall his other features. Was his beard grey or black, his nose straight or hooked, his complexion olive or pale. Even of the eyes themselves she could not remember their tint. He sat down beside her and in the same quiet almost reminiscent tone, remarked, 'You, are of course, sister to Dean Throcton. Further, you brought him here, by the mercy of the All Merciful, while time remained. When I left Egypt I questioned my soul why it should warn me that grave necessity lay behind my intention. I had duties in regard to my religious concerns which called for a visit to London, now that your country by the mysterious powers of money and machinery has reversed the miracle of Moses by joining two seas and so has made a water highway across the desert. I had the pleasure of this extemporised conference and generous hospitality to expect and my expectations have been more than met. But neither business nor pleasure could have given me that deep sense of urgency. Now I know. And this particular day—yes, it is fitting, lucky, as the ignorant say, auspicious as you might put it, blessed would be my term.'

'Who are you?' she asked directly: surely he would tell her a little more than had Dr. McPhail. He replied, 'A Sufi.' Whether he would have told her more or not, at that moment the easily-moving group of guests which had been circling the lawns, deserted the tea-tables as their pivot and began to approach that further end of the garden in which he and she were sitting. She saw her brother pass talking almost vivaciously with Dr. McPhail. 'You are relieved.' The voice beside her followed the change of her thought and added, 'Yes, we have a reprieve, a reprieve so that we may restate our case, offer, maybe, fresh surety and approach the Supreme Court with our appeal, and,' he added slowly, 'our promise to make a further...' He paused, then went on, 'Let me tell you what I now see straight before me on this quiet lawn in this place where ancient piety and learning have been refined until like a rich heavy wine too long kept it has become little more than a clear, thin, faintly flavoured, faintly coloured water. I see a fine and honoured presence, learning, yes, and learning made polished, finished, closed, as the pores of wood are closed when the cabinet worker has lacquered them. And so there is pride. And with pride always the danger of scorn, and with scorn, hatred, and with hatred, hell.' His voice had deepened until it was so low that she thought she had never heard a human tone so profound—but quiet, so that even as close as they were she could hardly catch the words. As she strained to catch what he was saying a sudden irritation swept into her mind: Surely, in spite of all Dr. McPhail's efforts—themselves rather absurd—to prepare her and to ally himself with her fears—all this was unhelpfully odd. How could it help her brother's mental difficulties for her to sit here and be lectured about his character by a complete stranger, an African, too, however learned he might be, and surely his learning could hardly be helpful in a case of brain-tension. She had heard the medical and hygienic state of Egypt was so low that those who travelled there in spite of every modern precaution often suffered severe upsets of the digestion and severe fevers. Her mind felt a colour-bar rising between her and this stranger who disconcertingly combined aloofness with personality. The voice beside her spoke again. But it was light now. 'You are right to resent a liberty if taken by one who is impertinent, though even then it would be more right to endure even that. I have no right certainly to lecture you, giving you a cheap form of character analysis of your closest relation, as a charlatan might do at a fair. So I will add, I see one of the finest works of God, a learned man who has industriously used his talent. And I see,' his voice hardly modified at all its same clear unstressed tone, 'I see, at this moment, following him, hardly a cubit behind his heels...' She had grasped the arm of her chair, and he interrupted himself to say kindly, 'No, don't feel panic. Practically everyone here is followed by a form or trail that would profoundly startle them and theirs, if these wraiths could be seen. And yet I do not see any but one who is in immediate danger of being overtaken. Indeed some are actually—how shall I put it—increasing the distance between themselves and that which follows, dogs them, don't you say. Of course that is not an accurate way of describing what is going on, but it will serve.'

'But that one, my brother?' Her voice was now tautly urgent. 'Well,' he spoke gravely but with no trace of alarm in his tone, 'that is why we are here. There is hope, I mean in this world. It will depend, must depend, on him. But if you are to understand and we are to do whatever may be permitted of us, you must grasp clearly what it is I am now seeing. I see that he is closely followed by a form that, because of its particular character, tells me,' again he paused, and concluded, 'tells me what he has done.' 'Are you sure?' It was all she could think to say. He closed the issue by saying quietly, 'A murderer alone is followed by that species and that particular variety follows those who have done murder through magic—or as you would put it not by deed but by intention. I need hardly, however, point out to you that your Prophet, Jeshua ben Miriam, may his name be blessed, has specifically told us that it is intention rather than act that establishes blood-guiltiness before the Throne of the Most High. Your brother is followed by what my predecessors in my land called the black form of Anubis, the dark and dreadful aspect of him who summons the dead before the Judge in the underworld. I see further that the creature is not only black with the shadow caused by murderous death, it is also leprous. He placed evil on another and then lied to himself when he had done it and while he did it. Therefore, not only has it returned on him, as it must: he is unable, because of his lie, to rid himself of it by expiation, by making the offering that, though it might not save his forfeited life of the body, would at least save his soul out of the hand of vengeance.'

They sat silent for some time. Time seemed to have stopped for her as she looked across from the pass to which he had brought her, the pass between two worlds, the unseen and the seen, and saw, as though she were already a stranger, a disembodied revenant, the bright innocent scene, where, as ignorant as children playing over a covered mine-shaft, the Conference members—her brother treated as one of them—chatted of their studies. She felt herself at last sighing, as coming to from fainting and then heard her voice saying, 'Can't anything be done? Can't I do anything?' '*That* offer is never useless.' He spoke as a fine judge of engravings turning over a large portfolio will select one and hold it up to the light. 'Next to its own act of trust in the Most High, the devotion of another can be the soul's greatest defence.' 'I would do anything for him.' 'I had judged that possible or it would have been little use our meeting.' 'Then can't I take this thing from him, for him—he is so helpless, so young, if the word does not sound absurd to you.' 'No,' and almost a smile could be suspected in the tone; 'No: years are made by the soul and its desire for growth. I am in my ninth decade, as it has been my duty to wait, and, if it might be, to grow inwardly. And others can refuse to grow, as he has. The folly of youth is the vice of old age, you know the phrase. So,' and his voice again let go its lightness, 'had he been really young, and not merely arrested, then you might have taken this for him. Parents, devoted and wise parents, can for their children. But very seldom a sister for her brother. For he acted with an adult intention and he can pay the price, the heavy price, if he will confess to his evil and throw himself on the mercy of the All Merciful. Therefore no one can do it for him. No man may make agreement for his brother nor take his guiltiness upon him. For it cost more to redeem their souls, so he must leave that alone for ever.' The Psalter quotation she had heard mumbled over so often and sometimes wondered about as the choir chanted all question out of it, now used by an Arab seemed to give a certain security to their conversation, a conversation that seemed to waver between incredible fantasy and hopeless despair. She felt a sudden strength of confidence come to her. This man knew. He knew with a precision about the things of the heart and soul that we had yet to achieve in things of the body and its hygiene. And with that, because her engrossed absorption with the present had been for the moment a little relieved, her memory began again to work. She recalled Dr. Wilkes, feeling his way, voicing his need for a true psychotherapy. That led to seeing again the young Chaplain under the limes. Could it be that her almost incredulous request for his prayers and the thing he had asked for—? Could he have actually, specifically prayed that the spiritual assistance he felt sure alone could help, should be sent? She realised with a sense of surprise that had, even in this atmosphere, a touch of the uncanny, how little she really believed that any understanding really listened to all sincere appeal. Like most good people when prayer seemed too specifically to be answered she was as much startled as reassured. 'Well,' and the voice was as undramatic as a surgeon's when he comes to the conclusion of an operation's first phase, 'I am glad that we have met and that I have been able to confirm what in your heart you already knew.'

He had risen from his chair. She looked up, with all her alarm returned. 'But, but what is to happen? You know. Please believe me I am absolutely sure now. You can help me. You will!' 'No, no. I have said that he must help himself if he is to be saved.' 'But surely you did suggest that I could help him, that I could be of use? And you must tell me what that is. I really am at my wits' end,' she suddenly recoiled into her lifelong poise, 'or I assure you I could never have spoken to a stranger as I have. What can I do—except make the offer which I have!'

He did not sit down again but bent slightly as he said, 'I wished you to say that again. You recall, in your tradition, that those who said they would drink the cup, were asked not once but three times if they could really know what they were declaring they would do.' He bent a little lower. He was now standing almost behind her, so that no one could have seen him touch her arm. Nor did she feel it. And, had she felt the touch, she would not have been able to turn round or attend. At that moment her brother was approaching. She heard him say, 'Well, Laetitia, we should be going. I am glad you have been able to meet our most distinguished guest. The Sheik is...' She heard his voice, thin and meaningless, as we hear the voices round us as an anaesthetic takes the brain. For her eyes saw her brother not three yards from her. And, not a foot behind him, she saw with equal clearness—there was nothing shadowy or wavering about it—padding over the lawn, following his every step, seeming to scent the imprint just left on the grass, a black leprous fox. She felt she must have screamed—some inarticulate, animal effort to warn him—had she not heard Sheik Khaldun's voice above her saying, 'Ah, Mr. Dean, we can have one more turn together,' and as she spoke he stepped between her and her brother. As they moved off together no shadow followed either of the tall figures. She was too exhausted to move: more, she was too exhausted to be roused even to dismay, when, after a couple of turns, she saw the two figures making for where she sat. The garden now was nearly empty. She could have heard their every word in the stillness. They were not speaking. The Sheik's face was calm with the silence that is waiting. Her brother's was tense with words he obviously still feared to release. Her presence was keen enough provocation to rupture his caution.

'You, certainly, are not slow to share your fancies with a complete stranger!' His voice was, if not under perfect control, still able to be repressed into a sneer. His lips, though, were trembling and white with frightened rage. Indeed, he whirled half round with something like a snarl when the Sheik put a hand on his shoulder. The hand, however, instead of letting go, completed for him the movement he had begun. He was turned in his tracks, and clearly saw there something that expunged from his mind any emotion as reassuring as a sense of insult. For when he turned again, so that she could see his face, it was still whiter; but all the defiance had vanished. He spoke in so low and unaccented a voice that had not the spot become as silent as a deserted church, she could not have heard. 'It is no use telling me to act. I am doomed. My one hope was that the whole thing must be subjective. I was building it up. If I could get away it must fade...' the voice died down. 'He is the All-Compassionate.' 'No. This is the Law. How can I believe in mercy when it would suit me. I believed in, I believe in Law. And now the Law has me in its grip.' 'Why dispute about terms. An algebraist uses *x*. He does not strive to define his efficacious symbol. You need mercy. It alone can save you. Why not then take it, why choose death?' The Dean stood beside the Sheik for some five minutes, then he began to sway. The Egyptian put his hand on the sick man's shoulder, again swung him round gently, but this time so that they were face to face.

'For the fourteen days' grace I have power to loan, Forget, Forget!' Miss Throcton saw her brother's face lose, first, its awful tension, then its fear, caution, circumspection. Layer by layer, the coats of defence that had been laid like a lacquer-varnish over it and hardened into a mask of pride, smoothed away, as over-painting disappears under the cleaner's solvents leaving the first fresh design and colour... She saw something of the boy she had known. True, the physiological age remained, but the psychological experience, the chosen and studied reaction to life, that was gone.

'Well,' he remarked in the vague friendly voice of someone who has forgotten the point of what they have been saying and gropes for the lost thread, 'Well, I must just go over and catch McPhail before he leaves. I want a last word with him. I'll be back in a moment for you. I am sure you'll enjoy every minute with the Sheik; a rare privilege, indeed; though perhaps only to be appreciated at its full worth by one who has borne the brunt of being called with ignorant patronage, a mere Arabian.' He nodded and smiled at them; then turned toward the further end of the lawn where Dr. McPhail was taking last counsel with the tea-staff who with their paraphernalia assembled were about to vacate the green. 'I cannot deliver him.' The Arab's voice went on in the same clear tone as it had spoken the word 'Forget,' clear and carrying, as though the Dean were not still, on his way across the lawn, within earshot. 'You have seen—his pride is still too passionately resistant. Pride can believe in Law: only humility can have trust in Mercy. But your affection—it permitted you to see, did it not!' She bowed. Then asked, 'But till this afternoon, till just now, I have been able to see, unless he touched me, and then I was still mercifully uncertain, never quite despairingly sure. And to-day, he was some distance from me, when, when I saw?' 'This time it was I who touched you, so that you might see, yes, as clearly as I saw and see. That I am now permitted to do to whom I please, for whom I believe it would serve. But the fact that you can see when you touch him (no one else could receive vision—light or dark—through him), that is because you are willing still to love him, in spite of your knowledge.'

'That means, then, that there is still a chance?' 'You realise what that may mean?' 'I repeat, I am willing. Could I endure to see him go down, if there remained any possible thing I might do to guard, screen him from that fate? How could I not be willing!' 'You have said it the third time. And now it is accepted. I will help. But my help will not appear to you, until the end.'

The Dean was already coming back for them, accompanied by Dr. McPhail. Together the quartet made for the college courts and passing through two of them finally reached the main gate leading to the street. The big doors were open and the small tunnel was dusty yellow with a sloping cone of sunlight. As they reached that Dr. McPhail stopped. 'I and the Sheik will say good-bye to you here.' He put out his hand, took Miss Throcton's and then the Dean's, bowed to them both and stepped back to make way for the Arab to make his farewell. He put out both his hands taking both the Dean's and his sister's at the same time. For a moment, as he did so, he brought the hand of the brother and sister together in his double hand-clasp. Then he bent his head murmuring, 'May the Power of the Most High overshadow you with his invincible protection,' and drew back toward the court whither his host was already leading the way.

'Rather touching, that gesture of oriental courtesy in farewell, and even the theological language, which is after all embedded in our laconic Good-bye, takes on a certain grace and almost conviction when said with such presence, don't you think?' her brother asked as they went along the street to their lodgings. Then added, as she had not replied, 'You mustn't mind that kind of elaboration of our simpler manners.' A slight touch of impatience rose, however, in his tone as he concluded, 'But I see my interest in the customs of other peoples cannot take your mind from the, of course, quite rightful observation of your own. I suppose ladies must wear these trains, better than the crinoline, but they seem to take if anything more management.' She looked up at him and seeing that he was looking at her, she smiled, 'Yes, I thought that the hem of my dress had caught.'

'Well, we managed to get quite a good deal off our hands at the Conference though it was an extemporised affair it was certainly well worth while.' He was following his obviously self-satisfied thoughts.

'Yes, yes.' Her agreement pleased him though he did not restrain himself from remarking that she could hardly estimate the amount of technical information that had been exchanged. 'I wonder,' he summed up, just as they came to their rooms, 'whether some time in the not too distant future it would be possible to obtain a long enough vacation to visit the Near East. Both McPhail and the Sheik tell me that not only is there so much worth seeing but that a scholar can find in the libraries of Cairo and Alexandria, now that they have been somewhat ordered, and in other places, documents that throw much light on linguistic and other problems. I have a feeling that the Sheik would find a visitor such as myself not at all unwelcome and of no little interest.'

CHAPTER FIFTEEN

Her brother's freedom from all apparent strain showed no sign of leaving him when they arrived back at the Deanery. Without question or explanation he went to the Cathedral, and he made no comments as to the way the stalls were being kept or the choir garnished. He spoke briefly to her about his work, remarked that he had received much encouragement—not merely refreshment—by attending the Conference, and would now prosecute his studies with renewed assurance as to their worth. He settled in to regular hours of study punctuated by as regular attendances in his Stall. Except that occasionally he would appear for a moment a little blank and ask her what he had just been saying, he seemed to her much as he had always been, perhaps a trifle less inclined to let satire tinge his accent or pride show through a phrase. She therefore expected that when she passed Dr. Wilkes in the street she would not be able to gain right of passage merely with a bow. He was honestly pleased with what he called complete improvement.

'Change,' he said brightly, 'is so often treated by moralists, and in most sermons, as something that must be always for the worse—until, of course, the final one for Heaven. And even then, we poor physicians are treated as having permitted one more failure! But change of air and change of place, as I think I mentioned to you earlier, I have found among the soundest allies of health. Here we are being given a vivid and most welcome example, are we not!' He paused and as she only bowed slightly, added, 'Indeed, I would venture further: Mr. Dean looks to me as though a weight had been lifted from him. He appears to me to be not only in his old health but actually to appear younger.' There was of course almost a question in his voice. The, 'I believe you are right' with which she closed their conference, disappointed him a little. As they went their ways he remarked to himself—'But can this be, as I had begun to suspect earlier it might be, a cyclic thing—as one subject gains resistance the next falls a prey, as one conquers the infection it passes it on to one who has so far escaped?'

He had no doubts that he had been right when after a fortnight he met Miss Throcton again in the Close. 'I wonder that she does not call me in?' was his not unnatural self-interrogation. The question never crossed her mind, though she was not unaware that it would probably occur to anyone who met her. She had not expected things to be otherwise and was indeed grateful that the two weeks that had been specified as the space during which the molestation would find no purchase on her brother had gone quietly. Both herself, as well as he, had seemed to be under the cover of a calm that was so secure as to feel almost anaesthetic. She had found herself incapable of thinking of past or future. She could not rouse either regret or foreboding so long as she was held in that almost animal peace. They had parted on a Friday afternoon in Cambridge from the Sheik. That had been the seventh of September.

The actual day of the Autumn Equinox opened as calm as its predecessors and even more still. The trees now were wearing considerable yellow, but as yet no touch of the frost-given red. 'It is even more peaceful than Cambridge,' her brother had remarked at breakfast. Cook, being more practical and food-absorbed, told her, when she went into the kitchen for the morning consultation, that harvest was yet to be lifted and rain was feared. She had answered that farmers were always pessimists and asked whether they oughtn't to be getting another cat. This brought out cook's own pessimism, 'We ought never to have lost Tiss. As fine a cat as ever I've seen; quite an "aristocrat".' It was all that horrid dog-fox coming in. When she had been with hunting folk they'd say, 'Fox in the covert, good; Fox in the house, bad.' Miss Throcton left the kitchen silently and when she was gone cook added herself to those who shook heads and said, 'Bad to start low with the leaf in the fall.'

Anyhow she and her farming friends did not have to wait long to be proved right about the weather. By noon it had clouded. The clouds did not roll up from the west. They formed first as a curdle of grey in the vault of blue, a curdle that grew steadily denser and darker while across it appeared still darker bands, almost black. Then, without hesitation, as though it had been timed and planned to a moment, as though the sound had precipitated it, just as the 2.45 chime sounded, the chime which set the bell tolling for evensong at 3, the rain began. It was from the first drop a steady deluge, straight, unswayed by draught or eddy, as though fine lines of unbroken water, and not drops, were running staunchlessly from the heavens, which had become a vast sagging perforated bag, onto the flooding earth. Through this grey curtain of ten thousand liquid threads, as Miss Throcton stood looking out of the south parlour window, it was now hardly possible to see with any distinctness the looming mass of the Cathedral's west front. The ear, too, received all other sounds—as happens when going under an anaesthetic—through a web of steady hissing. Though the sun must of course be still well above the horizon, the light under this depth of cloud had become no more than submerged shadow. She stood looking out at the great swamping cathedral lawn. She had rung for tea and to tell the servants to light a fire and the gas chandelier, and also to bring a couple of lamps. She had caught sight of her brother under a big umbrella, making his way from the north porch as evensong was ended. She noticed that the pallid gleam of the water running on the flat stretched dome of the umbrella, the tassels of rain that swept down from its edges as he strode through the downpour—all made his figure a confusion of greys and vague blacks. The full long coat which he was wearing over his clerical frock-coat and 'apron' flapped around his heels as he hurried across. The lining evidently must have caught in his foot some time, perhaps now, as he was almost trotting. She must look to it as soon as he came in, it might trip him. But, as he turned across the small cathedral lane, to gain the shelter of the house, she saw that the black moving object at his heels, though so close to him as to seem part of his coat or shadow, had a life of its own and a way of its own—every now and then, with a kind of playfulness, it would frisk up. Once or twice she thought that, as a puppy will, it almost had his hand in its mouth or at least could give him a lick. Still, as he entered the room, she was able to say to his not unexpected remark, 'This is the Deluge!', 'We are fortunate in having an Ark,' And a queer, perhaps desperate sense of humour made her go on to herself, 'And so must not refuse hospitality to the animals.' Surely it was better to joke as long as humour, that strange anaesthetic vapour, floated up through the mind. And surely there was some animal in the room. The lamps had been brought in, the chandelier spread its small bright fans of hissing gas, the fire had taken and was as radiant. Whatever had followed her brother into the room had no liking for the light. But it had not left. Through the hiss of the rain outside she could hear something panting close at hand and through the lapping of the flames the sound of a creature licking.

The drowning of the daylight and the disappearance of the dry earth under a quicksilver-like deposit of water had been similarly watched from the one other edifice in the Close that was higher in social status, though still closer to sea level, than the Deanery.

'One feels some flavour of Lot's relief as he entered Zoar and then was safely able to glance back at the mire-pit engulfment of his former home,' the Bishop remarked to his Chaplain, as, having won to the refuge of his Palace after a shower-bath scuttle from the Cathedral he now went to the window. 'This would have extinguished the Cities of the Plain!' Young Halliwell, like a good *alter-ego*, took what he judged to be his master's mood. 'I suppose it's better to be drowned than burnt,' the Bishop continued. Then the meteorological mood damping his spirits, he added, 'Dante enlarged the traditional high-temperature Hell with the contrast of a sub-zero inferno. But eschatological invention has yet to give us a submerged Satanic realm wherein the sinner will always be in utmost agony of suffocation and always sinking helplessly into a darker depth, a more awful and stygian abyss, crushed in upon and tormentingly constricted by ever-frightful pressures!'

'Sir!' Young Halliwell smilingly shuddered at the strange little verbal exercise in redemptorist rhetoric, 'May I ask could you be an incarnation of that poetical but minatory preacher, the late Dean of St. Paul's, Dr. John Donne? I had not suspected from your gentle sway of the pastoral staff, a very sceptre of peace in your hand, that you could turn and let fly such a bolt of apocalyptic thunder!'

The Bishop took the remark amiably and patting his lieutenant on the shoulder, 'That style, my son, won't come back as long as we are prosperous. Yet maybe we are more neurotic than were godly folk in my father's time. They took their brimstone with very little treacle, kept it down and thrived on it—when our light digestions would never stomach such hot salve. But I often wonder,' he sighed looking with unfocused eyes at the sight-dazing rain-curtains, 'I often wonder whether we have been wholly right in going over so heartily, so uncritically to progress, gradualism and inevitable amelioration. The weather and our lives are both of them more cataclysmic than we like to allow. Yes, I sometimes wonder whether the pathetic fallacy itself may not be less a fallacy than we allow and less pathetic than grim. These sudden meteorological breakdowns of customary balance and restraint, no one seems able to foresee them but only to be wise after the event, and so we tend to overlook them or quickly forget them. And in the process of our lives—the same spastic factor. We had a lengthy summer of longevities, almost a drought of deaths. And now in the last few months a veritable cloudburst of casualties, carrying away not only those overdue, but invading the levels where life expectation seemed still secure. Perhaps it has not stopped even now.' He looked up at the sky that seemed black and massive, then at the earth greyly shimmering in semi-inundation. 'Perhaps this time it won't stop and a second Deluge engulf this island. We here would certainly be first to be submerged.' The Cathedral clock chimed, 'Why, the very bells sound water-borne or water-logged. A charming fancy, that huge man-made rockery become the haunt of fishes, the vast tendril of the Kraken tolling at the bells and no doubt,' he could not resist a small private joke at his ritualist trouble-maker's expense, 'No doubt the sepia of some censer-like-swinging octopus rising as an obfuscating incense to the seaweed-shrouded roof. But time is time,' he pulled himself with a shrug into business trim. 'Till we go under, the captain must stay on the bridge. Come, our desk calls. Kindle our modern answer to darkness, the gas, sulphurous, explosive, burning and asphyxiating, with which Plutonic vapour—the stifling breath of Cerberus himself—we keep at bay his daylight-fearing presence. By the way,' he went on, his vague mood of malaise relieved by the burst of half-humorous rhetoric, 'The Dean does seem quite all right now?' 'Yes,' Halliwell answered, 'Yes. You recall I wrote you that note while you were away, just saying that he was leaving for a Conference for a week in Cambridge. I thought I wouldn't bother your bigger business with misgivings but wait and see if the change would work.' 'You did find him in poor shape?' 'You see I didn't find him, I failed to see him. As I was going across to the Deanery I ran into Miss Throcton seated in the Close. I know every doctor would say, never diagnose without seeing the patient, so I had no right to an opinion. Miss Throcton clearly showed me that she felt I should not call...' He paused and then went on, 'But she spoke to me frankly. She made no concealment of the fact that he was under some severe strain, but not one that medicine or, or clerical assistance, could mitigate. Change, acting with a fine constitution, was her hope. It seems to have been sufficiently well grounded...' Again, he paused. 'He is a strange man,' the Bishop was endorsing the matter and filing it in his mind with a couple of phrases, 'And she is a fine woman. Both of them go deeper than their surface appearances would suggest.' He was sorting papers for the next point on their agenda. 'She up and he down. And further, I somehow can't get out of my mind that there's some element in this sequence of undulant exhaustions that has escaped diagnosis?' The last comment turned almost into a question. Indeed, the Bishop, his capable hands still dealing papers like a practised whist-player deals cards, glanced up at his Chaplain standing attentive at his shoulder. The Chaplain looked down into the wide wary eyes that, he knew, saw far more questions than that firmly urbane mouth would ever verbalise. 'No,' the younger counselled his own administrator-learning spirit, 'No: when a man is become really capable he plays the game so well because he never looks beyond the board.' Aloud he expressed the thought in administrative language, 'Yes, and I see in your hands, Sir, the correspondence about the *locum tenens* difficulty at Parva Saltcote, again the problem of whether to wait resignedly for a recovery or move to recover freedom of choice by a resignation.' 'Maybe you're going to turn into a fashionable epigrammatic preacher of a rich "Proprietary Chapel!"' The Bishop smiled, his feeling-tone pleasantly altered by the slight unexpected play of words and his mind turned to a practical issue. 'Yes, I think we had better ourselves take action and call for a resignation.' He smiled and a moment after was dictating a letter, kind, discreet, firm and, because it had to get a sick man out of a cure of souls he could no longer serve and yet not hurt his feelings—a nice and not uninteresting task—the letter cleared comfortably all other vaguer thoughts out of the dictating diocesan mind.

The rain lasted three days. The little river on which the tiny city stood flooded, and the Close became not a sink but a reservoir. It was impossible to keep even a house so defended as was the Deanery, even moderately clean. Mud came in everywhere, muddy footprints. Miss Throcton sent for her defending staff of maids so often that, though well drilled, they began to murmur. Nor did cook's advice to them, though it was meant to be soothing—her counsel that the poor lady was none too well—succeed in rousing their sympathy. 'There's no cat now', they protested, 'so why should she send for us to-day to wipe up paw-marks. Why can't she tell the Master not to trail his dirty umbrella and that torn hem of his coat after him when he comes in. Just making work, it is, these days, when sense would know that nothing could be kept clean. She shouldn't do it! And we willing as willing for anything that's in our duty, and with right weather and not a judgment like this and all that! She shouldn't do it!'

Miss Throcton knew that as well as they. But it was one of the retreat points in the desperate rear action she was fighting. She could not resist seeing whether they could see. It was so painfully, foully, filthily—she used the strong words with care so as to be sure she was not shirking or stinting her rational clearly-defined estimate—so grossly plain to her, those footsteps. Big-game hunters called them 'spoor' didn't they? And in the slimy pounce of mud were, she felt sure, black hairs and round their hair bases clots of flaked skin. She had done her share of that sick nursing that falls to every kindly and efficient woman. She wasn't a molly-coddle that went white and into the vapours at blood or vomit. But she felt a nausea that almost gave her vertigo when, forcing herself to bend down and certify these clots of mud that almost ran into the broad stain of her brother's shoes, she found she could not doubt the evidence of her eyes. She did not dare touch; or even be found—like a witch peering for omens. Nor could she ask anyone else. Didn't they see what she saw, in the mud-stains. She remembered her old Scotch nurse seeing the oddest things in the leaves at the bottom of her teacup. No one else could see them, but time and again the queer old Highland body did seem, in this homely, ridiculous way, to get some hint of oncoming events—generally uncanny. The only possible way was to provoke the maids to question. They were certainly provoked, but only to question her considerateness of them. Even telling them to use carefully a mop with disinfectant, and to wash it in boiling water after, aroused no curiosity. But only conviction that she had become cantankerous and was taking out her pains at their expense. The vain hope that one of them would turn to her and ask, was her last attempt, the only way left open to bring along with her a contingent of humanity, the sane, kindly, grumbling-at-trifles, mercifully blind humanity whom she was leaving; to urge them a little further along with her on the dark way she must now go.

Naturally, she left till the last her brother. Then one evening—it was dark, still, foggy, the air supersaturated—he had come in and remarked, 'All Saints to-morrow—that is a feast in which all can join, Arabians and Christians. For it is the feast of those who have gone beyond controversy.' She waited, and then asked, 'Do you recall the last Dean's installation? It was on All Saints, I remember.' He looked at her oddly and then with a smile in which question overlaid irritation—'Well, are you raising that because to-night it is All Hallows Eve?' She could see the slight twist of sarcasm that spoilt the smile at the corners of his mouth and the finer narrowed lines round the eye that revealed a deeper uneasiness. And, with the same clearness, she could see the small, dark sorely-diseased animal—that no longer seemed to fear the light so much, so long as it might keep close in his shadow. It lay close by his respectably gaitered foot and at this moment as she watched it, it lifted its bloodshot eyes to watch him, then settled down slowly to lick running ulcers. He passed one fine scholarly hand over another. Then smoothed from his face the slight pucker of fretfulness and, feeling that he had shown an irrational irritation, added: 'The Feast is archaeologically very interesting—far more ancient, of course, than the Christian Church.' While, to himself he reflected, 'Women need anniversaries. Their minds live—at least when they are mature—so much in the past. Religion is their necessity, and our profession. A professional's attitude is confessedly better than the best amateur's. Though amateur means lover, obviously the good-sense of mankind has seen that understanding is superior to devotion.' Then, feeling that so much educative insight should not be denied where it was clearly needed, he completed his reverie aloud. 'The Christian Church's strength lay in its emotional appeal to slaves and barbarians. As soon as it would win the educated, it had to ally itself with Platonism. Further, it is now clear that Aristotelianism was incorporated into our theological thinking, precisely because the Arabians, possessing themselves of "The Philosopher" whom we had lost, compelled us in the nineteenth century to arm ourselves with the same intellectual equipment. No: religion cannot live on emotionalism. Indeed is there anything so tedious—even disquieting—as the devotion of others! If calm, it appears as perfunctory; if fervent, histrionic.'

He was enjoying himself at two levels of consciousness. There was the almost self-conscious pleasure of practising periods. Since he had been Dean, his preaching schedule being increased, he had found to his surprise that he enjoyed seeing whether he could transpose his writer's style into telling speech. Just below this level, that was using his sister as a sounding-board, was concealed a secondary, less recognised, more satisfying feeling, that he was demonstrating the superiority of his intellectual Laodiceanism to her uninformed faith, the ascendancy of ability over character. He did notice that she did not, as he had expected, reply. She surely should have? When had he last failed, when he tried, to make her retort? He liked her to, for lately he had begun to be entertained by her defences. They showed that irrelevance, that lack of real insight that must be present in a mind unschooled in logic but which had its quaint humour, and gave him further opening for his wit. The misgiving however was deep enough only to reach the surface as irritability. 'And, remember, our emotional faith found, as an administrative fact, that the fire of love was far below the temperature required to make men's wills and minds plastic. Resolution and intelligence were bent into orthodoxy not by a metaphorical but a very real flame.'

With a pulpit gesture he pointed his hand at the blazing hearth, then let open palm and fingers fall, to show that the issue was settled and might be let drop. She might be silent now. There was no answer to that. It was a telling close. He felt, therefore, actually a twinge of surprised irritability when he heard his sister check an exclamation and then say, 'Your fingers nearly touched the floor!' 'Well, you have always, if not boasted, been prepared to prove that, as we used to say, "you could eat off that lady's floors".' Again he tried to be nice but he could not help feeling that she was oddly on edge. 'At her age,' he sub-whispered to himself, 'Natural, natural.' 'Charles!' Her voice, there was no doubt of it, was not normal. Besides, she never called him by his name unless there was something that she was steeling herself to tell him. That was the tone in which she had spoken when she came with the telegram in her hand to say that their mother was dead. 'Charles, are you sure that everything is all right? I mean, are you certain that your improvement has been complete, complete recovery? That you shouldn't, couldn't, do something more?' It was, of necessity, a desperate cast, to reach out and make contact with him. But she was amazed at the completeness of his reaction.

'Laetitia, what are you talking about?' 'I mean,' she stumbled on, 'I mean...'—the wretched little word that always signals the breakdown of understanding between two minds, two spirits who have nothing but words with which to touch each other—'I only mean that just before we went away and indeed for some time previous you had been terribly run-down, and I was just a little anxious...'

'Of course, I naturally remember that I was overtired after all the changes which we had to effect here. That I haven't referred to the matter is, you must know, natural to me. It is wholly out of character for a nature such as mine to complain. Minor ills are only aggravated by speaking of them. He was a weak character or a poor observer—probably both—who gave us the counsel, feeble and inaccurate, that a sorrow shared—still less a nervous vexation—is by sharing halved!' He shifted complacently but did not trouble to look at her. 'And I think I may say that it argues well for my natural resilience that a brief week—and not of rest but active other-interest—the intellectual's real recreation—brought me back to complete tone. It is you, my dear'—he half-turned toward her and his voice did show concern of a sort, the sort that very little analysis is needed to find its root in self-love's fear of losing a servant hard to replace—'It is you who should watch your spirits. Anxiety is the demon of our age. You should have the strength of mind to settle down to your duties, as I do to mine. And you would do well to have an avocation as I have mine. Yours might be gardening when the summer returns. Meanwhile I prescribe a little needlework to keep your mind off gloomy reveries. You must not be cast down by the pathetic fallacy that Nature's seasonal Fall should affect our spirits. Here in this spacious, seemly security'—his eye swept the stately proportions of the room—'we can smile at the hobgoblin fancies that haunted man confined in such weather to a cave, or even to an unheated, ill-glazed cathedral! Put aside these lurking, substanceless misgivings. Black care does not only ride behind the horseman as Horace says. Just as much he sits beside the woman in her all-too-easy chair by the bright hearth. Drive him away.' And again he made one of those finished conclusive pulpit gestures that his hands almost fell into as he closed a sentence. This time she did however check any outward sign of her shudder. It shook her then all the more. For not only had that fine white hand brushed along the filthy, pus-streaked coat of the thing that was sitting beside him, but, as his hand swept, as though stroking down the leprous pelt, the creature rose, arched its back, and, as though it had received a message and dismissal from him, it slowly hobbled over. It came limping across and sat down at her side.

CHAPTER SIXTEEN

She did not see it every day. Once for a whole week she did not catch a glimpse of it. She could, however, nearly always hear it, whenever the house was still, snuffling at the door, or from behind some piece of furniture in the room, gobbling at its sores. It became almost impossible for her to swallow any food, such nausea took her, when, under the dining-table, with its long white damask that reached nearly to the floor, she heard the sound. Next, she could feel its touch: it would lean against her foot. Once or twice she could not resist the temptation—she raised the hem of the table-cloth to see. There was nothing her eye could find. Her brother noticed though.

'"To Whom the Heavens are not clean"—Job's idea of the Almighty is appealing to you?' he asked with that irritable humour, that watchful hyper-criticism that masked in him real insight. 'Surely,' he concluded, 'the inspection could be carried out earlier?' She lied feebly, 'I thought I'd dropped my napkin,' and then wondered was it worth the effort, did it really deceive, was he, under his simmering of complaint, trying to rid a curiosity that could only be answered by his putting a question he dared not ask; would it be better if the truth came out? The last query did however rouse her. She saw how she had been drifting. This was happening to her—the whole range of misery from his exasperating nagging miscomprehension right down into the horrible dark of the molestation itself—because the alternative was that he would be swept away, engulfed. She was standing—she had chosen to stand—between him and it. Because she had so chosen he was able to show this contemptuous complacence—he had to. His petty irritability was the transmuted expression of a knowledge, of a responsibility and a punishment that his surface mind would not endure.

Once this knowledge became clear in her mind—as after a day of fog, the sun setting, the night is cloudless—she found her courage had returned. But the suffering became worse. The attack now seemed to have become tidal, sweeping in first by one aperture and then by another. She realised that when she could see it she could not feel it and vice versa. The senses were being assaulted alternately. For three days she saw the jackal, it was everywhere she went on her household duties, as though the entity, if such it was, felt that it must not let her out of its sight. She could escape it for a while by going out. The weather was however very raw, the shortest walk seemed to bring on a miserable chill and exhaustion. She knew enough of sickness to realise, however short a time she consulted her mirror, that it was signalling back one word to her, anaemia. Her brother, too, showed his same scolding concern and practically ordered her to stay indoors. He even forbade her to go to evensong. On Sunday, however, she insisted on attending Morning Prayer. He was preaching. As he came down from his study, his sermon case in his hand, and found her waiting in the hall, dressed to accompany him, she noticed on his face the inter-play of protest and complacence. The Cathedral audience, he had begun to notice, was small: every contribution, of a listener, was therefore welcome. 'I observe,' he said, 'that you insist on your major religious duties. And perhaps I need not insist on your obeying my dispensation. The morning is mild, the earth more viscid than fluid. The Anthem, too, is a charming one, by Purcell, and may serve to raise your spirits. After all, the original, putative author of the Psalms, we are told, had his initial success in relieving the acute mental distress of Israel's first monarch.' He added, as they passed out over the Deanery threshold, and she glanced down and back, 'Yes, you would do well to carry your train. The mud has now set to the consistency of a mucilage!' He did not ask had she any other reason for that final glance.

In the choir, as the Dean's sister, she was seated in the sub-stall immediately under his curtained and canopied chief-seat. Taking the massive choir copy of the Book of Common Prayer, she turned over the pages to find and mark the day's psalms. Her eye caught the Latin captions—'*De Profundis, Domine!*' '*Adhesit Pavimento!*' '*Deus, Deus, Meus!*' How often divine inspiration seemed to have spoken through human desperation! Yet, to-day, these cries of terror and agonised appeal would be chanted and carolled into a mild aesthetic pattern—as the demon faces clustered on the canopies around her—and meant to remind the faithful that even in prayer, even more in prayer, were the soul's invisible enemies alert and roused—had been turned by the medieval carver, weary of a zeal he could not understand and maybe never saw practised, into comic gargoyles. Her eye, glancing back at the psalter, was caught by a verse in the full English text—'My darling from the power of the dog!' She had often wondered why with the whole menagerie for his imagination to draw upon and with lions and unicorns ramping in this very psalm the psalmist suddenly found his terror fixed on a mere dog. Perhaps he, too, had found himself exposed? She prayed the appeal with the intensity its first utterer had evidently felt. But as deep fear spurred her mind she recognised at a still deeper level that she was glad that the author in this passage had not asked deliverance for himself but for someone he loved.

The service ran its smooth course worn by immemorial repetition to a perfectly memorised almost-inattention. Then, the divine courtesies discharged, acknowledgements made and reassurance uttered, there came discourse. Her brother, fetched and verger-led like a priest-king to the pulpit, mounted the ornate scaffold and unfolded his argument. She certainly wished to attend as much as he desired to be attended to. She was, however, exhausted; her sleep at home was of course a travesty; for this brief twenty minutes—while she was 'in sanctuary' in the real if not in the architectural sense—sleep with its overdue account came down like a gaoler. It wrapt her round with the suffocating force of an anaesthetic. She struggled, experiencing that curious, acute distress—worse, though rarer, than its opposite, insomnia—that misery when sleep becomes an enemy, a tyrant, and tortures us if we would forbid it taking over our consciousness. She tried the usual stimulants, pinching her finger, then putting her hand to her face and biting lip and finger-tip. Her head simply declined on her hand, welcoming the offered support and disguise. 'In conclusion, therefore...' It was Charles's voice. What was ended? Something terrible had been finished. Charles was safe, she was sure, from the certainty in his voice and he was telling her. A great refreshment and relief rose in her. She was rested, she felt. She was being raised from where she had been bent down, intolerably oppressed, down in the dark mire with foul creatures... She felt her hand against her bowed face, smelt the scent of her glove, heard her brother's voice, 'We see...'

Her orientation in time and space flashed on her. She must rouse herself cautiously. She put out her free hand, smoothed her dress, then touched the hymn-book lying before her, open for the final hymn. Finally she glanced up at the pulpit. Already he had wheeled round to the East for the Ascription. 'And now,' his voice boomed, while with a rustle of recollection the congregation rose to restore its circulation and clear its throat with a good tune.

As he threw open the Deanery door for her to enter, he remarked, 'You were mistaken in disregarding my advice. You would have had better slumber here than in the choir.' She would have not made a retort or even a reply, even had she not, the moment they crossed the threshold, been met.

She had thought of actually calling on young Halliwell. Their short talk had convinced her that at least if he could not answer he would understand her problem. Of course, she could not ask him to the house. Quite apart from the fact that her brother would certainly be subconsciously suspicious and so discourteous, it was utterly out of the question that she should suddenly request this junior to visit them and, or what was the use, find an occasion for a private conference! Almost for the last time the involuntary mouth-tension careless people call a smile twisted her lips. First the Cambridge assignation, and then, the habit formed abroad, she now at home takes the initiative. And if she did go out and call on him—he lived in the Palace—would Mrs. Bendwell understand, just by woman's famed intuition, her wish for a *tête à tête*? She bit her lip, so painful was the hopeless silliness of the idea. Yet this young and already disappointed but not yet discouraged chaplain alone seemed to have even the ghost of an idea about the actual situation. He was the one person who might at least listen. All the rest would simply look on her as insane, an insanity prompted, no doubt, by an unrecognised jealousy of her brother. But even with this one acquaintance, it was now too late. If she was going to speak she should have done so as soon as she came back, when there seemed to be a respite and even some dim dawn of hope. Now she was no longer sure herself that the strange visitor at Cambridge had possessed any more gift or power than—his own phrase, she remembered—a clever character-reader at a fair!

It was clear also that every day the power became stronger, that the crisis, in whatever form it would finally manifest itself, was quickly approaching. That was shown by the growing familiarity of the Familiar. Once, when she came in to tea, it had run ahead and leapt, like a spoiled pet, into her chair. She had tried to take another, though it sprang out as soon as she came close. Her brother, was, however, as usual, incomprehendingly vigilant, 'That's your chair, Laetitia, the throne of the lady of the house, as she presides over the mystery of tea-brewing, the stall of the Decaness—not deaconness. None of this wrongful humility in the home—taking the lesser, lower seat. None of this outward mortification, even though we have entered Advent. "Rend your hearts and not your garments," as we heard in the Anthem to-day. Mortify your spirit, and not, as our very unhygienic spiritual predecessors did their flesh...' and he launched into a peculiarly apposite description of medieval filth, Catholic austerities and the odour of unwashed sanctity, of Thomas of Canterbury whose—the Dean called them 'garment companions'—fell from his sleeves onto the table as he ate: of Teresa of Avila who wore a tight-lacing corset but with holes in it through which her merit-gaining flesh protruded suppurating. Then, seeing that his sister's face had become ghastly, he added, 'You must forgive my male toughness. I was only trying to laugh you into a little rational self-indulgence.' But in spite of this kindly explanation she failed to rally to his offer to be amiable and, feeling that she had better be left to sulk alone—the nursery phrase came to his lips, though he held it back—he went to his study.

Her constant companion, too, seemed to have entered a 'dark-cycle.' She could not see him though she could hear him snuffling at his disgusting grooming. Then he was so lost to sight and sound also that she found herself repeating the text, 'And Satan departed for a season.' If it was so it was no more than to change costume for soon her attention was caught by signs that some other plan of approach was being prepared. She realised that her brother must not notice her attempts to sound the unseen dark tide that was flowing in and rising up around her. So she would wait till he left the room—and the long silences that now came down upon them were sufficient to drive him away after comparatively short visits—then she could not resist getting down on her knees. She knew it was no use sending for the servants. Indeed she felt she must, by touch, prove whether sight was deceiving her. Always there were those little balls of fuzz and hair rolling along in an imperceptible draught where the wainscot touched the polished floor-boards. In the evening, too, the light would time and again show large black cobwebs in the corners. She kept a long cane concealed in the big parlour cupboard. 'Like an eczemic that must scratch his sores'—the phrase came into her mind—it was so pat that the words seemed given, not composed by her. Finally, to sight, sound and touch, came the fourth sense.

It was near the year's end. It was at dinner. She was surprised into sending her plate from the table saying that it had not been washed. She saw the oil on it and smelt the sickly scent. As she raised her eyes, however, she caught sight of her brother's eye upon her. She left the room, gained her breath for a moment outside the door and came back saying, 'I may have been mistaken.' Wisely attempting no further explanation she gave all her attention to making herself swallow some mouthfuls, though on the substituted plate also she saw and could smell the greenish smear of oil. Nor would she change her bedroom, not even when on going there on New Year's Eve she found the jackal returned. As she entered with her candle he was there seated on the foot of the bed. She did take the pillow away and noticed that none of the long greasy hairs and the oil-stains that were in a patch on it had spread to the sheet under. She got ready. Then turned back resolutely to the bed. The jackal leapt off and cowered beside it. All night long she heard it licking itself. Once it put its front feet upon the edge of the eiderdown and its green eyes seemed not more than a couple of feet from hers. The sight shook her, but worse, she felt, was the stench. Yet though outwardly she felt her mind must be going, inwardly she could recognise that she was experiencing not a mad disgust and horror, but rather an immense tiredness, as of someone who has carried a load to the very limit of their strength and now knows that the next furlong must either see them home or they must fall in their tracks. So it was with a relief when a few mornings after, as the light came, she noticed an unmistakable, objective change. The light came slowly. She would lie through the night without a candle, for she could see her companion in the dark quite as well as in the light. But as the dusk that was acting as day's substitute stole through the curtains she noticed that her hand lying on the sheets showed up more distinctly than it should by such illumination on such a background. She had always had white hands and they had been very pale these last two months. Now they were dark. She did nothing for the time being about it, lying quietly, for she had told the servants not to call her or to bring her anything. As the light gained she saw, raising her hand, that there could be no doubt. Then she touched lightly her face. Of course if the hands were already involved the face would be more affected. As she put her hand down onto the sheet again, the jackal, which had been out of sight, leapt onto the bed. It made the small gesture that dogs do, when, uncertain of their reception, they wish to make advances. It bowed down its head and made a diffident, caressing movement with its paw. The light was now good enough that she could see the paw's nails. They were clear because the rotting flesh had left them bare almost to their roots. She put out her hand and stroked its head. She could feel it quite firmly under her touch, every detail, the moulting skin, the tubercular lumps of the sores and the skull underneath. It twisted round and licked her hand. Then it leapt from the bed.

She never saw it again. She never saw anything very clearly after that. The eczema spreading like a flush rapidly attacked all the face and the eye-sockets and the lids became involved.

At last her brother, through the callousness that seemed spread over all his emotions, appeared to realise that she was gravely ill—not merely tired and, maybe owing to lassitude, apt to give way to the sloth that attacks those with too few intellectual interests. Inevitably, however, his fear could only win expression as resentment. Visiting her as she lay in bed—she had sent down a message that she must keep to her room—he remarked that he hoped she now realised the wisdom of his former disregarded advice. He also felt some reassuring satisfaction in informing her that, though she might object, he had already sent for Dr. Wilkes. 'A prophet we know is disregarded in his own country, and so the advice of a brother who is only a scholar may be denied the attention granted an outsider.' Her failure to protest still did not add to his reassurance. Nor did Dr. Wilkes. Not that the physician was so poor a psychologist as to trust the Dean (whom he had already diagnosed far more than he had observed the sister) with his medical misgivings. All he said, when asked, was the truth.

'There has been strain, and, as we know, in this climatic phase which we seem to be in, there appears to be what might be called an endemic tendency to pre-eczemic nerve-ending irritability. In this house, too, there might be a co-ordinate of some environmental influence together with an associational element of what might be called suggestive force.' Dr. Wilkes was not unpleased in his surface loquational mind with the flow of the sentence, guarded yet ample, truthful but non-committal. In any case it served to cover over with an apparent self-assurance—which surely must be helpful to his patients (he used the plural term to himself)—a feeling almost of dismay that was rising in him.

The Dean's verdict, as he watched the doctor go, 'Pretentious polysyllabic verbiage to disguise ignorance,' might have had an even uneasier rider if he could have heard the doctor's self-unburdening of his own anxiety. 'Coincidence can't cover it. What a curse it is that we physicians can't have real colleagues of the psyche, in the clergy. Then there would be some hope of our dealing with the mind-body problem.'

Perhaps, then, it was no coincidence but an answer to his 'left-handed' prayer that put the Bishop's Chaplain in his homeward path. Nor did he have to verge on unprofessionality by opening the subject himself. The intellectual excuse to do what emotionally he desired, was given by Halliwell's unguarded concern. It came, too, with Palatial authorisation: 'I've just come from the Bishop. I don't want to trouble the Dean. You've just come from the Deanery. I do trust that Miss Throcton is not laid low. She has looked so very poorly of late. There has been so much ill health these last months.

The Bishop is puzzled, concerned. It makes him anxious.' 'So am I; so am I.' Dr. Wilkes felt quite safe in ranging his doubts alongside mitred misgivings. Besides, this boy looked frank, sincere, kindly, concerned. 'You know Miss Throcton?' he asked. After all, often an observant acquaintance can give you insights that help diagnosis. The younger man hesitated. 'Tell the truth, I have only had one personal conversation with her.' He paused. 'But perhaps I should tell you, as at the time, I must own it did make me uneasy and now I understand she is ill and under your care?' The doctor nodded to the half-question. And a few moments later when Halliwell concluded his account of the session under the limes, Dr. Wilkes again encouraged him, seconding him with, 'You are right, evidently the condition was in an initial, undifferentiated stage then. And, as I have to note so often, once the strain was lifted, once her brother threw off what I would almost venture to call the vaccination reaction—or the initiation ordeal if you like that phrase better—a reaction which taking office in this Close would now seem to exact—his repressed anxiety—that he might fail, like his predecessor—takes toll of her. As in so many families she pays his forfeit. I know it sounds strange but it is really only a legitimate extension of the basic idea of infection. One of my colleagues knew a surgeon in Manchester—a surgeon, mark you—called Braid, who used—as of course did that strange disqualified crank, Dr. Elliotson—mesmerism, or as he re-christened it, hypnotism, to produce sustained and deep anaesthesia. But the interesting point to me, to us, is that, I understand, this surgeon held he had proof that states of mental strain did often transfer themselves into physical diseases. If only we could be called in before the disturbed function has deranged the organ!'

'Would then?' Halliwell decided on the question. 'Could then mental methods affect bodily condition?' 'Of course, in a way,' the doctor spoke with a light touch of defensive superiority, 'Even the most conservative of our profession would allow as much. The trouble is our old friend *l'idée fixe*. Ideas are necessary but dangerous things. They tend to capture the mind that would use them. That's the trouble with mesmerism as far as I can see. It's because we medicos, engrossed with the body, incline to materialism, when we are forced to consider the mind we tend to fall into magic. The mind, the spirit is your province, really...' Then finding himself for once with an intelligent cleric who was his junior, he added, 'And may I venture to add prophecy to my prescription? If the Church neglects the deep mind then some materialistically-minded doctor will take over and start "ministering to minds diseased".'

To Dr. Wilkes's surprise young Halliwell showed not a trace of counter-defensiveness to this challenge. On the contrary, he seemed eager to contribute to their conference. 'I'm sure,' he said, 'indeed it is quite clear from what you have told me, that it must have been some sort of hypnosis, as you call it, that my father witnessed and was so impressed by in Persia!' 'In Persia?' Dr. Wilkes questioned. As do all defensive moods, his fear of being considered too credulous by the conservative had had as its converse the apprehension that he might concede the credulous too much. Dr. Esdaile who had been disqualified from practice about the same time as Dr. Elliotson, because of his employment of mesmerism, Dr. Esdaile had picked up his questionable and censurable method in the East—he had practised in Calcutta, hadn't he?

'I am afraid,' and the courtesy apprehension, that stiffened his open good will into caution, though it used the word fear condescendingly, was really inspired by misgiving, 'I am afraid that my outlook is limited by the Greeks and their clarity of thought. Our source master is Hippocrates, you know.' He smiled, but young Halliwell was not so young as not to be able to recognise a rapidly closed door. The two parted. Two almost open minds had failed in their mutual invitation to explore each other's findings. Miss Throcton was to have no help from any around her.

CHAPTER SEVENTEEN

Dr. Wilkes had prescribed that the face should be bandaged. Warm boric acid dressings covering the eyelids would, he believed, give relief. The patient accepted them and certainly did not say they were unhelpful. The world came to her now through hearing. She waited as someone caught in a cave that has collapsed waits in the dark, sometimes trying to construe the sounds without, sometimes wondering what must befall if help cannot get through. Sometimes the calm was that of complete shock. She remembered once in their earlier garden finding, just as Tissaphernes had caught sight of it, a fledgling on the lawn. She snatched it up in her hand. It was quite still, making no effort to get away from the hold of her fingers. You might have thought it indifferent or even content if you had not felt the frantic heart-beat and seen the feeble little gasping of its mouth. At other times she was let sink beyond this contact with the utter physical dismay. Then she listened to and construed sounds with the patient indifference with which a reporter takes down *in extenso* a speech, the meaning of which is of little or no personal interest to him. She found she could judge the state of mind of her few visitors by their step, their tempo of movement. The two maids, yes, they were concerned and sympathetic—she could judge that by their diffident tread. The doctor, too, he was increasingly cautious, tentative, yes, and sympathetic, too, in his more guarded way. Her brother, he was becoming increasingly nervous. He spoke to her little. The doctor had anyhow advised that she should not speak. But she could hear him as he paced up and down, say perhaps to himself as much as to her, 'Make an effort, it all depends on making an effort—a good constitution always can respond to the moral will to recovery.' She felt her face begin to hurt not merely dully but sharply—she recognised she was smiling. Oh, of course, her brother was repeating Mr. Dombey's recipe for his wife, when her labour had been too much for her and though she had met his primary demand by giving him a son, in regard to herself she had failed to respond to his wise advice. He came in for a spell morning and evening. One evening, she thought that he must have changed this small routine and after leaving with a murmured Goodnight—which certainly could not be expected to effect what it wished—had come back again. But after a moment she realised that it could not be he—he always walked up and down, quietly, but with the incessant restlessness of an animal in too small a cage. Could it be the doctor? He would ask after her condition, quietly to himself, she was not meant to answer, but he would stand by her bed and question. She could hear his mind, she found; and now she could not hear its doubts. The nurse he had sent in, she had asked that this attendant might stay outside the door, only coming in when summoned by the bedside bell. Someone, however, was there. It was only when she had become quite interested as to why her listening could not construe who was present that she suddenly remembered. Why, had she forgotten. Of course that would happen. It was as natural, as inevitable as the going of the jackal. She kept her mind, after that in an even deeper quietness, deeper than that which she had found would let her hear the thoughts of the few people who alone attended on her now. After quite a little while she found she could hear clearly. 'Daughter, I have served you as far as I might. I have not sent myself to you to say that. I have sent it, it can reach you, because you have sent strength to me, not I to you. I have only to confirm to you what already your spirit knows with sure hope. Tetelestai.'

It was one of the few Greek words she knew. It had been used, she remembered, when she was a girl by a fine Greek scholar who was said to be one of the dangerously High-Church mystics. He had preached on the Seven Last Words at a Good Friday service. She had been deeply moved. He had used that long word of finality with deep effect, saying that some had thought it might actually be the very word—the very Greek word—that was used at the moment when redemption became for ever an accomplished fact. Now she could hear that word again, Tetelestai. 'It is finished,' she said as quietly as someone who has completed a long and difficult piece of work tells one who set it. Then, rousing herself from her tired content that was too complete to have either memory or expectation in it, she asked, 'But have I turned it from him?' 'It has no power now but what he may give it. That is all that any may do for another.' She realised that was the truth. She was too finished, too completed to wish for anything else. The content increased until it took up, as the sun takes water from a dark lake and leaves it empty, all the flux of memories and fears, all the flow of time. She felt completely present at last, for she did not know where or when or who she was. All she had to do was to stay still, to wait, to continue present always.

Dean Throcton had knocked quietly at the door once, then waited. But the Bishop himself having come over at once in haste should not be kept waiting. He opened the door. Bishop Bendwell had brought with him a book of prayers. He had it always on his table. Meditation did not come easily to him—administrative problems would recur. He kept them more or less at bay with the double-ditch of good thoughts and holy requests set and faced with the Elizabethan English which has now almost the patina of good Latin. He was first and foremost an administrator but knew that the concept of an Episcopus, the overseership of a Father in God, covers more than what the Church advisedly calls the ecclesiastical 'temporalities,' and he had no fear of incompetence if he felt no particular inspiration when called on to death-beds. He had said not long before—as the intimacy between himself and his chaplain grew—and said it with a modesty that had in it so much real humility that the saying carried conviction, 'I know I am not high in the Church Invisible—perhaps Bishops seldom can be, if the first here are to be last there. But I am striving to be a faithful door-keeper in the House of my God. And as I am kind to, like, and indeed not only value but admire my Butler's competence in his station, so I dare to believe the Master of all masters, the infinite Overseer will feel and act toward me.' But neither was this sane, responsible man in anywise a sentimentalist. So he felt no need with this cold Dean of his to show emotion, still less any alarm when, looking at the bed, his not unpractised eye saw that the sheet was perfectly still. He turned, and, putting his hand on the other man's shoulder, he remarked in the tone that one admirer of their county cricket team would say to another when a sound member of the eleven has just been bowled after netting a creditable number of runs: 'We have all been proud of her and shall be. She will not be forgotten.' Whether the latter part of the sentence was kindly rhetoric or no, certainly the first part was more of an understatement than the Bishop could have known or, had he known, his taste for truth desired. It would have been highly improbable, however, if anyone could have made him grasp what in particular had been admirable in a life that seemed more quiet than most, and maybe even more comfortable than quiet.

When the Dean was left alone his expression was stronger, in the end. At first he seemed quiet. Then, evidently thinking that he ought to kneel down, the attitude, as attitudes often will, seemed to release a current of feeling. He felt his throat. It seemed as though it must split, as though a wedge were being forced into his larynx. He gasped. 'Laetitia' was all he could whisper. Then a spasm of grief twisted him like a cramp. The pain was so sudden and intense that part of him seemed to be split off, to wander off, as though it were seeking down the ranges of his quiet past to find if it could pick out another stretch of emotion among the long lengths of easy enjoyment and hardly memorable routines, another span or band to match the present acuteness of feeling. He found it. Yes, there was another, but it wasn't grief. He hadn't had much grief, very little, really, in his life. But this other buried pain that was as sharp as this present cut? It was hatred. But when had he had any real hatred? Slowly, like a person coming gradually to wakefulness in a strange room after thinking he was in his own bedroom—he remembered. That one bright patch of feeling, bright as a very hot sunbeam, seemed to thaw the landscape of his memory. Fact after fact emerged from the white snow-cover of amnesia, and the ugly things, which the blizzard of forgetfulness had made into one broad, unfactual sheet, came staring through. He forgot that he was with the dead. He forgot where he was or when he was. He had now been swept by the thaw-stream down to the spot from which he had escaped. How long this clear restored memory lasted he couldn't say. For he was not recalling the past to himself in the present. The past had called him away from the present. As soon, then, as he became aware of where he was his memory sank under. To remember and at the same time live was still impossible. After a while his rigid position began to relax; he shifted and fidgeted a little, feeling stiff. He looked up and around him. He raised himself clumsily from his knees. '"My words—" Why, they haven't even flown up! "My thoughts remain below?" Where? Pure wool-gathering, can't even recall what I was thinking of, and here and now! Worrying over some worthless small matter of my own concern!'

He stood close beside the bed. He raised the bandage that lay across the face. Death, as it so often does, had not only removed age and expression, it had taken away the physical damage. The skin had again become smooth with the congested blood gone from beneath it and had the texture of alabaster. As he continued to look at it, this face that he had known best in all his life and which now already was no longer the lifelong friend but the likeness of some unnamed woman, the cold quietness in it seemed to surround him. He felt something in his heart as cold, incapable of movement as the body on the bed. Moment after moment, as he stood still looking down at the white figure, his whole memory was sinking deeper under the renewed snowfall of forgetfulness. He noticed faintly that everything seemed as quiet as it was still. Though he heard now and then a distant sound from the outside world, it awoke no echo of meaning, no significance in his consciousness. Only once was his mind roused to question-point by his ear. Suddenly, from the direction of the garden below, came a small, sharp, querulous bark. 'We have no dog?' he questioned himself perfunctorily. He listened a moment more. The silence was not again challenged. He found a new handkerchief and spread it over the face. Then he went to the door. Outside, the nurse was waiting. 'I will see to everything,' she said, moving past him into the room. He nodded and went downstairs.

He slept well that night, only waking a few times and then not because of any restlessness of mind—it was a dog's barking that each time roused him. And each time, as soon as it stopped its quarrelsome little protest, he fell to sleep again. In the morning, after writing the necessary notes to announce his bereavement and sending them out he rang the bell for the cook to come to him. Cook, a glance made clear, had had a worse night and indeed clearly eyed his composure and lack of any apparent exhaustion with the disapproving surprise with which those who belong to an earlier and more expressive social pattern view the apparently heartless stoicism of their employers. She had taken the admonitory precaution of coming to the interview equipped with a large, fresh, fully-unfurled handkerchief, held at half-mast across her bosom, in instant readiness for the moment when the tide of her feelings would swamp her controls and she would be, as she told the head-housemaid, when that comforter was patting her heaving shoulders, 'awash with tears.'

The Dean's presence and attitude proved, at least at the beginning of the interview, astringent—a fact for which he was considerably more grateful than she. He was coldly business-like: did not refer to the death; told her what he wished for himself and gave her the main control of the house—she was elevated from cook to housekeeper. She was left neither puzzled as to what he might want, nor unpleased by the recognition and promotion, both in rank and salary that she now had received. On his side he now knew, with a feeling of complacency at his own adroitness, that he had reached the point when he ought, having pointed her mind to a far from unpleasing prospect, to be able to get her out of the room. Then the return of her grief—which quite clearly was getting ready for a come-back—would submerge her when and where she would have more suitable, more equal aid than he would or could supply. Yet to say, 'That is all, Mrs. Binyon,' might have about it just that touch of finality and dismissal that would give her emotions their cue, recalling the final finality. She would feel it was her duty to refer to it—as 'Happy Christmas' must be said when meeting anyone on the Feast. An innocent stratagem came to him. Rising, he went to the window, from which a glimpse of the garden could be obtained, for his study had the same outlook as his bedroom next to it—they were both over the great parlour and so, from a higher level, shared its view. 'I thought, Mrs. Binyon,' he remarked over his shoulder, 'that last night a dog had managed to get shut up in the garden. Will you tell Silas to see that neither he nor the boy leave the garden gate open. I was roused a couple of times by some yapping. Please see that he gets that message from me as soon as he comes in with the vegetables.' That would necessitate her leaving at once. For, as it happened as he looked down from the window he had been able to glance at the figure of the gardener in the kitchen garden making his way toward the back of the house with his daily offering from his stores of winter vegetables. He speeded her with this watch-tower information and then turned back to his desk, certain that she too must have begun her turn toward the door. She had not, and his look of annoyed question was not left unanswered long enough for him to put it into words. He was answered by a question, 'Ah, then, Sir, you heard it, too?' Before he could retort 'You'd have to be deaf...' or had to check himself from the irritated but unfortunate addition, 'it would disturb the dead...' she had added, 'You know, Sir, what it was!' He certainly knew that he did not want her explanations. 'I've told you. Please go at once and tell Silas to lock the iron gate at the end of the garden. If you don't go at once, you'll miss him!' 'Oh, no Sir! No! No locking of gates nor bolting of doors, no, nor high walls round them and glass set on the top of them—no, that sort is not stopped by that sort of thing or order. If you yourself, Sir, instead of Silas—if you yourself, Sir, with all your linen and satin, your robes and your rites were to go instead of him—poor fellow with his key and his spade—why, Sir, it would make not a difference nor a dimming of that din than if I in my kitchen with the kettle over-boiling and the frying-pan afire just spoke eloquent and courteous-like to the red-hot kitchen-range!'

He saw with a dismay that under its irritation had still some humour, that his effort to get rid of her and forestall the emotional outburst had evidently, for some obscure reason, been the actual trigger that had sprung the mine. 'Well,' he cut in, 'that dog can be kept out of the garden. Please don't argue but go and give my instructions!' 'But that's the point, Sir, as you've just said—a dog, yes, and then very well. But Sir, I've been with hunting people and I know the countryside. That's no dog, at least it's not a dog you could have in the house. It's a dog-fox that was barking on and off all last night. And I know why: when I was in Ireland with the household of the Master of Thomondstone, well, we knew that sound. And well, on such a night as we've now been through, we knew what it meant. As long as one of that race was lying "in wake," as they would say, there would never be a fox in any of the coverts, and ever there would be a fox round the house barking, calling at him, they would say!'

'Mrs. Binyon!' His voice was raised, 'I will not have that kind of superstitious and insane nonsense spoken in a Protestant Christian household!' For a moment he felt ashamed at having used such a term and such a method. His shame was however instantly expunged by relief. Mrs. Binyon, accused of unchristian, unprotestant views, recollected herself. Of course she could not deny to herself that she had picked up those theories and fancies over in Catholic Ireland where anything, as you might say, might take place. The gale of her conviction suddenly fell. But that, as might have been expected, by a better student of humanity than the Dean, permitted the deluge of her grief to break. 'I am indeed sorry, Sir, that I should have repeated such things, but, Sir, with poor dear Miss Laetitia, lying as you might say...' He was determined that nothing more should be said by her or him. He swung open the door and pointed to the stairs. Already the handkerchief had been mounted to mast-head so that cook's mouth and nose were covered, and wiping her now pouring eyes she picked her way to her kitchen, her chair and a strong cup of tea.

Still, she had been right. And the Dean himself, with a suppressed bewilderment, realised that there was nothing now that he or his staff could do about it. The two nights before the funeral, he heard the rapid barks as though they were peremptory calls, repeated knocks summoning a door-keeper to open or take the consequences. After the funeral there was silence. Indeed, nothing happened till a February day which was calm, still and sunny. He took a turn in the garden. Half-way down against the south-looking wall was a fine Forsythia, the first thing to bloom. He had gone over to examine the hundreds of bright yellow blossoms, almost like small gold flames in the level sunlight. Then, turning back to the long alley of mown grass that led up to the house, he glanced its whole length, for it ran from the house to the wrought-iron gate in the brick wall that terminated the formal garden. The design was finished off down at that end by a sundial set on an ample paved base. Evidently, on a day as mild as this, the few hours of sunlight had been sufficient to warm the stone pleasantly. For stretched on it lay a small dark fox. It certainly was not very shy for, though it looked wary, it did not make at once for the shrubbery, but watched him with its head on one side. He went quietly, slowly, toward it until he could see that the thick hair of its coat was really a dark walnut tint. It rose then but stood its ground and when he paused not half a dozen yards from it, it stretched itself and actually took a step in his direction. Then it, too, paused. It turned its head even more on one side as it watched and held one of its forepaws raised, as though wondering whether it might come closer. He could see the bright amber of its eyes. Suddenly he raised his arm. It darted across the strip of lawn and into the thick yew-hedge. He did not cross the herbaceous border to look into the hedge. But after he had had his tea in the great parlour he went to the window, drew aside the curtain that the maid had already pulled to and looked out into the garden. A fox was standing some three yards outside.

That night was as still as the day had been. But though he was awake several times he did not hear any barking. In the end he nearly overslept himself, waking with a start, not certain that the housemaid had not knocked at the door with his tea and shaving water. He sat up—no, he had not overslept—the room was still in dusk; outside the day could not have come fully. The house, too, was still. Then he was aware that someone might be, must be standing just outside the bedroom door. He nearly called out 'Come in.' But a moment after he felt a sharp relief that he had not done so, when down at the door threshold he heard a long breath being drawn. He bent toward the side of the bed nearer the door and listened. Perhaps a minute later he heard steps coming up the stairs. When they reached the landing they stopped for a moment and he was not sure that he did not catch a suppressed exclamation. Then they came on till they were at the door. There came a low tap. He answered with relief. Yes, now it was the maid. He thought that after her 'good-morning' she might be about to add something. If so, she thought better of it. He lay for a while sipping his tea and wondering whether in this case it was well or ill that the silence, which he had done so much to teach his household, had been observed. He could not make up his mind for his mind was not clear as to the matter of fact. To decide whether or not he would like to be informed it would be necessary surely that one should know whether there was information to be had?

That point at least settled itself without undue delay. First he saw the intruder at the end of the entrance hall, a large almost empty space but not too well lit. Then a couple of evenings after he was sure it was in his study. He heard something move and looking up from the circle of bright light given by his reading lamp caught sight of two small bright eyes. They seemed to have been caught by the sudden movement of his head. The animal was not grooming itself. He and it regarded each other, his face as expressionless as its mask. Then it moved off into the shadow. He remained looking for some while at the spot. He did not get up to investigate. At dinner that night, when, as he liked, the dishes had been put on the table and he had been left, he was reading a book. Looking over the top of it he saw the fire burning pleasantly and seated in front of it, not looking at him, sat this dark-haired fox. He could see the sheen of the flames on its thick glossy coat. 'A fine little animal,' he remarked in a low voice. It did not stir at the sound of his voice nor did he stir to come near it. He bent his eyes to go on reading. After a little while, when he put out his hand to touch the bell, he saw that the hearth-rug was vacant.

This absence was not more than some three days. Then, though the snuffling did not come at his bedroom door again, he saw the creature in most of the other rooms and in fairly good light. It appeared last of all in his bedroom. He had gone to sleep but woke up, he judged, before long. The waking was of that sort that he felt not the slightest drowsiness left in him. On the contrary, he was restless and, acting on the impulse, got out of bed. The moonlight was coming through a chink left by the curtains not being close-drawn. He went across and looked out at the night. The moon was still fairly high—a partial moon, the incomplete disk made by sections of two convex curves. He looked at it for some time, as though he were trying to recall something. Then he drew to the curtains and turned back toward the bed. The room naturally now appeared to him completely dark. But knowing his position and that the dressing-table was near him, he put out his hand. A box of matches was kept there to light the two candles which stood each side of the big mirror. His hand found it and he struck a light. He saw himself looming in the long glass and behind his white figure the white glimmering surface of the bed with the sheets thrown back. On this vague whiteness there was a small dark body. He whirled round so fast that the match in the draught went out. He felt behind him—he did not dare to turn his back—found the matches again, succeeded in lighting one and this time looked directly at the bed. There was nothing there but the rumpled sheeting. Carefully he turned again and lit one of the candles, peering into the glass as soon as he had done so. Again the bed was obviously vacant. He did not dare, though, to go to it. He lit the other candle, went to the wardrobe, took out a heavy dressing-gown and sat himself in an easy chair. The candles burnt down to the socket but at last the dawn came. He had not dozed for a moment. He drew the curtains and looked out at the grey morning. Then he looked in the mirror at a face far more grey and dismal, a face that became almost ghastly as he involuntarily looked over the mirror-image's shoulder and scanned the empty bed. He brought himself to go and look directly at the sheets. No, there was nothing there, no trace, no imprint, not a hair. He sat down utterly exhausted after that, with his eyes closed. At last he said one word—'Laetitia!'

CHAPTER EIGHTEEN

The Dean left his house as soon as he had made a pretence of breakfasting and conducting family prayers. Outside he started in the direction of the Palace but after a few steps he changed his course and went towards the town. He met Dr. Wilkes just leaving on an early round and asked him if he could spare him a minute. Still he needed the doctor to begin the interview for him. 'Mr. Dean, remember the old advice—a stitch in time—to which I would tack on a later saw, Better a little now than nothing soon!'

'You think I have become tired again so soon!' 'This is to be expected. You have been through much!' He added as complementary inquiry, 'Don't you find that those who can best show least must feel most? No one can practise the care and cure of bodies and not realise how the mind takes it out of the body.' 'But,' the Dean disregarded the personal reference, 'the Dean's task is not that of a rest-taker whether lying abed in the Deanery or "lying abroad" as the old phrase was about ambassadors.' The minimal joke eased a little their exchange. The doctor was able to press his point, 'I don't think you realised how tired you were last time and therefore how remarkable was your resilience and the benefit you won from such short change. If I may say so, sooner or later a man of flawless health is confronted with a problem weaker humanity is prepared for by a lifetime of intermittent ailing. There comes a day when the best of us discover that we must give ourselves more time, must wait while nature makes necessary time-taking replacements. As I say, this knowledge tends to come suddenly on the outstandingly hale. An unexpected external shock precipitates...' He left the sentence uncompleted. He felt genuinely sorry for this stiff, finely-minded, withered-hearted man, now left in that complete loneliness that in the end envelopes those who have only permitted as much intimacy and affection as they can use for their own convenience.

'Well, that's my advice. And I'm making it for the Close as much as for yourself.' He felt a certain pleasure in being able to advise one so aloof, the genial patronage of the expert called in to speak as a special witness. 'We are proud of you, Mr. Dean, and we want our scholar who gives this quiet little place its prestige, to live out finely his full allotment of years. I think you will agree with me that scholarship is a fruit which like the fig, depends on a late warm summer.' A friendliness which certainly had in it an assumption of at least temporary equality and would certainly at any other time have been resented now seemed almost welcome. 'Well,' and the Dean tried to keep his tone at the same officially unanxious level, 'to-day you of the lancet and the bottle speak with the authority once possessed by the pastoral staff and the mitre. I'll think it over.' 'He'd better,' Dr. Wilkes said aloud as he watched the tall-back figure stride black toward the Cathedral gate. 'That walk is too rigid. He's brittle. If he wasn't a Dean you'd think that masked nervous hurry showed a bad conscience. Well, he may blame himself for his sister's death and maybe has some right. Steady selfishness probably accounts for more murders—by causing a kind of anaemia of the spirit in the kindly—than arsenic.'

The Dean, however, at that moment was thinking what he would say to the Bishop. Arriving at the Palace he was shown up at once.

Bishop Bendwell was at work at his desk with young Halliwell, who withdrew. The Bishop rose and put his hand on his visitor's shoulder. 'Sit down, sit down.' Then, having done so himself, he looked, with his head on one side, at the figure which certainly showed a slackness that was as uncharacteristic as it was significant. And with a snap-judgment speed that was as uncharacteristic of himself the Bishop found himself saying, 'Easter will give us time this year. Do you know, just before we get into Lent it strikes me it would be wise for you to run off and have a week at Cambridge or Brighton if it suits you better. Cambridge did you so much good last year, and now with this sorrow—yes, I advise it as your spiritual physician.' 'Well,' there was a faint relief in the voice, 'do you know that was the very question on which I came to consult you. The man of the body has just pressed the same counsel on me.'

'"Out of the mouth of two witnesses shall everything be established",' the Bishop quoted with kindly unction, then rose. 'I'm as busy as a banker at a quarter-day. You get off as soon as you can and be back as fresh as you were on your last return so we can get through Lent and Easter all right. You know there can be no help from me once the confirmations begin!'

Halliwell, hearing the visitor go, returned. 'Well,' remarked his master, not looking up as the assistant resumed his place, 'at least I didn't waste any time with the inevitable and on the irrelevant. It's nerves, of course. He's obviously physically as strong and probably as temperamentally touchy, as one of his Arabs' horses. A good deal of remorse, no doubt, and aperture of expression atrophied. My oculist told me if the tear-duct is blocked and you want to weep it may be quite painful. You have no comment? Well, discretion, Anglicanism's pet virtue, has been called the silent hyphen between Charity and

Truth.' He smiled now, looking across at his re-seated Chaplain. The smile, however, was reflected only as far as the mouth's courtesy-contour. It did not rise to the eyes. They were questioning. The Bishop did not wish to disturb his deeper doubts with questions of obscure motive. He turned to some patronage requests—the psychology there was simple enough. The Dean went back to the Deanery, not comforted, but (the penultimate word the Bishop had used came sounding apt to his mind) confirmed. The mail was now laid out. He had forgotten to look at it before he had left after breakfast. He ran it through his hands as he stood in the hall—it was composed of local messages, most of them no doubt conventional condolences. Ah! there was one with the Cambridge postmark. He looked round the hall for a moment before tearing it open. No, he was quite alone in the empty stone place. He glanced again at the handwriting—of course, how absent-minded he was becoming, it was McPhail's. 'My dear Dean,' it ran, 'I should have written to you before. But, as I was able after those days last summer to judge to some extent the degree of your bereavement, I felt I should wait until, as the Scriptures say, the days of mourning were accomplished. Please do not think that I am suggesting that a sorrow such as yours will disappear with time. My intention only is to say that it will, as we know, clarify into an acceptance and though in the first days there is a numbing shock, after that—if I may put it so—the voice of a friend and his company need not prove that "vinegar upon nitre" of which the Book of Proverbs speaks. I am writing this letter, then, for two reasons: First, to express to you the deepest sympathy for the loss of so fine and indeed I would say advisedly, so noble a character and companion as Miss Throcton (for though I had the pleasure of but a short acquaintance, I had the opportunity of forming the highest estimate of her worth) and, secondly, to ask whether you would not consider coming to stay with me for a few days. It may be that we might turn our minds to those studies which, because they deal with the great insights of philosophy, need not, and I believe should not, be considered as distractions from sorrow but rather as true anodynes from grief.'

'That which is said three times should not be neglected,' was all the Dean remarked as he put the letter in his pocket. He acted however with dispatch. A note to the doctor and another to the Bishop were written, while his orders for his clothes to be packed and a 'fly' booked to take him to the afternoon express were being carried out. He had still some hours so he went over to the Cathedral to speak to the canon in residence. He also had a few words with the minor canon who was on duty and the verger. The big Gothic machine was turning over its cogs efficiently enough, slow but sure, if left to its own pace, like the monster late-medieval clock whose giant pendulum swung with a soothing cluck to and fro on the west wall of the north transept, winnowing away the spirits of men and letting the gross grain of their bodies fall under the dated slabs that paved the Cathedral floor. As he turned from watching it, where he had paused, crossing the nave to return to the house, young Halliwell came up to him, 'Excuse me, Mr. Dean. I wanted personally to offer you my condolences. I delayed writing. I thought I might speak to you. Miss Throcton was...' 'Thank you, thank you.' The Dean did not offer his hand, and made the slight bow of acknowledgement an opportunity to withdraw. 'I would like...' Halliwell was continuing, but already the elder man had turned his back, his dark figure moving into the shadows of the north aisle. The younger sighed.

But as far as the Dean could see, and he kept his eyes fixed on the immediate agenda, everything was going with speed and directness, with the kind of rapid foregone completeness that marks a dream in its final stages. Time and again as he walked about making his final dispositions he would glance sharply behind him, but nothing caught his eye. Yet his mood appeared not to be one of relief. His face showed a settled urgency, that was all. Mrs. Binyon, who was motherly and felt herself now to be really the mother of the house, knocked and came in when he had sent his lunch out nearly untasted. He would excuse her, she was sure, but might she put up a little something for him in the train seeing that he had eaten hardly a crumb all day and it would be late ere the train came to Cambridge. And might she be so bold but would he rest a little as there was yet the best part of an hour before the fly would be round. Her concern irritated him so much that he could not resist quoting the reply of the Lord Protector Cromwell, as he lay waiting for his call and the attendants asked him to eat something or sleep a little, 'I am concerned neither to eat nor to sleep but to be gone.' She looked at him a little queerly at that and then asked might she know when he would be back. 'Certainly, certainly,' he said, but added nothing, so that she had to leave in the confidence that he would not come back 'and she with not a thing in the house.'

When he arrived late that night at Cambridge, Dr. McPhail was on the platform. They drove in silence to the doctor's house, said no more than was necessary when they were there—the Dean refused refreshment—and parted to their rooms. Again the night, for the Dean, was uninterrupted. He came down to breakfast and Dr. McPhail, to make conversation, pointed out to him the birds that came round the french window to be fed. They took out crumbs to them and were feeding them when Dr. McPhail remarked, 'The cats never grant an armistice. Birds have to snatch their livings, poor little febrile things. Look there, in the damp earth of that bed is the mark of a prowler. I'm afraid I've often, by this attempt at charity, given one of those carnivores a meal he or she would never otherwise have had.' He pointed down to small paw-prints that came close up to the threshold window-ledge. The Dean looked. 'Those aren't...' he began. Then went on, 'I think I'll go inside. It's a little chilly. May I help myself to another cup of coffee?'

His host waited till he had finished it and then left him, suggesting as he reached the door, 'Shall we meet in half an hour in my study? I have a few papers I would like to go over with you!' The Dean nodded, waited till the door was closed, then went over to the french window. He made no attempt to reopen it but he peered down through the glass for some time.

The half-hour over he went up and knocked on his host's door. They were soon settled by his fire. But Dr. McPhail seemed to have gone into a brown study looking at the coals. Finally he turned round and unlocking a side drawer of his desk, reached back inside, bringing out a largish envelope of parchment-coloured paper. Without looking at Dean Throcton, he remarked, 'This letter came for you from Sheik Ibn Khaldun.'

'But could he have heard and written so soon? Very kind, very prompt, but, no, I don't see how he could have had time? Oh, but I see it has not been through the mail,' he added as he put out his hand for it. 'It was,' the hander remarked, yielding it, 'I should have said, enclosed in one to me.' 'But when did it arrive?' The voice was half curious, half peremptory. The reply seemed to be unaware of the tone in which the question had been put, 'It came with the Sheik's courtesy letter as soon as he returned to Cairo—he had enjoyed, he said, the visit and had found the long journey profoundly worth while.'

'But why, why then was I... I mean, why did you delay...?' 'I was, of course, acting on his instructions...' 'But what strange behaviour. Surely even an Oriental would know our customs of courtesy—at least such a man...' 'Yes, I do not think we need have any doubt of that. He is a man of both worlds, of this as much as of the other.'

'Then why...? Surely I have a need, a right to be answered!'

'I think, indeed, I am as sure as I can be, short of not having seen a word of its contents, that the best answer would be found in that envelope which you now hold.' Dr. McPhail said no more but turned his attention wholly to the fire. The only sounds in the room were the gentle crackling of its flames and the rustle of the stiff paper as the envelope was torn and the enclosed sheets spread. Then nothing but the licking of the fire relieved the silence for perhaps half an hour. At last the Dean's voice began, though the tone was unlike any that McPhail had ever heard him use. There was in it an urgency and what was even stranger something that might have been humility. 'I am told to read you this. After reading it myself half a dozen times I see nothing to do but to obey.' And, without change of tone he read on:

'Dear Mr. Dean.—This letter will be delivered to you when it is due. That date will be settled not by us but by the strength of resistance and power of what I shall call absorption that resides in an heroic soul. The extent of that, the capacity for spiritual endurance, is known only to Allah, Whose dooms be hid. We know that He succours His servants, when, through them, He combats evil. Therefore, with them, as with Him, time is not to be held as we hold it. That at some time He will deliver his servant, as the Scripture says, "out of the power of the Dog," we know. Because there will then have been accomplished all that the dedicated human will may do for another.' The Dean's voice became lower but remained clear. 'When that is done, then, I would dare to judge that the evil which has been roused and permitted entry, by folly disguising itself as learning and pride pretending that it is understanding, will have been brought to an arrest. I use the term advisedly, for I would warn most strongly against any shallow hope that would now believe that there has been worked a final cure, a true exorcism. The actual precipitate is temporarily dissolved and has to re-form itself. A blend of scorn, hatred, pride and folly had created the atmosphere in which evil could—I use the chemical analogy—ignite. You must also, perhaps inadvertently, have used some physical, some material expression of your rage, some incompetent and accidental aping of one of the psychophysical techniques which you call—and dismiss as—magic. This acted as the spark. I need attempt no further to explain this to you. For this instant, precipitate and aggressive form of the molestation has been cancelled. It was nullified by the extent to which devotion and purity of intention could be expressed by one in touch with him who made the criminal mistake. Therefore are you now, at the price of your sister's death, freed from the immediate and almost successful assault of the enemy. Your freedom has been given back to you. That is all that Allah ever gives even to His chosen. Therefore it is all that the most loving may win, even for those to whom they would gladly give all. For you to complete and perpetuate what has been begun for you, you must make her sacrifice effective. There is forgiveness at the hands of the supreme justice. But only if true reparation has been made. As one who has chosen to be a teacher in religion, you should not need this initial instruction. But I have known you resist all effort to help you. Had you not so spurned that help when first offered, she whom you now begin to rate at her true worth, might still be alive.'

The Dean's voice was now a whisper, but Dr. McPhail could hear it. 'Here is the simple formula that you should have known as a child and observed all your days: Contrition, to be the effective acid that can clean away the crust under which the soul is decaying, must be three-fold: You must own that you have done and wished to do evil; you must vow that never again will you do so, nor put yourself in that situation where it might befall you so that you would so act; and thirdly, it is incumbent on you to make all the reparation that it still lies within your power to make. Thus, and thus only, may you escape that which is contained but not turned from you, and which, should you delay, then one day or another you will be persuaded yourself to summon back—when, as it is written, "The last state of that man is worse than the first".'

The letter fell from his hands. Dr. McPhail took it up, only remarking, 'I can but repeat what I said to your sister when I had to assure her—with such heroic results—that she could trust the Sheik: I have never known him to be mistaken and I have known him, I should add to you now, give such judgments as that which you have now just read!'

'But what am I to do?' All the pride, a lifelong incrustation, seemed to have been flayed off the man and to have left exposed under the raw surface a terribly afflicted child.

'He sent further instruction to me in his covering letter. Here it is.' Dr. McPhail had turned to the desk drawer and brought out a couple of similar sheets. He read in as low and accentless a tone as had the Dean, 'If this unhappy man shall, when you have given him my letter, really wish to save his life, the course, though it will test his intention, is open and simple, owing to the aid already given. All he has to do is to resign that which he gained by evil. That is reparation. Thereafter, I am prepared, because of the greatness of the sacrifice already made for him on my instruction, and to assure that nothing should be lacking to consummate it, I offer to take him, should he come out here, and to teach him if it be the Will of Allah, the rudiments of that knowledge beside which all learning of the tongue and the brain is but withered bark on the tree of life.'

The Dean sat quiet for another half-hour. Dr. McPhail only moved once to replenish the fire. Then his guest rose. 'There is no other course. I have sufficient funds to do as he orders and to comply by attending on him. Thereafter he will have to decide.' He stood silent and then went on more to himself than to his listener, 'And I, who in vanity used to taunt my colleagues about the great learning of the Arabians, so sane, so simple, so stylistically satisfying—now Justice in its merciful wish to save me from the degradation of madness sends me, a disgraced, detected imposter, to sit in poverty at the feet of a teacher whom I would have dismissed as a fraud but who now will spare me no knowledge.'

Dr. McPhail also stood up. 'Then I may tell you one more thing, something which, until you had decided of yourself, I might not say. Our instructor told me also that so long as you stayed here you would never be safe from the molestation which you had wantonly admitted onto your track. Here is what he says, "In this matter of the mind and the body, the spirit and matter, we have to be pure empiricists. What we do know from practical and tragic experience, is that the only safety that may be relied upon by one who has torn the veil is to flee the land where that disaster befell him. It has been found that if he puts water between himself and his tracker, then he may find some rest. If he should also accept instruction, then he may hope for peace and live to thank the All-Merciful for the judgment that fell upon him. Allah is the All-Merciful but He is the God of Law. He gives a way out through which the soul may escape. If it will not then it must endure the terror of being overtaken".'

CHAPTER NINETEEN

Two days afterwards the two lobes of the Diocesan brain were working at the big study table under the oriel window that commanded the Palace garden. The larger lobe turned for a moment from the close-up of correspondence to the larger lovelier view seen through the glass. 'There's Jevons with the mail. More letters and these still to be dispatched! Halliwell, I wish I had that man's composure. Every day he becomes more episcopal. Look at him now. The Archbishop himself, carrying the Crown Imperial, could not be more majestic.'

The figure disappeared through the arched door beneath them. But the ear now took up the tale, the stateliness of his approach being conveyed by the discreet boom of his measured step. 'I often wonder whether even the Last Day could discompose him. I expect him to rise saying "Dinner is served".'

The door, still vibrating from the knock requesting entry, swung open. 'The mail, My Lord,' Jevons announced, and deposited a large silver salver almost hidden under its white skilfully-piled load, wheeled and was gone. So, too, under this heaping cloud of further correspondence, was the Bishop's struggling humour. He took up the letter that had been given pride of place, glanced across the table and saw that his colleague had gone back to the earlier deposits they had been working. Then after a couple of minutes' reading of the latest news, 'Halliwell,' he asked, 'Do you know what I have just learnt?' 'News of the Dean?' 'How did you guess that?' 'I don't know.

He came into my mind the moment you looked up and saw Jevons approaching—perhaps association of ideas—they're both what I'd call "unapproachables".' 'Above pity and above reproach, a modern parody of the medieval ideal!' The bishop's humour gleamed faintly over the rising cloud of care, 'Well, he's got consumption.' 'He can't have!' 'There's no doubt he has. Why did you say he hasn't?' 'Well, really, Sir, I don't know. I just felt that couldn't be the—the... reason: just as I felt sure Jevons was bringing you a letter from him.'

'Well, listen to this, "I have to-day received advice as to my condition. I am informed by an eminent consultant whose diagnosis I am in no position to challenge and whose judgment is very highly rated by competent authorities, that I am in an unsuspectedly advanced state of decline. So acute has the condition been found to be that instant action is demanded of me, if the gravest consequences are to be avoided. I am instructed that I must leave the country for the south without any delay, otherwise I am in momentary danger of a fatal attack".' The Bishop looked up over the letter's edge, 'You see, it is consumption, not a shadow of doubt.' Then he went on. '"About the length of absence that this recuperation must require, I have been unable to obtain any judgment. I am informed that recovery itself cannot even now be assured. In these circumstances I have no choice but to leave without returning to Norminster, and I am therefore writing this letter to place with deepest regret my resignation of the Deanery in your hands." Well,' the Bishop sighed more conclusively than sadly, 'we must be thankful for the mercies that can be detected. On the whole it is certainly better to have a clean vacancy, "an extraction" as our dentists put it, than that condition from which this Close has so long suffered, slow decay *in situ*. It's tuberculosis without a doubt and without a doubt our doubly damp

Close is no place for such a patient. A highly polished Arabic style is no compensation for a highly infectious cough! I think we may trust the Prime Minister to do well by us. He certainly meant well last time. We may have to go outside the diocese but there are two or three names I might suggest to his Secretary...' The Bishop's own secretary seemed a couple of times about to say something but instead dipped his pen. 'Here's an addressed envelope,' he concluded, 'You'll be writing him a note by this mail, won't you.' He looked at his senior officer in the army of faith. This was the way his father-in-God carried things. Maybe it was the way to face mysteries, to face them over with practical applications and next steps to be taken, to look at the brighter side of things, brighter because it came on top, because it didn't penetrate down.

'I've a feeling, too,' the Bishop went on, 'that our crisis, epidemic, call it what you will, may be over. You're surprised at my having hunches, no doubt. Oh yes, I have them. But, like Samuel Rogers with his religious views, I keep them to myself.'

The quizzical play of the elder man's features gradually converted the younger's expression of puzzled query into an answering smile. 'And when you're my age, and no doubt of equal if not superior ecclesiastical elevation, you will be as cautious about publishing them—not because they have proved so often wrong—but because they may have turned out to be so largely, so disconcertingly right.'

He dived down on the still disconcertingly large heap of mail. It kept them busy on the bubbling surface of things till lunch—and after, until as the Cathedral clock struck 2.45 the Bishop exclaimed, 'I must take a turn in the Close and get a breathful of fresh air before evensong.' He had time for half a dozen turns. Completing the third he saw that Dr. Wilkes was coming up behind him. There would be just time for a genial greeting and not enough to be detained. It would be interesting, too, to see the physician's reaction. 'I think I should inform you, doctor, that the Dean has suddenly been ordered abroad.' 'Abroad?' 'Yes, I understand a consulting specialist—I think that is the term, is it not—is convinced that an acute consumptive condition has suddenly intervened.' 'Tuberculosis?' The question had in it something of Halliwell's incredulity. But a moment after the physician corrected his surprise. 'Well, well,' he added, 'Of course T.B. cases can and do suddenly spring themselves on us. And, further, there can be little doubt that many end-processes of conditions that up to the point of sudden crisis are purely functional, purely nervous, if I may put it that way.'

The slower summons of the larger Cathedral bell was at that moment exchanged for the thin nervous rapidity of the five-minutes warning. The Bishop waved his hand: the doctor saluted.

* * *

Besides his letter to the Palace, the Dean had mailed another to the Close, one to the Deanery. 'There, I knew it,' cried out Mrs. Binyon, for she was the recipient, 'I knew it, from the moment that fox came into the house, from that moment...' Nor when she read them the rest of the letter—a month's wages for all, a lawyer coming down to see about the things being moved—could they hope to move her from her dark conviction. Indeed the more they thought the whole thing over, the more they felt that though it didn't sound a bit likely or Protestant, there might be something in it.

ALSO AVAILABLE

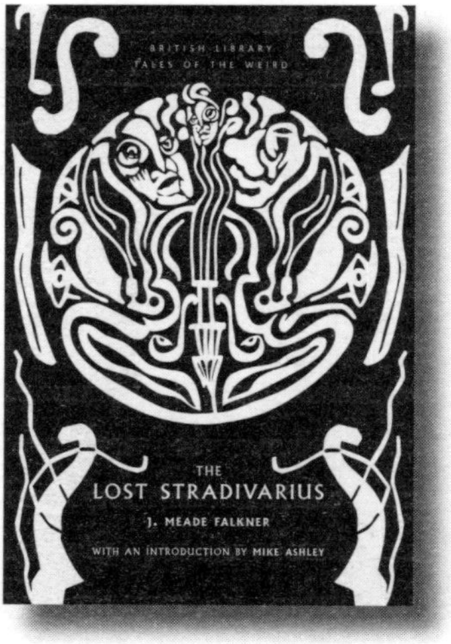

Oxford, 1842. After a summer spent obsessing over a bewitching new piece for the violin, John Maltravers discovers a beautiful Stradivarius in a secret panel of his student rooms at Magdalen Hall. But as the instrument leads John towards virtuosity, his sister Sophia begins to suspect something sinister lurking in the violin's history. As Maltravers plays and replays the wicked and irresistible tune of a debauched and bygone era, a corrupting force is closing in.

First published in 1895, *The Lost Stradivarius* is a true classic of strange fiction, sometimes described as the novel the great short story writer M. R. James might have written, for its evocation of the powers of the past that endure to haunt us through time.

ALSO AVAILABLE

A festering evil lurks in the grotesque carvings of a cathedral's hallowed inner sanctum; sheltering in an Alpine chapel, a young libertine confronts his eerie monastic doppelgänger; locked in a Spanish cathedral, a honeymooning couple bears witness to a fatal procession.

Churches and other sacred sites have inspired writers of the weird and uncanny for centuries as spaces in which death and the afterlife are within touching distance—where ghosts, demons and possessed effigies remain to haunt the living. Through eleven stories spanning the years from 1851 to 1935, this new anthology revives a throng of undying spirits from a host of lesser-known and classic authors including Elizabeth Gaskell, M. R. James, John Wyndham, and Edith Wharton.

For more Tales of the Weird titles
visit the British Library Shop (shop.bl.uk)

We welcome any suggestions, corrections or feedback you may have, and will aim to respond to all items addressed to the following:

The Editor (Tales of the Weird), British Library Publishing,
The British Library, 96 Euston Road, London NW1 2DB

We also welcome enquiries through our social media accounts, @BL_Publishing.